THE GIRL WHO
MARRIED AN EAGLE

THE GIRL WHO MARRIED AN EAGLE

Tamar Myers

WILLIAM MORROW
An Imprint of HarperCollins*Publishers*

THE GIRL WHO MARRIED AN EAGLE. Copyright © 2013 by Tamar Myers. All rights reserved. Printed in the United States of America. No part of this book may be used or reproduced in any manner whatsoever without written permission except in the case of brief quotations embodied in critical articles and reviews. For information address HarperCollins Publishers, 10 East 53rd Street, New York, NY 10022.

HarperCollins books may be purchased for educational, business, or sales promotional use. For information please write: Special Markets Department, HarperCollins Publishers, 10 East 53rd Street, New York, NY 10022.

FIRST EDITION

Designed by Yvonne Chan

Library of Congress Cataloging-in-Publication Data has been applied for.

ISBN 978-0-06-220385-4

13 14 15 16 17   OV/RRD   10 9 8 7 6 5 4 3 2 1

This book is dedicated to the memory of Robert Gordon Chambers.

Mr. Chambers, sixty-two, of Charlotte died on October 18, 2011, at Levine & Dickson Hospice House in Huntersville, North Carolina, following a valiant and vigorous fight against melanoma in consort with the extraordinary care provided by the Blumenthal Cancer Center at Carolinas Medical Center, Charlotte.

Bob was born September 13, 1949, in the Philadelphia area to the late Gordon Harispe Chambers and Marjorie Chambers Nicholson. He graduated from Chestnut Hill Academy (PA) in 1967, Princeton University in 1971, and Villanova University School of Law in 1975.

He was preceded in death by his wife of thirty years, Lynne Meyerberg Chambers, in 2003 and his nephew Keithly Jones.

In addition to his mother, Bob is survived by his daughter, Nicole McCormick (Michael) of Florence, Alabama, and her children: Sophie Lynne, Michael Aloysius, John King, Lila Carol, and Matthew Hawkins McCormick; son, Robert Gordon Chambers Jr. (Gina); sister Joyce Chambers; sister-in-law, Priscilla Dugdale (Bill); seven nieces and nephews; a grandniece and grandnephew; and his beloved friend, Becky Rizzo.

Bob was a partner with McGuire Woods in Charlotte and previously a partner with Montgomery, McCracken, Walker and Rhoads, and Duane Morris LLP (both of Philadelphia). He was a member of the board of directors of the World Affairs Council of Charlotte, past chairman of the American Benefits Council, chairman emeritus of the Board of Trustees of Chestnut Hill Academy, past president and director of the St. Andrews Society of Philadelphia and past trustee of the Foundation of the St. Andrew's Society of Philadelphia, Saunders House, the Cap and Gown Club, and other nonprofit organizations. Bob was a competitive and avid member of the Varsity Squash Team at Princeton University and a freshman coach.

Bob's family is grateful for the care given by his superb oncology team, Dr. Richard White, Dr. Asim Amin, and Denise Hogan, PA, and the incredible, indefatigable IL2 nursing staff on ICU Floor 11 at Carolinas Medical Center.

ACKNOWLEDGMENTS

This novel contains more fact than fiction. For research I mined the painful depths of my memory, which often led to nightmares. Despite having been treated for posttraumatic shock syndrome, I often scream aloud just as I fall asleep. My fear is that I will be hacked to death by a machete.

My mother *did* run a boarding school for the runaway child brides of head-hunting warriors. One day the chief, along with six of his machete-wielding warriors, appeared on our verandah as we were having dinner. My father excused himself from the table to greet the chief.

When my father returned to the dinner table, the following conversation ensued (to the best of my memory, for I was age eleven).

Mother: "What did the chief want?"

Father: "He said that when independence comes, he is going to live in our house and take our daughters for his wives."

Mother: "Oh, no! What did you say?"

Father: "I told him that he was crazy."

Mother: "Then what did he say?"

Father: "He said that he would burn us out."

Older sister: "Daddy, what are we going to *do*?"

Father: "Eat your soup."

Me: "Daddy, will you protect us with your double-gauge shotgun?"

Father: "I cannot." He looked at Mother. "I cannot because we are pacifists. We do not take human life."

The subtext, however, would seem to be that pacifists stand by and allow their children to be slaughtered—or worse. Indeed, such is the stuff of nightmares.

PREFACE

There once was a girl who married an eagle. To be sure, this eagle was no bird with feathers, beak, and talons. This eagle was a powerful chief of the Bashilele people, who resided in the Kasai district of the Belgian Congo, in Africa. His mother, who was a chief's wife, claimed that he was conceived when she heard an eagle scream, looked up, and the eagle's seed entered through her mouth. Who was there so brave as to call one of the chief's wives a liar? And anyway, when the boy was born, he emerged screaming like an eagle, and his fingernails were long like talons. Therefore, he was given the name Tshiminyi, which means eagle.

In due course of time, Tshiminyi inherited his human father's position, and he was thereafter known to all as Chief Eagle. Tshiminyi was fearless in battle and thus was able to lead his warriors to victory in countless raiding parties. Soon he became a very wealthy man and was able to afford many wives. By the white man's year of 1960, Chief Eagle had twenty-two wives and was in the process of acquiring his twenty-third. Her name was Buakane.

Because of its special meaning, one must take care to pronounce Buakane correctly. Phonetically, it might be spelled thusly: Bwa-kah-neh, with each syllable receiving the same amount of emphasis. This word translates as goodness, excellence, purity, holiness, elegance, handsomeness, beauty, fairness of color, honor, honesty, integrity, justice, righteousness, sanctification, uprightness, virtue, worthiness, and right. Indeed, this was far too big a name with which to saddle the average child, but the girl who was about to marry Chief Eagle was far from average.

Even in her mother's womb, Buakane had been exceptional. Never once had she caused her mother to be sick in the morning, nor given her a moment of discomfort. When it came time to deliver, Buakane slipped out as easily as that which one does in the privacy of the tall grass on a daily basis. That is the truth, *mene mene*.

What about labor pains, one might ask, and rightfully so? The answer would be: of these there were but three. These pains were a blessing sent by Buakane's maternal grandmother who had long ago returned to the Spirit World. She had been bitten by a deadly poisonous mamba snake when Buakane's mother was only an infant. Without these three labor pains, Buakane's mother, whose name was Tshibetu, would not have known it was time to return to her hut, and there to squat above her birthing mat.

The word *tshibetu*, it should be mentioned, means "grasshopper swatter," and it is a noun. The Bashilele sometimes hunt by lighting circular fires, with diameters of several miles across. The men use their bows and arrows to kill the mammals that escape the flames, while the women and children swat at grasshoppers that are the size of sparrows and that are capable of flight. The giant insects are knocked out of the air from a height of about ten feet using the grasshopper swatters. These consist of foot-long paddles woven from palm fronds that are attached to the ends of skinny poles that are six or more feet long.

Grasshopper Swatter had been given that name because a misplaced swat to her mother's abdomen had sent her mother into an early but successful labor. Since the name Grasshopper Paddle rolls off the tongue with more ease than Grasshopper Swatter, that is what she could be called from now on, but even that is too cumbersome. So just Paddle will suffice.

At any rate, so easy was Buakane's birth that Paddle attended to everything herself. In fact, given that her husband was away hunting, and her mother-in-law disliked her enough to stay away at the slightest excuse, Paddle was able to appear in the doorway of her hut holding her newborn before anyone in the village even realized that she was missing.

"Come, friends," Paddle called in a voice as strong as ever. "Come and see what I have made!"

The ancient crone who lived next door, a woman of least fifty Belgian years, had been peeling manioc tubers with a sliver of sharpened iron that might once have been a machete blade. Slowly she set her work aside, used a nearby tree stump to pull herself erect, and hobbled over.

"What is it?" she lisped, for she was entirely toothless. "Is that a monkey you have?"

"*Kah!* Be silent, you fool," Paddle cried. "This is my daughter."

"Now who is the fool?" the crone said. "I saw you enter your hut, and you were with child. The midwife did not follow you. Now but a short time has passed, and you wish me to believe that you have given birth."

"*Tch!* Look, old woman, put your hand on my belly, and feel for a child; you will not find her there. Put your hand between my legs and feel that I am still bleeding."

The crone did what she was bade, for she was past the age of embarrassment. Satisfied that Paddle was telling the truth, she took a closer look at the newborn.

"Please, neighbor," she said, "hold the child this way and that, so that I might see all of her, for never have I seen a more perfect child."

Now it was that Paddle and her husband, Bad Odor, had yet to select a name for their child. The name was to reflect some aspect connected to the child's birth, or perhaps some omen foreseen by the village witch doctor. But when the old lady made this strange request, Paddle sensed something momentous was about to happen, and she joyfully complied.

As Paddle lovingly held her naked infant up and turned her this way and that, even spreading her tiny legs in order that the crone might inspect her daughter's genitals, Paddle was totally unaware that a crowd had gathered and was murmuring in one voice. "*Buakane, buakane, buakane!*"

"This child is perfect in every way," the ancient crone said. "It is as if she was carved in ivory by a master craftsman, and then dipped in the pink juice of *mbelebele* berries. Do you hear how the village chants her name?"

"*E*, I hear!" a man said. It was Bad Odor, the girl's father, just returned from his hunt, and slung over his broad right shoulder was a nice plump antelope. "By the spirits of my ancestors, I swear that from this day forward our daughter will be called Buakane."

Truly, Buakane was deserving of her name. Not only did she take to the breast immediately, but she never cried, never once gave her parents a reason to feel anxious. In the fierce sun of the upland plains, her skin turned as black as obsidian, and every bit as glossy and smooth. Her limbs grew long and strong, her neck graceful, and her features were finely chiseled. Although Buakane was exceptionally beautiful, one could tell at once by these characteristics that she was a member of the Bashilele tribe. It was said that even the Belgians admired these "savage headhunters" for their beauty.

But to become a full-fledged member of the tribe, a *Mushilele* (that is the singular form of Bashilele) must bear on his or her body certain physical signs of belonging. The most obvious of these is that the two upper front teeth must be knocked out. In addition, beautiful patterns are created on the skin by inserting small lumps of charcoal into shallow cuts. The charcoal is sterile, which usually precludes severe infection. Eventually, very attractive keloid scars form. The higher the scar, the more exquisite it is considered to be.

Patterns are created on the cheeks of course, but it is a woman's back that is surely her best feature. On a wealthy woman one might see an astonishing array of swirls and curlicues. Yes, of course, all these things are quite painful, but never are they done to a small girl. These are the rituals of one who is about to become available for marriage.

Unfortunately, Buakane was born at a difficult time in the tribe's history. Polygamy had caused such a shortage of marriageable women that the average age of marriage for a girl was as young as nine Belgian years. The husbands were sometimes four or five times that old. Many men, anticipating this long wait, were making provisional contracts with pregnant women. They were putting down payments on unborn babies, knowing that they would not get a refund if the baby happened to be a boy. The full bride-prices were also being driven up to ridiculous heights. By the time Buakane reached her ninth Belgian year, or thereabouts (the Bashilele do not keep track of such nonsense), her father had already been the recipient of many marriage offers. After all, who among the Bashilele would not want this most remarkable girl to be the progenitor of their descendants?

But Bad Odor would not even listen to their offers, for he was confident that the longer he waited, the higher the dowry his daughter could command. Then, when Buakane had grown as tall as her mother, and had still to sprout the beginnings of breasts, or womanly vegetation, Bad Odor demanded that his daughter have her two front teeth knocked out. She would also have her cheeks scarred, the scars that would mark her as a Mushilele. Her back, however, would remain smooth until after marriage; her husband could pay for that.

Thus it was done. But never once did Buakane cry out in pain. Not one tear did she shed. Not even the oldest crone could remember a girl as brave as Buakane.

Truly, truly—*bulelela*—the girl who was given a name that meant eighteen wonderful qualities lived up to every single one of them. There was no one in the village of Mushihi, the village of Chief Eagle, who could say a bad word about her. Normally, one might expect something like this to engender jealousy among her peers, but there was something so special about Buakane that the opposite thing happened: everyone vied to be her friend.

Then one day Buakane's father noticed that his daughter's body had begun to change. Where once her chest had gleamed as flat as a boy's, buds formed almost overnight, and soon swelled into guavas. Already she'd been wearing the loincloth for the span of three long dry seasons, so he did not know for sure her complete state of development.

"Grasshopper Paddle," he said to his wife one fine morning after breakfast, "concerning our daughter, Buakane, does thatch now grow in the shade?"

"What?"

He pointed at his own loins.

"The thatch is now a jungle," Paddle said. Then she threw back her head and laughed so loud that Buakane, who had meandered off with some friends, came running back in alarm.

"*Baba*, what is wrong?" she demanded.

Paddle contained herself immediately. "Nothing is wrong, Beautiful One. It is quite the opposite. Your father just informed me that this morning he will begin entertaining offers from your suitors."

"*Baba*," Buakane said calmly, "I have yet to commence the bleeding."

"*Aiyee!*" Paddle cried in mock agitation. "This is not a matter to discuss in front of a man."

"I am not a man!" Bad Odor shouted. "I am your father; I must know these things. Nevertheless, Buakane, you are turning into a beautiful young woman, with hips that will accommodate the passage of many babies. As the old adage says: do not hesitate to release your arrow when you are close enough to shoot; you may not have a second chance."

Buakane nodded. Rather than be resentful that she was about to be bartered like a goat or a basket of chickens, she was instead grateful that she had a father who cared enough about her to fetch the highest price. After all, if a man paid a good deal for something, was he not more likely to treat it better than something of lesser value? To show her appreciation, she excused herself from the hut and resumed talking with her friends. It was much better to let her parents discuss the details without her being there, she thought. Too many details would cause her to worry, and Buakane wanted only to be happy.

Days passed, and Buakane convinced herself that she still had plenty of carefree days ahead of her. For in addition to all the good qualities that she possessed, Buakane was in possession of one very unfortunate quality: optimism. In a society where only two out of ten children survived to reach adulthood, it was pessimism, doubt, fear, and wariness that were needed to outsmart the Grim Reaper. If a village thought that it had enough food and water to outlast the coming dry season (a full three months without a drop of rain), then surely it did not. If a warrior thought that he was skilled enough with that bow that he need practice no more, then surely he was not. Simply put, doubt led to improvement.

One day, when Buakane returned from sauntering about with her peers, she was alarmed to discover that the door of the hut had been secured from the inside with a wooden peg. This was a most unusual circumstance in the middle of the day. Given that Bashilele huts lacked windows, the doors were normally kept open to catch what little breeze was available. A closed door usually meant that something intensely personal—although not necessarily sexual—was taking place within the four palm-thatch walls.

It was a good thing that the old crone was no longer alive, for to be sure, she would have found a spot where the thatch was thin and pressed a large but wrinkled ear against it. The old crone had been a busybody and loved nothing better than to spread gossip. Some might think that Buakane, the faithful and discreet daughter, had a right to hear the conversation too. At any rate, this is what she heard.

"Grasshopper Paddle," Bad Odor said in a hoarse whisper, "earlier this morning, when I washed at the stream with the men, Chief Eagle signaled that he wished to speak to me alone. So I followed him up the stream a ways, to the pool where the manioc soaks. It was there that he told me that he wishes to purchase our Buakane to be his twenty-third wife."

"*Aiyee*," cried Paddle softly. She shuddered. "What did you tell him?"

"What *could* I tell him? He said that she will have her own hut, meat once every ten days, and when he beats her, he will not hit her in the face. And as for us, we will receive ten goats, five sheep, nine chickens, and five ducks."

"*Kah!* That is nothing! Bad Odor, do you not agree that she is the fairest maiden in the village? Her face scars are the thickest and most evenly spaced. Her front teeth were extracted without any damage to her palate. And where until just two moons ago she sported guavas on her chest, are they not mangoes now? Husband, I tell you that she will bleed when I cycle next. Believe my words, for I can smell it rising on her now. Tell the chief that he must deliver fifteen goats—all under two years of age, and twenty hens. No roosters!"

Bad Odor could but pace for the excitement. "Yes, yes, but then we have a deal. Yes?"

In reality Bad Odor did not even *have* to ask Paddle her opinion—not on anything—but Grasshopper Paddle descended from a clan of much higher rank than that of Bad Odor. Not only was she a member of the nobility, but she was a cousin of the chief. Therefore she was automatically considered to be the brighter of the pair. As usual, there had been a shortage of available females when he chose a wife, and she had cost him dearly. One values that for which one has paid dearly. One even values that thing's opinions—even if that thing is just a wife.

"Then we will have a deal," Paddle said. "But remember, Bad Odor, that when Chief Eagle dies—as is the case when any chief dies—all his wives must be buried alive with him, in order to escort him into the next world. Are you prepared for that to happen?"

Bad Odor froze. "*Yala!* Why must you always throw gravel in my path?" He thought for a moment. "Then it is our duty to see that Chief Eagle lives an especially long life. You personally will taste every one of his meals in order to guard against poisoning."

"Excellent," said Paddle, "for I am a small eater. Now I shall no longer have to cook!"

"*Kah!* I should box your ears, foolish woman."

"*Aiyee,*" cried Buakane from outside her listening hole.

"You spoke of ears," Paddle said, "and behold, now the walls have grown some. Quick, hand me an arrow, husband, that I might pierce the ears of our nosy neighbors—they who have taken the old crone's place."

"*Aiyee,*" Buakane cried again. "*Baba,* it is only me—she who must now be buried alive, her arms and legs broken, dirt filling her mouth and nostrils, as she gasps for her last breath. *Baba,* do you hear me?"

"I hear you well, you foolish child. Now get in here at once before the entire village hears you."

Buakane moved as fast as a pouncing leopard, so that she virtually fell into the hut just as her father opened the door. He slammed it shut behind her and then picked her up by the armpits.

"Your mother is right; you are indeed a foolish child," he said. "You possess many good qualities, but I am not so sure that discernment is one of them. Did you honestly think that your mother and I would let Chief Eagle's men do that which you described? Indeed, we would not! Your mother—she who comes from the higher-caste clan—has relatives up in Basongo who will hide you."

"*Tatu,* do you mean that I am *not* to marry Chief Eagle?"

"*Tch,* your simplicity tries my patience, daughter. Of course you will marry Chief Eagle. As long as he lives you will be well fed and you will have your own hut."

"And you will be rich," Paddle said pointedly to her husband.

Bad Odor glared at his wife. "Higher clan or not," he said, "your mouth offends me." He turned back to Buakane. "You will be Chief Eagle's twenty-third wife, but you must run into the bush immediately that the chief shows signs of a serious illness. If you are questioned, say that it is to relieve yourself. Do you understand, daughter?"

Buakane nodded, her gentle eyes now large with fear. "But, *Tatu,*" she said to her father, "I do not understand why Chief Eagle would want to marry me. Ours is a large village, so that there are many other girls that the chief could have selected instead. I can think of several who would be much better suited to his taste than I."

Paddle and Bad Odor exchanged knowing glances. Was not the daughter whom they had created together truly a marvel? Any other girl, even one only half as beautiful as she, would have been unbearably conceited. By now, such a girl would have been driven out of the village by a flock of jealous harpies. Or else such a girl might have met a disastrous end at the hand of an oversexed bachelor.

Truly, truly, *bulelele,* so far it had been Buakane's innocence and attendant good nature that had protected her from folly. Clearly, she must marry Chief Eagle as soon as possible and be under his protection. He was still a young man—as far as chiefs went (albeit not young altogether)—and as for the future, that would sort itself out.

"You must hurry to the women's place along the stream and bathe," Bad Odor said. "Your mother will go with you. Then you will rub your body with palm oil until it glistens."

"But, Bad Odor," Paddle said, "we have just enough palm oil left for the evening meal."

"Shut up, wife," Bad Odor said. "Why must you always think like a woman? Tomorrow we will be rich! Now what was I saying?"

"You were being harsh to the mother of the chief's future wife," Buakane said.

Bad Odor glared at his daughter, but he dared not reprimand her, for he knew how obstinate she could be. "Yes, that is it exactly," he said. "And while you are at the stream bathing, I must go and speak with the chief."

ONE

Julia Elaine Newton was young and naive, but she was not altogether stupid. She had come to the mission field fully aware that, while God was the Supreme Judge, the only one whose opinion really mattered, she was going to be judged left and right anyway. So be it; she had nothing to hide.

She'd been born and raised in Oxford, Ohio, the home of Miami University. Her father was a professor of European History at MU, and her mother was a grammar school teacher in the public school system. Her mother was also active in the PTA, and both her parents were avid bowlers. The family belonged to a middle-of-the-road Protestant denomination, and they considered themselves to be as midwestern as one could get. In other words, Julia Newton came from a *normal* American family, and she probably would have stayed just "plain boring Julia," had it not been for the Missions Day program the summer after she graduated from college.

Julia had already been hired to teach at the high school in Oxford when the family's minister fortuitously invited a missionary from Africa to give the guest sermon at their church. This was a highly controversial gesture on the minister's part, because this particular middle-of-the-road Protestant church was notoriously lukewarm on the idea of foreign missions. It was a subject that made a lot of people uncomfortable, and since being comfortable was the American Dream, anything negative was to be left at the doorway of the church.

After all, every year the congregation took up a special offering, to collect a few dollars to feed some starving children with bloated bellies in far-off Africa. Some years the offerings were diverted to emaciated children (with hollow eyes) in India. And, of course, with the money went some religious literature that was to be translated, in hopes of saving a soul or two. This was enough to make everyone feel like he or she had done their part until the following year, when the next Missions Sunday rolled around again.

But this year was different. The guest speaker on Missions Sunday was a man by the name of Brother Zug. Oddly enough, Brother Zug did not even belong to the same pleasant middle-of-the-road denomination. Whether his visit was fate, happenstance, or God's will, what he had to say changed the young woman's life.

"True disciples of Jesus," he said, "don't spend their evenings sitting on overstuffed sofas watching Ed Sullivan on TV. Neither do they spend their weekends at the bowling alley drinking beer with their friends, or out playing golf. No sir, true disciples give everything they have to the poor, and then they follow Jesus to the ends of the earth. If you don't believe me, then look it up in your bibles. In the Book of Luke, verse three, Jesus tells his disciples that they shouldn't even pack an extra set of clothes."

Brother Zug smelled his armpits and wrinkled his nose, carried on like nobody's business, but not a soul had laughed. The citizens of Oxford, Ohio, in 1959 were civilized people. They bathed or showered daily. They also changed their clothes frequently. Some, but not all of them, changed their underwear daily—just in case they were to be hit by a car.

"I know what you're thinking," Brother Zug said.

"Oh, yeah," Professor Newton grunted. "I just bet you do."

"Shhh," Mrs. Newton said.

"You're wondering what the disciples did about their under-wear."

A nervous twitter rippled through the congregation. It happened so fast, however, that Julia couldn't tell which of the many stony faces had reacted to Brother Zug's surprisingly off-color humor.

"Well, I'll tell you," the visiting preacher shouted in a voice that rumbled like thunder. "They probably wore *nothing* under their tunics—just like the Scots wear nothing under their kilts. But now that I have your full attention again, let me remind you of something: it is our responsibility, as Christians, to see to it that every person, in every distant land, has the opportunity to hear the good news of salvation before they die. If not—well, those who die in sin will spend all of eternity in hell, screaming in agony as they dodge flame after flame. Tell me something, do you want that on your conscience?"

Brother Zug pointed to Mrs. Crabtree, who always insisted on sitting in the front, center pew, even though she wasn't hard of hearing. Mrs. Newton claimed that it was because Viola Crabtree had the vanity of a peacock and spent hours getting ready for church every Sunday morning. After she'd gone to all that trouble, she damn well better be seen. Especially by the reverend.

"*You*," Brother Zug said, still picking on Viola Crabtree, "are *you* prepared to pick up your cross and follow Jesus?"

Viola whimpered something to which neither Julia nor anyone in her family was privy. She was probably asking if there were hair dryers in Africa.

Brother Zug continued to press his point. "Are you prepared to follow him through mosquito-filled swamps, where the trees are festooned with snakes and where cannibals lurk in the shadows, armed with their bows and poisonous arrows?"

Poor Viola. Julia almost felt sorry for her. Mrs. Crabtree was squirming like a worm on a hook and had actually managed to scrunch down about two inches. At the same time, Julia was growing intensely envious of the old lady. How she would love to be asked those same questions! A quick disclaimer, though: Julia detested both snakes and mosquitoes, but the words *festooned* and *lurk*—oh my stars, were they ever so romantic!

Now you can bet that most of these middle-of-the-road church members, many of whom were already thinking of Sunday dinners followed by afternoon naps, did not want to have a guilt trip thrust down their throats. A few of them were polite enough to stick it out until the end, but the majority of them simply got up and walked out. To be fair, Julia would hasten to add, no one booed, and not one of those who stayed said anything rude to Brother Zug.

All right, that's not quite true. Julia's mother did say, "How very interesting," as she shook the visiting preacher's hand. Anyone who knew Mrs. Newton well would recall that she was originally from Charleston, South Carolina, and therefore recognize her comment as a scathing rebuke clothed in velvet.

Of course Julia didn't know what Brother Zug thought about this, just that he smiled at her mother and nodded. Julia's father shook the guest preacher's hand but said nothing. Julia, however, babbled like a maniac, because suddenly it seemed like she'd found her life's purpose—the reason God had put her on this earth.

Julia begged off eating her mother's Sunday pot roast—which she dearly loved, by the way—and joined her preacher's family for dinner, since they were hosting Brother Zug. It was common knowledge that the preacher's wife was a terrible cook, but strange as this may sound, it too may have been part of God's plan. Instead of eating, Julia and Brother Zug talked about the grave need for missionaries in deepest, darkest Africa.

There was a tribe of former headhunters called the Bashilele, Brother Zug said, that practiced both polygamy and polyandry. Julia knew what polygamy meant, but Brother Zug had to explain that polyandry meant that a woman was allowed to marry more than one husband. Apparently this practice was a response to the fact that the powerful, rich men like the chief and his elders could afford many wives. The result was that other men had to be content with sharing wives. In fact, because of the shortage of available single women, it had become the practice to marry children.

The Bashilele were a tribe of warriors who'd resisted outside influence until 1950. That was when a courageous Mennonite family, Russell and Helen Schnell and their four children, leased land from the Belgian government upon which to build a mission station from scratch. Not only did they build a church, but a school, and Mrs. Schnell presided over a boarding school for the runaway child brides of these fierce Bashilele warriors.

"She is a very kind, gentle woman, with a heart of gold," Brother Zug said. "There is no doubt that the Lord has his angels guarding her every step."

Julia expressed her deepest admiration for Mrs. Schnell, declaring her a true heroine for modern times. Brother Zug waved his fork with great excitement, oblivious to the piece of rubbery roast that clung precariously to the tines of his fork.

"Yes, yes, and you can be the next Helen Schnell, don't you see?"

"How?"

"We have built a new station to the north, perhaps some sixty kilometers distant. That territory is still Bashilele, but it is ruled by a different chief—one who claims to be half eagle, and that is his name: Eagle. Chief Eagle.

"We had two couples assigned to that mission station. One of the men is the station's builder and mechanic, plus runs the boys' school, and the other missionary handles most of the preaching and evangelizing. In the Belgian Congo, boys take precedence, I'm afraid.

"The preacher's wife is a nurse—oh my, is she ever kept busy handing out sulfa pills and what have you—and the other woman *was* the girls' school principal."

Julia's minister gently pulled the hand wielding the waving fork down to the table. "Brother Zug, what do you mean by *was*?"

"This woman—her name was Elizabeth—died two years ago, and we've had a hard time keeping a replacement. You see, this is a very primitive, remote mission, and the job is not without its potential perils."

"Perhaps you should help us see better," said Julia's minister.

"With God's help," said Brother Zug. He closed his eyes briefly. "Bear in mind that these little girls who are taken in and sheltered are also the wives of grown men. And these men are warriors, who are armed to the teeth with machetes and carry six-foot bows that shoot razor-sharp arrows. They also live by hunting. Believe me, these Bashilele men know how to kill."

"Brother Zug, *please*," said the preacher's wife said with a shudder. "Do you really think this sort of blunt talk is appropriate in front of a young lady?"

"Yes, sister, I do," Brother Zug said. "We are discussing female children half her age, who are forced to engage in sexual relations with men in their forties. If I can convince this young lady to go to Mushihi Station and save a few of these girls from their so-called husbands, then maybe we can stand a chance at saving their souls."

The preacher's wife turned the color of rhubarb pie before fleeing the table. Julia felt awful for her, but really, Brother Zug was right. If Jesus had called on his followers to save souls, then surely that was more important than having a pleasant dinner conversation. And to be honest, it was also more important than sparing one's hostess's feelings. After all, no one could be more blunt about it than the Lord himself in chapter 14 of the Book of Luke.

"I'll go," Julia said. She'd needed surprisingly little persuasion. It just felt so *right*, somehow. Maybe the Holy Spirit really was moving in her heart, and this was that "call" she'd heard so much about.

"Whoa, there!" said her minister, he of the middle-of-the-road church. "Julia, you haven't even asked your parents—or me!"

"I don't have to; I'm twenty-one."

Brother Zug beamed. "I always said that when God moves, he works incredibly fast. Praise the Lord!"

"Amen," Julia's minister said, "but really, Brother Zug, this isn't the place to recruit your foot soldiers."

"Foot soldiers?" Julia asked.

"For the Lord's army," Brother Zug said. He winked. "Although I see you rising through the ranks to lieutenant in no time at all. What are you doing this summer?"

Julia's face burned with embarrassment. "Uh—I still haven't lined up a summer job."

"Perfect," Brother Zug said. "We have a missionary on loan who can handle things until the end of the year. In the meantime, you should go to Cincinnati to study the Tshiluba language—that is the regional tribal language—with one of the retired missionaries who was born and brought up in the Congo. The natives call her Mamu One of Us, because she speaks the language without any accent. I can arrange this if you like—at no cost, I assure you."

Julia's heart raced. She was so filled with joy and anticipation that she wanted to burst out singing. So when Brother Zug, who was either a mind reader or a superbly gifted manipulator, began to sing "Onward, Christian Soldiers" in his rich baritone, the young woman joined in without hesitation in her warbling soprano.

TWO

Julia Newton's first stop in the Belgian Congo was Leopoldville, the capital city. However, she was to remember almost nothing of that place because she slept like a hibernating woodchuck for two days. On the third she awoke drenched in sweat under a mosquito net and was so disoriented that she wished either to wake up from this nightmare of her own creation or else to find a hidden door in the room that would allow her to step into nothingness. Unfortunately, this feeling of "what I have gotten myself into?" was a familiar one, for Julia Elaine Newton's most outstanding talent seemed to be that of getting herself into trouble.

Julia had been taught to pray away her troubles, and she was attempting to do just that when a woman who quite resembled her very own aunt Irene in temperament knocked sharply on her door and then entered without waiting to be admitted.

"You have five minutes," the strange woman said without preamble.

"I beg your pardon?"

"To gather your things and get downstairs."

"But where am I?"

"You're in Leopoldville, of course. The Interdenominational Missionary Guesthouse."

Julia stared at the woman, waiting for an introduction.

But instead, the woman consulted a tiny silver watch, which was her only adornment, and tapped her foot impatiently. "Time's awasting. No time to chitchat."

"What happens in five minutes?"

"Hurry." She glanced around, and seeing that Julia's largest valise had not even been opened, she picked it up and carried it out with her. This was the same suitcase that Julia's father had joked contained the Colossus of Rhodes. That was before he'd asked her seventeen-year-old brother, Willard, to help him load it into the back of their wood-paneled Chevrolet station wagon. How that same valise managed to get to the third floor of the Leopoldville guesthouse would forever remain a mystery.

Sure enough, only a minute or two later, a pickup truck came roaring into the compound of the guesthouse. The driver leaned on the horn, and within seconds the ridiculously strong woman was back again. This time she grabbed Julia by one of her biceps and began leading her downstairs.

"Please," Julia protested. "You don't need to be so rude."

"It's a small plane," the hostess said. "Downdrafts are building up. You'll see."

Julia was then pushed up into the cab of a battered blue pickup truck. The driver, who cheerfully introduced himself as Hank, was a white man—but a very rude white man as well, because he couldn't even trouble himself to hop out of his precious truck and say hello properly. *So much for manners in the Belgian Congo,* Julia thought.

But then her feelings of rebuke faded almost as soon as they drove away from the guesthouse, because a world of magic began opening up outside its gates. The Belgian sector of Leopold-ville consisted of wide, tree-lined boulevards. The exotic trees—mango, banyan, jacaranda—had whitewashed trunks and they arched over the streets in places, creating tunnels of foliage and offering blessed shade. On either side of the boulevards, practically hidden by bougainvillea, lantana, and hibiscus, stood the stately garden villas of the government elite and the well-off merchants.

But even the homes of the less important whites benefited from the verdant splendor, although no doubt this mantle of tropical foliage was cared for by a coterie of native servants. Thus it was that all the white-occupied zone of Leopoldville appeared to Julia's eyes—bloodshot and jet-lagged though they were—as tidy and prosperous.

Therefore it came as a rude awakening, a total shock even, to suddenly find that they had driven across an invisible line and into a shantytown of the worst description. Even in Hamilton (which is the city nearest to Oxford, Ohio), there did not exist a slum to equal one as horrible as the one Julia beheld on her first outing in the Congo. The structures that lined both sides of the road could not be called houses; the word *shack* was even too grandiose for them.

These "things" had been built from empty wooden beer crates and sheets of corrugated iron. They were tied together with torn strips of plastic and dirty bandages. Cardboard covered the gaps and cement blocks held things down—or up. Whatever became available was put to use as shelter material, which in one case *did* include a kitchen sink.

Julia was furious at the Belgians for allowing this. "This is unbelievable," she said. "Shame on the Belgians yet again."

"This isn't the Belgians' fault," Hank, the driver, said. "These people don't have jobs. These people are here on their own volition to sponge off their relatives."

"That, sir, is the exact sort of racism I heard back home in Ohio. I certainly did not expect to hear it from the lips of a missionary."

Hank had the nerve to chuckle at that. "This is a first," he said. "I was born here in the Congo, at a mission called Djoka Punda. I have lived here most of my life, and I have never been called a racist before. Anyway, what you see around you is the product of a system of entitlement based on bloodlines. It exists in many tribes, and it can be beneficial for an individual's survival.

"It goes like this. A person who has something is expected to share his resources with his relatives who are without. The closer the relatives are—that is, the more blood that they share—the more it is that the fortunate person is expected to share. *But* this sharing thing not only extends to half siblings; in some tribes it extends to cousins and their children as well. For example, if a hunter kills an antelope, he will receive only a small piece of meat, because the rest will all have to be shared. It is possible even that his wife—or wives—will get none."

Julia waved her hands impatiently. "But this? This is just poverty. What explains this? I don't understand."

"Lady, you fire questions off like a machine gun," Hank said.

"Do you, or do you not, have the answer?"

"Yes, in a minute."

Julia's ears burned. Mother and Dad, Minister Jones, everyone whom she knew and genuinely cared for, had at one time or another lovingly beseeched her to leave her famous temper behind in the United States when she set out for Africa. It wasn't that Julia was intentionally mean; to the contrary, she was known for her kind heart. It was that Julia was passionate—particularly about matters of justice. "A modern-day Deborah," her minister once called her.

"The Africans who work as domestics for the Belgians live in little cement block houses behind the villas," Hank explained. "Trust me, those servants' quarters are palaces compared to anything that you see here. But the law of sharing brings relatives by droves to the big city, and since they are not allowed to join their relative on his master's estate, and there is often no work for them, here they congregate, forming slums. No water, no toilets, no rules, lots of beer, lots of prostitutes—one working person will sometimes be supporting as many as sixty relatives who do nothing but beg for trouble."

"Well, it still sounds like it's the Belgians' fault," Julia cried indignantly. "Why *don't* the white owners allow their servants' relatives to live behind their mansions—hidden, of course—in some halfway decent quarters? It wouldn't be any skin off their noses!"

"They don't do it because they don't want to encourage the people to leave the traditional way of life. At least not until the tribal people have had some education and are prepared to make the transition. And anyway, how about you, Miss Julia? Would you care to have sixty half-naked people and their goats, sheep, pigs, chickens, dogs, turkeys, pigeons, drums—the whole kit and caboodle—move into a string of rooms behind your house? You'd have to watch where you step because every living thing—people as well—would use your backyard as their toilet."

"Perhaps I've spoken too hastily," Julia said, her cheeks burning yet again.

She really did try to be an agreeable person, but the people she'd met so far had not made it easy. The Belgian officials at the N'Djili International Airport had been curt, the Africans had seemed subservient, the hostess at the Interdenominational Missionary Guesthouse far from welcoming, and as for Hank—he was uncomfortably handsome.

He had dark curly hair, a deep golden tan, and the greenest eyes she had ever seen on a human being. Starting from the soles of his bare feet, to his narrow hips, moving up to his deep chest and impossibly broad shoulders and then even mashing down his curls, Hank stood a good six feet two inches tall. A strong chin, a Roman nose, and straight white teeth were also components of the picture.

In short, this was not what she had expected in a missionary; they were supposed to look more like Brother Zug. Proper missionary men were supposed to be doughy and somewhat androgynous, due to their multiple chins and distended paunches. They certainly weren't supposed to have *sex* appeal.

How utterly unfair of God to allow the Evil One to put a stumbling block like Hank in her path on day one of her ministry. Just don't look at him, she kept telling herself. Try not to inhale his scent either. His *scent*? *For crying out loud,* she thought, *how debased have I become? Hank's not an animal!* Yet the harder she tried not to sneak a peek or accidentally get a whiff of his manly odor, the harder it became to ignore Hank. This was especially the case since he had apparently decided to appoint himself as her tour guide.

"See those mountains outside your window?" he said. "Those are the infamous Crystal Mountains. They are what prevents oceangoing ships from steaming up the Congo River as far inland as Stanleyville. You'll be flying over them on your way up-country."

"Up-country?"

She glanced at him just as he grinned. "Yeah, that's what we call anyplace *but* Leopoldville. This really isn't the Congo, you know."

Julia held her tongue. Aunt Marl, the woman who had taught her the Tshiluba language, had also been kind enough to clue Julia in on a few facts that she had better bear in mind if she wished to make her adjustment to the mission field as smooth as possible. First, she was to remember that missionaries were people too. Heat, hunger, thirst, exhaustion, loneliness—all those things could make them every bit as cross as the next person. However, being the good Christians that they professed to be, they took their troubles to the Lord in prayer, and usually did a fairly good job of reining in their emotions. When their emotions did get the best of them, however, they were more likely to act out against the natives than against their fellow missionaries.

Julia had been shocked by Aunt Marl's candor; no adult had ever spoken so honestly to her—and none had since. Julia's feelings must have shown on her face, because the dear woman had tried to put an arm around Julia. But stubborn Julia had pretended to suffer from claustrophobia.

Aunt Marl had been clueless. "Oh dear," she'd said. "That could be a problem as well. After they get over their initial fright, the children will want to crowd around you, touch your skin, feel your hair. You'll be like the Pied Piper wherever you go."

"But eventually they'll get used to my presence, right?"

"Mmm—possibly. Listen, dear, I want to warn you about something."

"Yes?"

"Sex."

Julia had laughed nervously. "Aunt Marl, I thought you said— well, it sounded like—"

"Let's hope it sounded like 'sex,' because that is what I said. Do you think that you could say that word, Julia?"

She'd squirmed. "No—not here. Not in front of *you*."

Aunt Marl had smiled. Ruefully, perhaps.

"As I understand it," she'd said, "you are to be posted at Mushihi Station, which is in Bashilele territory. The Bashilele are an extremely handsome people—both the men and the women. They are tall and long of limb, altogether well proportioned. The men have muscular chests, shoulders, and biceps, and flat abdomens. Correction: some of the young men have abdomens like washboards."

She'd emitted a deep, throaty sigh, almost a growl. "Ach, the women, such beauties! They have long, graceful necks and full breasts of the most pleasing shape. They too have small waists, but generous, wide hips that add to their allure. I warn you, young lady, and mark my words, and mark them well; it is impossible to look upon a Mushilele and not give God the glory for his creation."

"Amen," Julia said. What else should she have said? For she had just been privy to a heartfelt prayer from a humble missionary who could see God's artistry in a tribe of savages. Unfortunately, Aunt Marl was not quite through with her.

"Ah, but you see," Aunt Marl said as she paused to shake a bent, arthritic finger at Julia, "the other edge to this sword is that it is impossible to look at a healthy Mushilele of a certain age without having thoughts of lust flit through your mind like cirrus clouds on a windy spring day. The more you try to block out these thoughts, the harder it becomes, and they'll push into your mind like weeds—even during the most sacred moments.

"For example," Aunt Marl continued, "you might be on your knees praying—kneeling on cold, gritty concrete, mind you, and you will find yourself staring at a headhunter's loincloth just inches from your face. You will find yourself wondering what is behind that little curtain of woven palm fibers. Would the world end if you flicked that little curtain aside with your index finger? What harm is there in just looking?

"Surely that is not adultery—is it, Julia? Show me one place in the Bible where it says that just looking is adultery. And please don't mention Noah and his son, Ham. The Bashilele were not my children. Besides, this is hypothetical. You do understand that much, don't you?"

Julia was gobsmacked. It had never occurred to her that adults, *real* adults—the kind with wrinkles and liver spots—ever had these kind of thoughts, much less found them hard to resist. She had thought that she was the only person in the world who was so spiritually bankrupt that she couldn't manage to keep those sort of physical thoughts at bay. After all, Julia and her college room-mate had never even engaged in such intimate conversation.

"A penny for your thoughts," Hank said, and she could feel the color rushing to her cheeks.

It was amazing how fast the human brain could operate if it had to. In a nanosecond she thought up and discarded several plausible scenarios. In the end she settled on a much-scaled-down version of the truth.

"For some reason, I was thinking about what my Tshiluba

teacher, Aunt Marl, said in regard to the Bashilele tribe. She seems to think that they are an uncommonly attractive people."

That's when Julia became keenly aware that Hank's gaze was on her, instead of on the road. And it remained there until she was forced to speak again.

"Watch out for the goat!" she cried. "You almost hit that goat."

"Not by the hair on its chinny-chin-chin."

"You're still staring at me," she said, "instead of the road. Did I say something wrong?"

"Is this Marl Boatwright you're speaking of?"

"Yes, do you know her? I mean, she's been retired from mission work for centuries."

She stole a glance just in time to see Hank smile, but it was very short-lived.

"More like fifteen years," he said. "Julia, I'd like to think that I have limits, thresholds of behavior that I won't cross no matter what, and gossiping is one of them. I've seen the harm that gossip has done—is doing—to my own life, but in your case I am going to ask your permission to make an exception. I don't want you walking into a lion's den without being warned; you might step on its tail."

Julia may have been sexually naive, but she was quite an accomplished gossiper. *Everything* was grist for her gossip mill, which had been spinning like a hamster's wheel all through college. Granted, gossiping was not the Christian thing to do, but her friends had consoled one another with the thought that they were only young once, and that they were guaranteed to grow out of this phase (hadn't their parents?). Besides, they were saved; wasn't this all that mattered? After all, gossiping—if the stories that you passed around were true—was such a small sin that it didn't even appear on the list of the "big ten."

"You should definitely tell me," Julia said to Hank. "It is much better that I find out from you than from a complete stranger."

Hank nodded; oh sweet, sweet Hank. Did he not remember that the two of them had only met less than an hour ago?

He exhaled sharply before getting right down to business. "Marl Boatwright got *too* chummy with a native," he said.

Then Julia inhaled sharply. "Oh my gracious! I can't believe that."

"You better believe it," Hank said, "because every word of it is true. In the beginning, Marl was surprisingly discreet about it—they both were. In fact, the affair was ended, and it might never have come to light, except that she thought she was pregnant. So she arranged a trip to Luluabourg, the provincial capital, and had a test done at a Belgian hospital. The results were negative, but they were also leaked by the doctor, who happened to know our mission doctor. And there you have it, the only sin greater than murder in the eyes of the Mission Board: adultery with a native."

"And you don't believe that's wrong?"

"Forgive me, Miss Julia, but what I believe is none of your business, is it?"

Maybe so, but he didn't have to be so rude about it, thought Julia. As a consequence they rode in silence for the rest of the way. Therefore, she was quite relieved when they pulled off the main road and onto a wretched side lane. Soon after that Hank stopped to unlock a padlock that gave access to the world's shortest runway, bar none. If it was any comfort—which it was not—the plane in which Julia was to fly was also of Lilliputian proportions.

"I fueled her up last night," said Hank, "and the flight plan has already been radioed in to the tower at the main airport. That means we can leave at any time"—he glanced at his watch—"within the next six minutes."

Although Julia was still too annoyed at him to laugh at such foolishness, she did at least try hard not to be a stick in the mud. "Shouldn't we hang around until we see the whites of the pilot's eyes?"

"You already have," he said, laughing.

"I beg your pardon?"

"*Oui, mademoiselle,*" he said. "As luck would have it, I am not just your chauffeur, but your own personal pilot as well."

"*You?* A pilot?"

"Ah, now that hurts. What's the matter, don't I look the part? *S'il vous plaît, mademoiselle,* do not allow the lack of a proper uniform to put you off; no bush pilot worth his salt wears a uniform. Then again, I'm not even a proper bush pilot. I'm just a friend sitting in for a friend. The regular pilot assigned to this flight is Carl Naysinger, who happens to be suffering from another bout of malaria."

"Oh." Julia dreaded getting malaria; she knew that sooner or later it was inevitable. The fevers, the chills, the malaise—as a single person, who would be there to nurse her back to health? In the "old days," the Mission Board allowed only married couples to serve for just that reason.

Could it be that Julia Newton had gotten ahead of herself? Had she checked with God first before setting out on her adventure? *Really* checked? Because if she had, she might not be referring to it as an adventure, but as a "calling."

"Dear Lord," she prayed, "I'm forever getting myself in over my head and then relying on you to come to the rescue. This time I think I've jumped off the deep end. I might even have hit my head. In fact, I might have hit my head first, judging by what I've done. All I can say is help!"

"Miss Julia, are you all right?"

"Quite. Why do you ask?"

"You've been mumbling to yourself."

"I was *praying.*"

"Hey, I'm really not that bad of a pilot," Hank said, sounding hurt, but he grinned good-naturedly.

It was practically impossible to carry on a conversation when seated up front in a single-engine Cessna, and it was a totally impossible feat to pull off if one wished to simultaneously appear cool and urbane. Given that shouted witticisms rarely hit their mark and that Julia's verbal aim was poor, even under optimal circumstances, she decided that her best strategy was to keep her lips zipped for a change. Okay, so make that a first.

It was a wise choice, because it freed her up to enjoy the scenery. That very night, if she could, she was going to describe it all in a letter home.

Imagine, if you will, looking down upon millions of deep green broccoli heads, all facing dome side up. Each broccoli head represents the emergent crown of a massive rain forest tree. Here and there one catches glimpses of long strips of silver Christmas tree tinsel; these are streams. Sometimes the streams turn into frothing rivers of cola, rich with tannin, while others, no less swift, are the color of sun-dried bricks.

More than anything Julia wished to share this sight with someone to whom she was close. Jeepers creepers, she'd even be willing to share the moment with her little brother, Willard, who was seventeen and a know-it-all if there ever was one. In exchange, she'd have to listen to him spout off the scientific names of trees and geological formations and all that, but that would be okay. Outside of being boring as all heck and a bit stuck on himself, Willard really was an all right guy.

At least Julia had *Willard's* number, having known him since birth. Hank, on the other hand, was a total enigma. He seemed to know Africa quite well, but why shouldn't he? He was born here, after all! However, he did not know the first thing about women. Because if he did understand women, then he would have picked up on Julia's interest in him, which had begun the moment that they'd met. It was an interest that Julia could not squelch, no matter how hard she tried.

Even when Julia closed her eyes and tried to relive the day that she received a D as a semester grade for geology in college, or when she broke her metatarsal skiing and couldn't dance at her senior prom in high school, Hank insisted on entering the picture.

It was he who issued her the near-failing grade, and it was Hank's arms that she had envisioned wrapped around her as they swayed at the perimeter of the dance floor.

Of course these images were merely flickers of her imagination, the kind of experience an honest person might admit to having a zillion times a day. She didn't dwell on them, so they didn't count, inasmuch as a temptation didn't count if one didn't act on it. Still, it was irritating that these thoughts of Hank should intrude unbidden into her sphere of thinking.

It was precisely because of this that Julia never prayed with her eyes closed. Her entire life she'd been instructed, along with others in the room, to "bow your heads and close your eyes for a word of prayer." She'd been told this was to minimize distraction for the faithful. For her, however, it was tantamount to lowering a pair of movie screens upon which her very active brain (or was it the Devil, with a capital D?) would project unimaginable, and undoubtedly very sinful, images. Sometimes the images involved the minister himself—and in very compromising situations.

One thing for sure, you didn't want to waste any time praying with your eyes closed when you could be looking at Congo cloud formations. They were God's handiwork, and so totally awesome that just looking at them was the same as praying. In Africa, clouds pile up in the sky miles high in preparation for the afternoon thunderstorms. Julia mused that if one might climb the clouds, just as one climbs mountains, then it might be possible to climb right into the lap of God and gaze into his face. Surely these were the sort of clouds that the Lord would ride on when he returned someday in all his glory. One of those anemic clouds typical of Ohio would simply not be up for the job.

At any rate, there she was, captivated by the virgin landscape below her, enthralled by the sky all around her, and feeling physically pulled like a magnet to look at the man sitting next to her. All that changed in a flash when their tiny plane dropped from the sky, like a fish that had slipped free from an eagle's talons.

Julia had heard that old saw about having one's life pass before one's eyes when faced with death, but she later remembered having two thoughts, neither of which were connected to her past. One was whether or not her body would ever be found. Would it perhaps be eaten by animals? The other thought was whether she would be able to recognize her grandmother when she stepped into heaven. Or vice versa. After all, wouldn't they both be inhabiting new bodies?

Strange as it might seem, she was not afraid that she would feel pain when she actually crashed into the broccoli-top trees, which were fast becoming enormous. (By this point she could see black-and-white monkeys leaping about in the tree that would be her final resting place.) She'd been brought up to believe that the Lord instantly erased all memory of death so that one essentially felt nothing upon passing. This was his special gift to his martyrs throughout the centuries, like those Christians who'd been fed to the lions in the Roman coliseums.

Mercifully, Julia didn't recall screaming. With her heart squishing the air out of her lungs, it wouldn't have been much of a sound anyway. But then, just as surely as they'd plunged, the plane began to climb, just a whole lot slower. The engine caught and sputtered a bit at first, as if it couldn't quite believe its good fortune, and then gradually the rain forest disappeared from sight until all Julia could see were the clouds.

"Holy crap!" Hank said. "Now *that* was a close one."

Wow, Julia thought, *talk about a jolt to the senses!* They had just survived *something* awful together, hadn't they? In fact, it seemed like they'd almost crashed. But instead of saying "Hallelujah!" or breaking into prayer or song, the pilot, who was also supposed to be a missionary, had instead—sworn! Holy crap, indeed.

"What happened back there?" Julia asked between gasps.

"Downdraft," Hank said. "Those beautiful clouds can be lethal. Did you at least enjoy the ride?"

"Not one bit."

"Good," Hank said with a smile. "We like our new missionaries to start out sane and then have Congo drive them slowly crazy. If you were already loco upon arrival, you'd have nowhere else to go but right back to the States on the next banana boat."

THREE

It was just before dusk when the plane touched down in the town of Belle Vue. The *town*—ha! Forget all your preconceptions of what a town is or ought to be, because the Belgian Congo had its own peculiar definitions. A place was a town only if it had white residents; no matter how large an all-black settlement, it was always called a village. But give it a handful of whites and it was sure to pop up on the map like mushrooms after the first September rain.

Belle Vue, like all Congo towns was strictly segregated, so that even the whitest mulattoes had to live on the black side of town *unless* they were household employees. That is because each white residence had a servants' quarters behind the main house where a trusted servant, such as a watchman or a nanny, might stay, although most Belgians preferred to have their staff reside across the river in the workers' village.

The white population of Belle Vue, perhaps one hundred twenty souls, resided in hilltop villas on one side of the Kasai River, and on the other side, tucked out of sight behind the hilltops, lived the five hundred plus natives in their one-room concrete boxes.

"Do not feel bad for the African," the Belgians joked. "Who in Europe has a house with diamonds embedded in the walls?"

This feeble attempt to assuage their collective colonial conscience was based on the fact that there were indeed diamonds
embedded in the walls of the workers' houses. The sole reason
Belle Vue existed is that long ago Belgian prospectors had discovered that the land drained by the Kasai River and its tributaries
contained vast quantities of alluvial diamonds.

Unlike in South Africa, where the diamonds had to be dug
up from the earth's core in dangerous mines, the Kasai diamonds
were there for the picking. They were just another pretty stone
mixed in with the gravel, so that when the gravel was mixed
with cement to make concrete block—*voilà*, diamonds in the
walls!

The commercial removal, sorting, and exporting of diamonds
was all controlled by a single company: the Consortium. Virtually
everything in the town of Belle Vue, whether it had to do with
Africans or whites, was controlled by this company and its rules.
Even the airport was owned by the Consortium.

Although it was easy to arrive at Belle Vue, apparently it was
not so easy to leave. To do so, one had to report to the Office of
Colonial Departures. Someone of the appropriate gender would
then conduct a complete and very thorough cavity search. At
the same time, the contents of one's luggage would also undergo
extensive examination. For example, one's toothpaste would be
squeezed out of the tube and smeared around on a flat, nonporous
surface. The seams of one's clothing could be run through the
thumb and forefinger of an experienced agent, looking for small
diamonds squirreled away in the hem.

This knowledge was all part of the education Julia had received from Aunt Marl, along with her Tshiluba language lessons.
It was referred to as orientation, although Julia's boyfriend at the
time called it "indoctrination." The more that Julia learned about
the Belgian Congo, the more that she was hooked—an analogy
that she hated but that, again, her boyfriend used. Needless to say,
they broke up.

At any rate, no amount of education could have prepared her for the real experience of Africa: the fecund smell of the tropics as she stepped out of that small plane, jackals loping across the road the way into Belle Vue, and the roar of the falls as she and Hank crossed over to the black sector. Her jaw dropped some more when she saw the Missionary Rest House, which was to be her stop for the night. This hostelry clung to the side of a cliff, above the falls, as audaciously as a swallow's nest. The setting was so gorgeous that King Baudouin and Queen Fabiola had paid the Rest House a brief visit on their recent sweep through the colony.

It has been said that night falls on central Africa like a heavy velvet stage curtain with a broken pulley. One moment a person might be luxuriating in the gloaming; in the next moment, the same person could be stumbling about in the inky blackness of a starless sky. But if the stars were out, then a person's mind would reel from the brightness, for it is actually possible to read outside without additional light when the moon is full. Or so it was said.

At any rate, there was nothing to be seen at the Missionary Rest House, just much to be heard. The sound was the roar of the falls, accompanied by the pounding of Julia's heart. The hostess, Miss Amanda Brown, had left a detailed note stating that she had elected to cross over to the Belgian side of the river to view a romantic film at the Club, and then on to spend the night with her Belgian husband in his house.

Oh, the scandal of it all! Not that Julia would pass on a word of what was in the note, mind you. But *someone* would, and when the news got back to the Mission Board in the United States, Amanda Brown from Rock Hill, South Carolina, would surely be fired. Never mind that Amanda Brown and *Capitain* Pierre Jardin, of the Belle Vue police force, were legally married under Belgian law; they were *not* married in the eyes of God.

It was a shame, really, because the scandal wasn't even taking place in Belle Vue. Here the white population was composed pre-dominately of Roman Catholics, and Roman Catholics were sophisticated people like Brigitte Bardot and Grace Kelly. It was the folks back home, in the buckle of the Bible Belt, who didn't recognize Amanda's civil union. To folks like Brother Zug, she was simply carrying on an adulterous affair out in the open. A thing like that was sure to give Protestants a bad name.

To be fair, Amanda did leave a long list of instructions for Julia, and a huge pile of clean fluffy towels, so that the newcomer did feel very much cared for. That night she found that reading the Book of Leviticus—just a few verses even—put her quickly to sleep. Before Julia knew it, she awakened to the restorative smells of bacon and freshly brewed coffee. As her wonderful new day gradually came into focus she became increasingly— then fearfully—aware that something was standing at the end of her bed.

"What are you?" she gasped.

"I am not a *what*?" the creature said. "I am a woman."

Julia leaned forward, rubbing her eyes as she did so. Indeed, it was a woman, an African woman in traditional garb. But in her defense, this native was no taller than a six-year-old American, and as twisted as a Pennsylvania Dutch pretzel. Besides which, she had a small black monkey tied to her back.

"Then *who* are you, and what are you doing here?" Julia asked in amazement. They had been speaking in English, but now seamlessly switched to Tshiluba. It was the first time that Julia had ever spoken that language to anyone besides her teacher, Aunt Marl. She felt a rush of adrenaline. It was if she'd been learning to ride a bicycle with training wheels, and now magically they'd disappeared, but she was still managing to balance.

"My name is Cripple and I am the head housekeeper," said the woman. "Who are you, *Mamu*?"

Mamu! Oh the thrill of that word!

"I do not have a name in Tshiluba at this time," Julia said.

"Then what is your Christian name?" the strange little woman asked.

Thank heavens that Aunt Marl had explained some of the native customs to Julia, like the one about them not having any surnames. However, if they were baptized, she said, as many of the natives were, it was the custom to choose a name from the Bible as a second name. This was called one's "Christian" name, even if it was taken from the Old Testament.

"Uh—I do not have a Christian name," Julia was forced to confess.

The woman named Cripple twisted this way and that as she adjusted the monkey tied to her back. "*Mamu,* am I to hope, then, that you are a heathen like me?"

"*What?*" Julia cried in alarm. This was certainly not the way she had dreamed that her first contact with an actual African would take place.

"A Christian must have a Christian name, *Mamu.* It is not I who has made this rule, but you missionaries. One must be born again, you say to us—although such a thing is not possible—and then take on a new name, leaving our heathen names behind. Therefore, if you do not yet have a Christian name, you must still have a heathen name, and thus you are a heathen—like me." The little woman smiled in welcome.

"But I am not a heathen!"

"Most certainly you are, *Mamu.* Believe me, this is a matter for rejoicing, is it not? Tell me your heathen name so that I might address you properly from now on."

"I most certainly will *not* tell you my heathen name! My heathen name is my business—oh, never mind! I wish to be called by a Tshiluba name just like every other *mamu.* Tell me, Cripple, which Tshiluba name should I choose?"

"*Tch.* One does not choose their own name, *Mamu.* A name is a gift given by others, and always it is an observation of some characteristic, or behavior, of the recipient. Is my English good?"

"Yes, you speak it excellently. Now please, if you will, select something for me. I am so, so, anxious to start my adventure here in Africa!"

"Very well, I shall call you *Mamu Mukashiana*."

"Is that a good name, Cripple?"

"*Eh*, you are deserving of this name, *Mamu*. Come now, let us be going."

"Us? I am headed to Mushihi Station to run a girls' school. Where are you going?"

"I am going with you, Mamu Mukashiana. I am to be your housekeeper."

"Praise the Lord," Julia cried, and meant it. What were the odds of having a housekeeper who was fluent in English virtually fall into one's lap?

Oh what a joy-filled morning it promised to be for Julia. First, she raced to the window where she spent a few minutes taking in the majesty of the falls. Then, accompanied by a bit of groaning, she managed to haul her suitcase up onto the bed so that she could dress carefully for the trip. What fun it was to pull out a white cotton skirt and blouse, to prevent overheating in the broiling sun, a white cork helmet, white anklets, and white oxford shoes.

It wasn't until the new missionary was through dressing that Julia sensed that she was being watched. She jumped, dropping her heavy train case on her left foot.

"What are you still doing here? Have you been here the entire time? Watching me dress?"

"Trust me, *Mamu*, I have seen this white flesh before. *E*, it is indeed most unfortunate, but we too have albinos, *Mamu*."

"I am not an albino, Cripple. I am just a regular white person."

"*E*, perhaps." Cripple cocked her little head cheekily, as if she still hadn't made up her mind. "Tell me, *Mamu*, why is it that Protestant white women grow no hair under the arm, but the same cannot be said of Catholic white women?"

"Is this so? I hadn't noticed—oh, you must have noticed the difference between American and European women. Cripple, I do not know the reason, only that modern young American women such as myself, and apparently Mrs. Jardin, shave under the arm."

The native woman nodded. "You are both very foolish, *Mamu*. This place"—she tried in vain to smell her own armpits—"is where the gods have placed the woman scent. Clearly, in your case, you have offended the gods by removing the bushes upon which they spread the scent for attracting a mate."

Julia's cheeks burned, whether from anger or embarrassment, she wasn't sure. How dare this village woman, who was a bit on the ripe side and whom she had just met minutes ago, be giving her grooming advice. The very idea was ridiculous and insulting. Now that was an unexpected shower on her parade.

She set the rest of her things down. "*Shala bimpe* (stay well)," said Julia, and pushed past Cripple and out into the hallway.

"*Mamu*, remember to eat your porridge," Cripple called after her.

"I don't have to do anything," Julia shouted. "I'm free, white, and twenty-one."

She had barely gone the length of a tether ball cord when it hit her just how awful those words could sound to someone who wasn't all those things. Had Cripple even heard her? After all, she'd been practically running away from the maid. And even if Cripple had heard that unfortunate phrase, it was strictly an American idiom, and not something an African housekeeper was likely to have picked up on the job.

Then precisely because she *was* free, white, and twenty-one, with a head as strong as a bull elephant's, Julia continued to walk briskly through the Missionary Rest House, out the front door, then around the building to where she found a flagstone path that led to a terrace overlooking the falls. So these were the famous Belle Vue Falls as seen by morning's first light, when supposedly there were rainbows dancing in the mists that shrouded the fern-covered rocks. They were said to evoke awe in the hearts of every-one who saw them.

I'm sorry—but this is not that big a deal, really, Julia said to herself. She was only being honest; her parents had taken her to see Niagara Falls three times as a little girl. She'd seen them once in the dead of winter when the falls were a virtual fairyland of ice formations, and twice in the summer when the power and majesty of the great falls actually brought her to tears. Niagara Falls, as seen from the Canadian side, made this falls look like a mere trickle of water by comparison.

Then Julia stopped seeing the Belle Vue Falls altogether, for she'd focused on the figure of a small child sitting hunched forward on the terrace wall, her elbows on her knees. It was a white girl, of all things! Could she be a Belgian neighbor? Julia approached from the side so as to catch the girl's attention. Heaven help her if on this, her first *real* day in the Congo, she was responsible for some waif toppling off a wall and into the catchment basin of some second-rate waterfall.

"*Bon jour,*" Julia called just loud enough to be heard over the din of the water. "*Bon jour.*"

Praise the Lord, the child turned, swinging her legs back over the wall! Julia sprinted the rest of the way. It wasn't that far, and all downhill, but nonetheless when she got there Julia was panting like a husky in July. Meanwhile the child gazed at her with unbridled curiosity.

"You're wearing everything white," the imp said just as Julia was about to speak.

"Indeed I am. And what of it?"

"Because you'll be as black as sin when you get where we're going."

"Wait a second," Julia said. "You're not Belgian, are you?"

"No, of course not," the child said. "I'm African."

"Don't be silly; you're white."

"Yes, but I am a white African. I was born here, just like my papa. This makes me the second generation of my family to be born here, and the third generation to live in Africa."

"I see," Julia said. "What is your name?"

"My heathen name, my African name, or my Christian name?"

Julia couldn't help smiling. "So many choices? Well, first things first, I guess; let's start with your heathen name."

"It's Clementine—but just so you know, I'm nobody's darling."

"Hmm. Well, there is an orange called a clementine. Anyway, I think it's a beautiful name."

"You do?"

"Yes, I do."

"I think your name is beautiful too," Clementine said.

"*My* name? How do you know my name?"

"Because you're Auntie Julia, the new missionary coming to join us at Mushihi Station."

Auntie Julia! She'd arrived in Africa just two days prior, and already she was being addressed by the missionary honorific "aunt," which was the right of every Protestant white woman, just as "uncle" was for the men. The mission field was one big family, and finally to be included among that number thrilled Julia to the bone.

"Ah, so you're *that* little girl," Julia said at last.

"Yes, ma'am, that's me. I'm the Great Distraction. That's what Reverend and Mrs. Doyer call me on account of I'm wicked, deceitful, and an all-around distraction to them from doing the Lord's work. It's quite possible that I might be guilty of adultery as well, although I am not quite sure. I know that Auntie Verna certainly thinks so."

What an odd little creature Clementine Hayes was. Big brown eyes, dark brown hair that hung in tangles almost to her waist, skin as golden brown as buttered toast. A waif—that's the word that had first come to mind, and it was a good one. She was a waif who appeared to be drowning in a sea of khaki fabric. The sleeves of her shirt extended beyond her fingertips, and her skirt, which had been cinched at her child's waist with a man's belt, draped over the tops of her shoes. Clearly, these had been her mother's clothes.

Clementine must have read Julia's mind. "My mama is dead, you know," she said. "So she doesn't mind it when I borrow her clothes. Papa doesn't care either; it's only other adults who seem to care." She paused and fixed the large brown eyes on Julia. "Do *you* care, Auntie Julia?"

"Not in the least—although I wouldn't want you to trip on your skirt and go tumbling off the terrace."

"At least I wouldn't be the first to fall," Clementine said. "The last guy was eaten by a crocodile. I bet you it's that very same one that's there now."

"*What?*" Julia flushed. "Good one," she said. "Joke's on me, the newcomer. Just wait until I get settled in on the mission station and take you snipe hunting. You ever been snipe hunting?"

Clementine stood and pointed at something below them, but her eyes were on Julia. "There! Down there you'll see it, if you'll only look. Even an American like you can see it."

Julia peered cautiously over the edge. She hated being made a fool of, especially by children.

"Oh my God," she blurted involuntarily. "I mean, what *is* that?"

"Like I said—it's a croc. Papa says it's a twenty-footer. The Belgians call him Cyclops, on account of he only has one eye, but us missionaries call him—well, we just call him the croc."

"Huh. That's kind of sad."

"Don't worry, Auntie Julia, I don't think it hurts him anymore. Where his eye used to be. I can't remember him ever having two. Papa said it's against the law now to shoot him because it's impossible to get down there anymore, and that old croc has a job to do, which is eating the bodies of any Africans who might find themselves swept over the falls. Europeans too, but it doesn't happen much to them."

"I see. But I meant it was kind of sad that we missionaries don't have a name for such a magnificent beast."

Clementine cocked her head. Her dark eyes glittered.

"Mama was eaten by a crocodile," she said, without displaying the faintest trace of emotion.

"Are you serious?" Julia asked gently. On the face of it, her question was stupid and insensitive, but the girl's statement had been so bizarre, how else should Julia have responded?

"Oh, I'm quite positive," the child said. "You can ask Papa if you don't believe me. He shot the crocodile that ate Mama, and when he butchered it, he found her Timex watch in its tummy. He also found two iron bracelets that were from Bashilele women, and also one from a Mujembe woman."

"You don't say!" Julia said, although who was *she* kidding? Only cowards and truly kind people trot out that hackneyed phrase, and it was always a stand-in for disbelief.

Clementine's gaze didn't waver. "Of course, now I suppose you're going to ask him if I'm lying. Go ahead, see if I care, 'cause I'm telling the truth—I swear I am."

Julia had a younger brother; she could stare anyone down.

Clementine sighed dramatically. "No fair, I'm only ten years old." She paused. "Okay, I'm *almost* ten—which *is* double dig-its—so being *almost ten* has to count for something. And so maybe the crocodile didn't eat *all* of Mama, but it *did* eat her arm. And she did die from it, which, to hear Auntie Verna tell it, is all my fault."

"*What?* Verna Doyer—I mean, Mrs. Doyer actually said that?" Julia had heard rumors of discord at Mushihi Station, but this was shocking. Well, that is, if it was even true. It was difficult for even bright children to separate fact from fiction. And hadn't Julia learned in her Psychology 101 class that bereaved children often blamed themselves for the death of a parent?

But little Clementine stared at her with all the conviction of a martyr, never once blinking. "Yes, ma'am, Auntie Julia."

"'Auntie Julia' is sufficient. Go on."

"I heard her telling all her troubles to God during one of the weekly prayer meetings. I'm excused, you see, on account of I'm too young to hold still that long, and I'm supposed to be in bed. Auntie Julia, sometimes the grown-ups pray about boring stuff like getting more school supplies, or debts and fund-raising, but other times their voices get sharp—like knives—or cold—like ice—and that's when I creep close to hear what they're saying."

"Why, you little imp!"

"Does that mean you want me to stop?"

"Heavens, no," Julia said after only the slightest hesitation. Perhaps it was wrong to encourage gossip from a disobedient child, but on the other hand, it was readily apparent that the little girl very much needed a sympathetic ear.

"Well, you see, it was like this. One night, during all that praying—which can go on for hours and hours and such—I hear a woman crying, and I think that's Mama, but of course it wasn't, on account of Mama was dead and eaten by that crocodile. Anyway, I nearly fell back on my behind when I saw that crying woman was Auntie Verna, and that Papa was crying too. And Auntie Verna is saying things like 'I might have saved her if that child hadn't been so distracting.' And Papa was saying things like 'You can't blame a little girl for caring about her mother.' Then Auntie Verna says 'I might have saved her anyway if she hadn't been in the family way.'

"Ooh, Auntie Julia, you oughta have seen Papa's face. We're peace-a-fists, we don't believe in violence. But Papa was so mad that I thought he might actually give Auntie Verna the fist part. Then Reverend Doyer—he doesn't like to be called Uncle Arvin—jumped to his feet and said that the prayer meeting was over."

Just like that, Clementine's story was over as well. Julia counted to ten—*rapidly*.

"Then what happened?"

Clementine pursed her lips, two pink rose petals. "Before they left, Papa said that he couldn't help blaming Aunt Verna a little a bit if she was gonna have that attitude. But you know something, Auntie Julia?"

"What?"

"Reverend Doyer didn't cry or nothing."

"Cry or *anything*."

"Yeah. The next time he saw me, he grabbed me by the arm and looked me straight in the eye, like he was trying to dispose me of a demon. 'You are the great distraction to your father's work,' he said. 'You are why missionaries shouldn't have children.'"

"Oh, dear, dear Clementine," Julia said as she practically lunged for the child with open arms. After all, that was by far the saddest story the recent college graduate had ever heard.

Yet, with the agility of a trained boxer, Clementine feinted this way and that, managing to avoid all physical contact. "I *am* the Great Distraction," she said. "You are well advised to stay clear of me. Did you not hear a word I said?"

Julia fought to suppress a smile. At the same time, she was as mad as hops. She'd been played for a fool by a very disturbed little girl—very disturbed indeed. Julia was framing a rebuke in her mind when the child suddenly lost interest in her game and craned her neck to get a closer look at the new missionary's face.

"Auntie Julia, how old are you?"

Julia winced. "One doesn't ask a lady her age."

"Why not?"

"Because it's not polite."

"Mama didn't mind when I asked her," the child said. "And I didn't mind when you asked me. Aren't I a lady?"

"I didn't ask you; you volunteered," Julia said, but when she saw the child's expression—such innocence, such vulnerability—she felt awful. "I'm sorry, Clementine. I didn't mean to sound so harsh."

"I forgive you, Auntie Julia."

Oh my gracious, thought Julia, *what a cheeky thing to say*. Instead of speaking her thought, she smiled. "Thank you, dear. And yes, you are quite the young lady; you certainly don't seem like any child I have ever met. What grade are you in?"

"I don't go to school," Clementine said, "because I'm wicked and a misfit."

"*What* did you say?" Julia was sure she hadn't heard right.

"I'm wicked and a misfit; that's why I don't go to school."

"Where did you hear that? Who said that to you?"

"I'm not supposed to gossip," said Clementine.

"Fair enough. But isn't there a boarding school for missionary children?"

"Yes, but they won't take me on account of I'm wicked. Incorrigible, is what they tell Papa, but that's just on account of they're afraid of him. Besides, the housefather beats the students with an old fan belt taken from a diesel engine. He beats them until they are covered with black and purple stripes. The girls too. Papa would never allow that to happen to me. My flesh is too valuable, he said."

Julia gasped softly, a sound not even heard above the roar of the falls. Clementine, it seemed, needed no encouragement to continue on with her tale.

"You are not allowed to leave your bunk at night for any reason—not even to go to the bathroom. But if you wet your bed, then Uncle Derrick will thrash you with the fan belt and put your mattress in the schoolyard so that everyone can make fun of you. Papa would never hit me, and he won't allow anyone else to hit me either."

Julia, who had never even been spanked, was horrified. At the same time, she was trying to take what she heard with a grain of salt until she could have the girl's stories verified, perhaps by her father.

"Are you homeschooled then?" she asked the child.

"Ma'am?"

"Does you father teach you at home?"

"Oh yes, Papa makes sure that I study my two or three pages every day—except for Sunday. Then we study the Bible."

"What do you study the rest of the week?"

"The *Encyclopaedia Britannica*."

Julia had been advised—perhaps warned is really a better word—by the secretary of foreign missions that the child, Clementine Hayes, was something of a prodigy and perhaps deeply disturbed (*wicked* was not in the description). In retrospect, perhaps upon hearing those words, Julia should also have seen red flags pop up in her mind. Any sane person would have turned tail and run. Was it her youth, her infamous inherited stubbornness (from Grandma Jenny on her father's side), or her wanting to get on to the mission field while the colonial sun still shone that compelled her to accept this exceptionally difficult challenge?

Even now, having just met the precocious child, she was torn between feelings of sympathy for her and mounting dread that she had bitten off more than she could chew. Every word that issued from Clementine's mouth seemed preposterous, just more evidence that she was a psychopathic liar. Julia had signed on for a five-year term to serve as a teacher on a remote mission station where there was just Clementine and her father, Reverend Paul Hayes, and the Reverend Arvin Doyer and his wife, Verna, a nurse. She had done it to herself; she had no one to blame but herself.

"Auntie Julia, I know what you're thinking."

There was that thrill again, but this time it was tempered by worry. "What?"

"You're worried about me being wicked. But you're not to worry, you see. I don't need a new mama, and Papa doesn't need a new wife. So, even though you'll be living next door to us, you shouldn't be expecting to see very much of us at all—except for Wednesday-night prayer meetings, and Sunday at church, and then Sunday-night suppers together, and then more prayer. Oh, I forgot chapel every morning."

"My stars," Julia said, "you certainly are a praying brunch of folks."

Oops, in addition to having been born stubborn, Julia had

what her mother termed "a slippery tongue." That explained why so many things had trouble staying put in her mind where they belonged. In her defense, however, it was possible that her slippery tongue could be blamed on all the cod liver oil that her mother had forced her to down as a child.

"Don't get me wrong, Auntie Julia," Clementine said. "Due to my intense wickedness and my excessive immaturity, I'm not the least bit like the grown-ups; my mind wanders. Anyway, that's not what I meant about me being wicked. You see, it's like this; everyone—except for Papa—thinks that I'm a liar on account of I'm so smart. But I'm not a liar, Auntie Julia, I swear I'm not."

"But dear, you claim to study the *Encyclopaedia Britannica* for homework. Isn't that a little far-fetched?"

The little brown waif, weighed down by her mother's khaki shirt, attempted to shrug. "I guess so, but my papa said to always tell the truth. And anyway, it's the student version of the encyclopedia, so it's not like it's all that big of a deal."

Julia wanted to scoop up the child and hug her. That's how anxious she was for an easy fix of this problem of the enigmatic child with the vocabulary—and possibly the mind—of an adult. But surely the little girl lacked the wisdom of an adult, for that came about through accumulated life experiences and lessons learned, and there was simply no substitute for having put in one's time here on earth.

Julia extended her hand. "Come," she said gently, "they want us up on top. The truck will be here any minute, they said."

Clementine regarded her calmly. "Who is 'they,' Auntie Julia?"

"Mrs. Jardin, the really nice American woman in charge of the Missionary Rest House."

"Oh." Clementine slid to her feet and then clapped the white cork helmet back on her head. "Mr. Jardin is really Captain Jardin, the Belgian chief of police. He's a Roman Catholic, which means he's going to hell. Papa says that Aunt Amanda still stands a chance—if she confesses her sin of marrying a Catholic—but she better do it right now. After all, you never know which day is going to be your last. Uncle Arvin and Aunt Verna, on the other hand—well, they never did like Aunt Amanda, so they say that she is doomed with a capital D. What do you think, Auntie Julia?"

"I think that only God can judge us," Julia said.

FOUR

Meanwhile at Mushihi Station, which lay deep in headhunter territory, Nurse Verna Doyer literally popped out of bed. She had always been an annoyingly early riser, and to hear her husband tell it, her engine perpetually idled on high. She could go from zero to fifty in three seconds (fifty miles per hour was as fast as Reverend Doyer believed that anyone should ever drive).

What, one might rightfully ask, was Nurse Verna Doyer in such a ding-dong hurry to do every morning out in the middle of nowhere? After all, she had no little ones to feed, and it wasn't like she cooked her husband Arvin's breakfast, because she never did. (Cooking was the providence of houseboys.) Ah, but Nurse Verna Doyer was a nurse, an RN—practically a doctor by the unwritten laws of the bush—and she was needed, perhaps desperately needed, at the small clinic that the mission station maintained on the north side of the church.

The first thing that Nurse Verna did after landing on her feet was to properly clothe herself in her earthly garments. She did this even before she knelt beside her bed in morning prayer or relieved her full bladder. Only God knew when an African would pound at the door, having been bitten by a snake, or on behalf of a loved one in breech labor. Along with the sunrise came Nurse

Verna Doyer's duties, and she took them seriously. God had called her to be a missionary nurse in the Belgian Congo, then paid her way through nurse's training. She had complete faith in the Lord—just as long as she armed herself in both spiritual and earthly armor.

For her spiritual armor she reread the Book of Ephesians, chapter 6, each morning. Her earthly armor was a bit more involved. First she put on her brassiere (never referred to as a bra!). This contraption had been made by inserting dozens of tongue depressors into hand-stitched pockets along lengths of wide bands of surgical elastic. The end result was a brassiere that made it impossible for a native patient with fumbling hands to grab hold of the breasts of Mamu Snake.

With her breasts secured, Nurse Verna pulled on a pair of clean knee-length cotton underwear into which she had sewn an extra crotch. Nurse Verna firmly believed that suffering for the Lord was a virtue, and feeling virtuous gave her pleasure. Therefore, she did not mind at all her added discipline of wearing a whalebone girdle on even the hottest days. Only God knew for sure what those poor ladies had to suffer through back in biblical times, but it was a lot more yardage than women had to wear in the present day, that much was for sure.

After the girdle, Nurse Verna slipped a heavy wool tunic over her head. She had once been told that wool was a versatile material that served to keep out heat as well as cold, but she was no longer sure of that statement. Perhaps it was the nylon slip that she wore over the tunic that was the culprit, because to be truthful, there were many days on which Nurse Verna felt decidedly hot. However hot she felt, Nurse Verna constantly reminded herself that the fires of hell were even hotter.

All Verna's dresses were simple, homemade affairs in various shades of white, and they lacked buttons. Nurse Verna permitted herself the use of only hooks and eyes for closure. Her hair had never been cut, not once in her fifty-four years. She wore it in a pair of braids that she wound around and around atop her head like a grease-soaked crown.

Verna's legs were protected from the sun, from insect bites, and most of all, from unwanted stares by the length of her skirts and the thick woolen stockings she wore. These were held up by garters attached to her girdle. Her dainty size six feet were shod in sensible white leather tie-shoes with a bit of a heel and with thick soles, both to keep her out of the dirt and to give her some presence.

Nurse Doyer was only five feet two inches tall, but fully armored, which included her white pith helmet, she gave the impression of being a much larger woman.

"Oh Lord," she prayed the morning of Julia's arrival, "give us the strength to face this day. And we just ask that this new woman will not be seduced by the likes of Henry, and that she might actually have some positive influence on that urchin of his who runs amok—the Great Distraction."

By then both the Doyers were dressed and had just finished breakfast. Their habit was to read a few Bible verses aloud, discuss their meaning, and then offer their concerns up in prayer.

"Please, wife," Reverend Arvin Doyer said, "must we always be so hard on the man? He is a recent widower, after all. And as for that so-called urchin, I'll say this, not one of us can speak either the Bushilele, or Tshiluba, language as well as she can. Haven't there been hundreds of times when you've needed her to translate for you at the clinic?"

Preachers and their hyperbole! "Maybe dozens of times—at the most," Nurse Verna said.

Reverend Doyer nodded. "I'm sure you're right."

Nurse Verna stood. "Well? How do I look then?"

"You don't have a spot of jam on you! I'd say you look like a professional nurse."

"Which I *am*, Arvin. What I mean is, do I look like the perfect example of a Christian? In other words, someone whom this Miss Julia Newton would choose to emulate?"

"Indeed, wife, you do."

"Then I shall delegate my work today so that this frock remains immaculate."

Immediately Reverend Arvin Doyer began to shout his prayers up to heaven. "Heavenly Father," he said, "only Thou knowest what lies in store for my wife, and Thou knowest as well that she has rather limited patience. If it be Thy will, guard her tongue from speaking words that could wound. In Jesus's most holy name, amen."

Nurse Verna Doyer did not appreciate having her limited patience referenced to as if it were a fact, although indeed that was the case. What's more, she quite hated the mention of her tongue.

As it happened, no sooner had Reverend Doyer said the word *tongue* than out came Nurse Doyer's, flickering like a snake's, through the gap between her teeth. It was a habit that annoyed her husband to no end and made the natives think that the spirit of a snake lived within her. *Mamu Nyoka,* they called her—Mother Snake.

Yet the Bashilele people, whom she now served, and who ritually knocked out their two front teeth, were rather flattered by this gap, believing that its existence was somehow in appreciation of their culture. There you had it; everything that Nurse Verna did was to the glory of God, even if some of the things that she did seemed to get under the skin of Reverend Arvin Doyer.

So, having passed her husband's visual inspection, off Nurse Verna Doyer strode to face what was undoubtedly a very full clinic. Yet, despite her haste, it took a minute or two for Nurse Verna to escape her husband's loud prayer. She knew that Arvin didn't believe that the Lord had a hearing problem (except when it came to hearing the prayers of Catholics, Mohammedans, Hindus, and Jews). She believed that the prayer somehow involved her, but she had not a minute to spare.

The clinic, with its sick and dying, demanded every ounce of strength that she could muster. From first light to last light, she toiled there, as well as burning the "midnight oil" if she had the kerosene and a translator (Clementine's father would not let her stay up past nine).

Today, as every day, she followed the dirt path that led from her screened back verandah, past the carpenter shop where Henry worked, and on to the thatched roof church, and just around that, to the three-room clinic. Now that the rains had come, each step sent up waves of grasshoppers that settled, only to rise again in yet greater numbers. Up ahead, perhaps as close as thirty feet, a pair of enormous pied crows landed. They were monstrous birds, easily two feet tall, resembling hunched-back waiters in black tuxedos with white cummerbunds. Nurse Verna started to smile and even slowed her pace, before she remembered that she was on God's mission and had not been led to Africa for the sights.

She had only just rounded the church when it was instantly apparent that she had been right not to dawdle. The line today was almost as long as usual, stretching from the north clinic door, wrapping once around the building, and then halfway out to the supply road. Praise God there would be some kerosene arriving along with Miss Julia Newton.

Many Boils, her assistant, was standing by the clinic door in his starched white apron. Truly this man had been sent from God to give her a hand. A member of the Baluba tribe (known for their intelligence), Many Boils combined compassion and arrogance in just the right proportions needed to perform triage when so many people were in need.

"Life to you," Nurse Verna said as she unlocked the heavy wooden door.

"*Eyo,* life to you as well, Mamu Snake," Many Boils responded.

"What is our first case?" she called, as she threw open the heavy wooden shutters.

"*Mamu,* it is a woman who has been beaten by her husband."

"Many Boils, all these people waiting in line, and yet you bring me a beating? *Yai,* do not waste my time!"

"Mamu Snake, this woman has a broken arm, a broken jaw, and the bleeding thereof will not stop."

Nurse Verna leaped to the door. "Do not just stand there, Many Boils. Where is she?"

"She is under the mango tree, *Mamu*, with those Bashilele warriors."

"Oh, Heavenly Father," Nurse Verna prayed aloud in the Tshiluba language, "please do not let it be so. Not again."

"But, Mamu Snake, it is so; she is the seventh wife of Chief Eagle. It is she upon whom you had to perform the miracle of stitches the last time, as if her skin were but a torn blanket. It would appear that since she cannot keep her mouth shut, the chief has chosen to keep it shut for her."

Many Boils appeared to eye Nurse Verna warily as he spoke. No doubt he thought that he might have gone too far. This was often the case.

"You are right to think those thoughts," Nurse Verna said. "The mind of a man is superior to that of a woman; therefore, a husband must be master over his wife. Likewise, science has proven that the white brain is superior to the black brain, therefore the Belgian must be master over the Congolese. These things are all part of God's plan for us."

"*Tch*," said Many Boils, for he did not agree with the last part.

"*Tch*," said Verna, for although she believed that every word in her bible was true, even the ones that came out of St. Paul's mouth, she couldn't quite bring herself to concede that Arvin had the better mind.

After all, she was a graduate from a state school of nursing, holding a bachelor of science degree with a basic understanding of chemistry and mathematics. Arvin, on the other hand, had never *actually* graduated from seminary, but he *had* attended for a semester before "dropping out" to make room for somebody who had heard God calling in a louder and clearer voice. Then somehow, when the Mission Board found that there was a special need for a doctor/preacher team at a new mission station—well lo and behold, Arvin found himself suddenly ordained. The Lord did indeed work in mysterious ways.

"*Mamu!*"

Nurse Verna jumped in irritation. If there was one thing she didn't like, that was being barked at by a man.

"What is it, Many Boils? Can you not see that I am busy?"

"Were you praying, *Mamu*?"

"Grab the basin and the sack that contains the rags, and follow me," she said, and then did what she was best at, which was to stride.

When the warriors saw her approaching in such an aggressive manner, they fled. This is what they'd done the last time as well, for a woman with such courage was deranged. Possessed. A warrior might face a lion or a leopard—or even another man—and feel only the thrill of the hunt, but even a brave man fled in the face of a fool. Mamu Snake had lived in the Congo long enough to know that this was the case, and she used this bit of knowledge as if it were a medicine. The Lord, she was quite certain, had no problem with this.

But when she drew close to Chief Eagle's seventh wife, a woman grown exceptionally old before her time, Nurse Verna let out an involuntary yelp of dismay. Not only was the Mushilele woman's jaw broken, it had been pushed so far to the left side of her face that her tongue had been severed in the process. No wonder the bleeding would not stop. Even more alarming was the fact that the poor woman was totally unresponsive to touch. Perhaps she had fainted—although quite possibly she had suffered a severe concussion and had lost consciousness due to the buildup of fluids around her brain. To complicate matters, the woman was burning up. But whether her fever was a result of her injuries or from malaria, it was impossible to diagnose at this stage of treatment.

"Get me the drill," Nurse Verna said to Many Boils, when

he finally arrived with the basin and rags. (Many Boils believed that it demeaned him to be seen hurrying on orders of a white woman.)

"*Mamu,* do you wish the hand drill or the electric drill?"

"Many Boils, this is no time for games. Bring me the *hand* drill—please."

While he was gone, Nurse Verna cleaned the woman's skull. She used a rag cut from one of Arvin's old shirts, one that he had eaten his way out of, and dipped it in rubbing alcohol. Drilling into patients' skulls was nothing new: the Incas and the ancient Egyptians both did it. It was, however, a last-resort remedy for Nurse Verna, because her patients often died.

Killing the wife of a headhunter chief could have serious consequences, but what choice did Nurse Verna have? There wasn't a doctor within a hundred kilometers at the moment, and those kilometers were rutted dirt roads. But even such a trip was impossible at the moment, because Mushihi Station's only vehicle was in use, with Henry gone off to fetch his wife's replacement.

When Nurse Verna looked up and saw Many Boils virtually sauntering back with the carpenter's hand drill, she was justifiably furious. "Many Boils, light a fire under you," she yelled.

"*Mamu,*" said Many Boils, "*wa kufende mene, mene.*" You have grievously offended me.

The line of waiting people and those who had come to support them (sometimes literally) took great delight in Many Boils's humiliation. For what else had they to do but stand and endure their own pain? Behold, is not diversion some of the very best medicine? Knowing that it was, the people laughed and clapped, and some of them burst into snatches of song, some of it at Many Boils's expense, and some of it at Mamu Snake's expense.

But by the time Many Boils delivered the hand drill to Nurse Verna, the seventh wife of Chief Eagle had returned to the bosom of her ancestors, to be once more an authentic person in the *real* world. That is to say, she was no longer part of the illusion that is this world, for that is indeed what it is: just an illusion. Those who think otherwise are either Christians or other heathens; they are not Bashilele. Of course this was not Verna's take on the matter.

"Now look what you have done," she said to Many Boils. "Now that she is dead, we cannot save her soul. Now she will burn forever in hell with the Roman Catholics."

"*Tch*," said Many Boils. He was obviously still furious. "She was but one, a Mushilele, and a woman besides. Look, there is another with her daughter. We will save them both. But tell me, *Mamu*, is this hell of yours so vast that it can hold all of us Congolese?"

"*E*, I am sure of that," said Verna, for she too was angry. Yet at the same time her heart was heavy.

FIVE

When the Belgians levied taxes, they sent soldiers into every village that they could locate (indeed, some were well hidden) and rounded up every single male person who had hair growing beneath his arms. These were the adults, the people who must render unto Caesar. When Chief Eagle wanted to count the people in his very large and sprawling village, he counted heads—in a manner of speaking. That is because in those days the Bashilele men drank their wine from human skulls.

These skulls were trophies collected by the individual man when he set out on the verge of his manhood to take the life of someone from another tribe. Along with the skull, he often kept an ear. The ear was worn dried, on a leather thong, around his waist. Often when a Belgian official, or even just a powerless missionary, visited a Bashilele village, the skulls were carefully hidden (perhaps in the thatch of the hut's dark, smoky ceiling), so as not to get its new owner into trouble with colonial law. The ears, however, were often still blatantly worn, for how could one prove that such a thing was not a monkey ear, or perhaps from a deceased relative, or any other animistic symbol?

On this particular night, in 1959, in the very large and important Bashilele village of Mushihi, the great Chief Eagle was hosting all the warriors in good standing to a drinking party in the palaver hut, under the Tree of Life, at the center of the village. This special event was in honor of his having just acquired his twenty-third wife. Tomorrow the girl's father would slaughter all but two of the goats he'd been given in dowry, and then the men would eat meat. After that they would have the strength needed to set forth on a raiding party into Bapende territory looking for slaves.

They would take only a couple of slaves—a few sturdy children—so that the Belgians wouldn't be bothered with looking into the problem. If all went well, they would catch a small boy, who could be given to the elderly widow Sees Many Things. Her husband had once been a great warrior. The rest of the slaves would be taken up to Port Francqui and sold to the Arabs who plied the marketplace on the pretense of selling merchandise and looking for guides. It was rumored that the Arabs took the slaves back to their distant homeland and resold them there for more money than any Mushilele could ever comprehend. However, the money that Chief Eagle customarily received from these Arabs was enough to keep his twenty-three wives fed *and* supply his warriors with all the new machetes that they needed.

But this night in particular was not about slaves per se; it was about Buakane. Yet how does a wife differ from a slave? Or any woman for that matter? Well, some might say that a wife could complain to her husband, whereas a slave could not complain to his or her master—surely not without receiving a terrible beating. A wife could also be at the receiving end of her husband's fists, but there were also husbands who had been known to permit their wives a bit of discussion first. And rarely—yes, it had been known to happen more than once—a man was born so wise that he stooped to ask his wife her opinion. But all these thoughts were not normal for one so young as Buakane, so she struggled against them.

Tonight there was no point in struggling further; Buakane

had been sold into the harem of Chief Eagle. Buakane, daughter of Grasshopper Paddle and Bad Odor, was going to disappear from her own thoughts. She was going to do what she was told, without hearing anything else that was said. She was going to feel the things that she was supposed to feel, but never any pain. Buakane, the person, was going to be absent from Buakane, the body. *Forever.* That was the plan.

On the afternoon of that auspicious night, Paddle and Buakane's best friend, Withholds Famine, along with two of Chief Eagle's wives, accompanied Buakane down to the spring, to cleanse her properly as befits a bride, especially one of such importance. They brought with them a small gourd filled with palm kernel oil. This substance is clear and of considerable value. It is not to be confused with the orange oil used for cooking, which is much more easily obtained.

The wives of Chief Eagle could not have been more different. Breaks Wind While Walking had once been named Brings Good Luck. She was the chief's oldest wife, first in rank, and had a crusty exterior, although it was rumored that she was a wise woman who could listen to reason. Most unfortunately, she suffered from a painful knee condition, one that made walking almost impossible. As a result, she could get about only via a woven hammock carried by four slaves. As the senior wife, she also had a personal slave in attendance.

The other wife was quite literally, Other Wife. This was a name bestowed upon her by Chief Eagle, for she was second in seniority, and at the time of their marriage, that was indeed her position. After all, Chief Eagle did not have a reputation for being an especially imaginative man, nor was he one who was especially concerned about a woman's emotions. There were some in the village who concluded that Other Wife's sour disposition might be the result of her husband's lack of respect, given that Other Wife had once been a royal princess, the daughter of a Bakuba king.

First, the three adult women said prayers of blessings to the spirits in the rocks from which the spring emerged, then to the water itself, then the earth, the forest, and the sky, in that order. Next, they beckoned to the girl that she should join them as they stood knee-deep in a pool of water, water that was as clear as the finest diamond. Buakane did as she was bade, but she did so on the arm of Withholds Famine, for she was nervous.

It was cool under the canopy of trees, and the water was chilly, in and of itself. That was always the case. But on no other day had it ever caused Buakane's teeth to chatter. Today she shivered violently as well.

"We must hurry with the ceremony," Paddle said.

"No," Breaks Wind While Walking snapped. "If you wish to have your daughter marry a Bashilele chief, then you must see that she completes the entire ritual. Otherwise she will end up as just a concubine—a whore. Is that your wish, Grasshopper Paddle?"

Breaks Wind While Walking had only recently acquired her current name. Chief Eagle, who had never been a patient man, gave this most disgraceful name to her one day in a fit of rage. He was holding a feast for a visiting chief when his number one wife blew wind with the sound of a bleating ram. Whether or not she would have to live out her life with this disgraceful new name, only Chief Eagle knew. But there was one thing that Breaks Wind While Walking could count on: she would forever be the preeminent woman in the village. She had borne Chief Eagle many sons, and they in turn had fathered many sons; this legacy was there for all to see and admire.

"Then we will hurry," Buakane's friend, Withholds Famine, said.

Together Buakane's mother and her two future sisters-in-law dipped their gourds into the cold water, and together they bathed and purified every part of the girl—this girl who was already pure in spirit and who was without physical blemish of any kind. When it came time to wash her feet, they took handfuls of sand from the bed of the pool and rubbed it against the soles of Buakane's feet to remove the dead, dry skin. The result was that even her heels were as soft and smooth as the powder to be found on moth wings.

While they were all yet standing in the water, before Buakane's skin had a chance to dry completely, the two adult women poured small amounts of palm oil on their hands and took to massaging every square centimeter of the betrothed. They took the most trouble with her face, and the swellings that would someday be full breasts, polishing them gently until they glistened. As they worked they spoke of the things that a wife must know about the sexual act, such as the husband will always approach from behind.

"*Yala*," Buakane said, "do you think that I do not know this thing? Have I no eyes?"

The women howled with laughter.

Even the eldest, Breaks Wind While Walking, joined in the ribaldry. "I have it on good authority that the white men prefer to do it from the front."

"*Aiyee*," cried Other Wife.

"Perverts," Grasshopper Paddle muttered. She too had heard such a rumor and would have been keen to try it, but of course a proper wife would never make such an immodest proposal. Only a prostitute would dare suggest such a thing—and even then at the risk of receiving a much-deserved cuffing.

"But there is one thing that you really must be told, little one," said Breaks Wind While Walking.

"What is that?" Buakane asked respectfully.

"You must never, ever, turn down our husband's requests—whatever they may be."

"Never, ever," the other women chorused. Only Withholds Famine remained silent, for she was Buakane's friend, and like her, she was innocent.

Breaks Wind While Walking pointed a finger at Buakane. "If you tell anyone the words that I am about to tell you, I will send my personal slave into your hut at night and he will slit your throat. Do you understand?"

The girl nodded.

"Good. I will tell you these things only because your mother and I are from the same highborn clan, and we were like sisters growing up, were we not, Paddle?"

"We were like goat turds to a crawling baby. Impossible to keep apart."

"*E*, and ever I was the baby. So I will come right out and say this: there are times when our husband behaves as a man possessed. These times are impossible to predict. He can change from the man who loves his family above all things, to the man who feels nothing but the most intense rage and the deepest despair. During these periods of darkness, he will lash out at the closest person—be it a slave, or a beloved wife, or even a child."

"I understand," Buakane said, feeling that indeed she had a new understanding of the human side of this handsome man who had such a huge burden placed upon his shoulders. He was, after all, responsible for the lives of almost a thousand people. His was one of *the* largest Bashilele villages.

"*Tch*. I am afraid that you do not. If you did, you could not have answered so quickly. Whatever it is that overcomes Chief Eagle in these dark moments, it is like nothing else I have ever seen."

"Perhaps it is witchcraft," Withholds Famine said. Perhaps she said it as an aside, meant just for her friend, but of course everyone heard it—even the slaves waiting on the bank.

"Silly little girl," said Other Wife. "Do you really think that someone as experienced in the ways of the world as Breaks Wind While Walking does not recognize the signs of witchcraft in her own family?"

Buakane, who had ceased shivering from the cold, now shivered with apprehension. "Mother," she said, "how can it be that you and Father would wed me to someone who is so troubled?"

"*Aiyee!* Buakane," her mother said sharply, "do not be so impertinent. Do you not remember the number of goats that were given to your father and me in exchange?"

"How many?" said Other Wife.

"There was much haggling," Paddle said. "But in the end we settled on twenty goats, a basenji bitch, ten chickens, and six pairs of breeding pigeons. But eighteen of those goats must be killed for the feast tonight."

"*Tch,*" said Other Wife. "This skinny child is not worth the two remaining goats. Plus, you still have ten chickens and a bitch."

Breaks Wind While Walking snorted. "You say that because her bride-price exceeds yours." She turned to Buakane. "And pigeons," she said. "Now, do as you are told and produce many sons. Then one day, if you are very lucky, our husband will give you your own personal slave. Remember to ask for a eunuch, in case the village moves yet again, and you must take apart your hut and carry it with you."

Withholds Famine nodded. "You see, Buakane, there will be many advantages to being a chief's wife: having your own hut, the assurance of food, and the possibility of owning a slave one day."

"All true," said Other Wife, "but you forgot to mention one very important privilege, which will be given to Buakane once she has consummated the marriage."

"What is that?" Withholds Famine said.

Other Wife hooted and slapped her thigh. "It will then be her privilege to be buried alive with our husband, the great Chief Eagle of Mushihi Village, the largest village between here and Basongo. And perhaps if you treat him well, your eunuch will do the honor of breaking your arms and legs before you are tossed into the grave."

"Where will she be tossed?" Withholds Famine said. "On top of you?"

At this point, Breaks Wind While Walking and Paddle were

the ones who hooted and slapped their thighs. But even the five slaves present, eunuchs all, who were waiting wordlessly on the bank, were shaking with mirth. As for Other Wife, she too was shaking, but with anger at the young girl's impudence. And of course Withholds Famine did not laugh, for she had not meant her words to be taken in jest. Never had Buakane had a more loyal friend.

To Buakane, it seemed as if all the world came to a stop at that moment. The birdsong in the trees above stilled. The spring ceased to flow. Her heart stopped beating. This custom of burying a woman alive was but part of the whole experience of being a chief's wife. It was one thread in a cloth that she had yet to examine, filament by filament. Chief Eagle was an old man, despite what her father said. What if he died in just a few years? What if he was bitten by a mamba tomorrow? Buakane was not prepared to die; she was not prepared to suffocate, her lungs filling with dirt while her limbs screamed out in agony.

"*Baba, Baba, Baba!*" she cried. Mother, Mother, Mother! Buakane's knees buckled, and she sank into the clear, cold waters of the pool like a woman already dead. Immediately she popped back to her feet, unable to bear the temperature.

Only Paddle reached to warm her distraught daughter with her arms. Breaks Wind While Walking, Other Wife, and the slaves were laughing hysterically. Even Withholds Famine could not control herself. However, neither Buakane nor her mother, Paddle, took offense at their behavior, for that was the way of the Bashilele people.

Life was often very short and always filled with danger. Therefore it behooved one always to laugh whenever one could. Bad Odor, who'd been to the mission station, said that this behavior baffled the Christian missionaries, who were always quick to judge.

"Do not worry yourself so, little one," said Breaks Wind While Walking when she could breathe normally again. "When that time comes, the witch doctor will give you a potion first, to dull the senses."

Other Wife wagged a finger to punctuate her next words. "True. But only if you have taken care to stay on his good side."

"*Kah,*" said Buakane, "what does that mean?"

"We adults have a proverb," Other Wife said, "that you would do well to live by, now that you are a woman."

"What is that?" said Paddle angrily. "Buakane is still my daughter; I am the one to instruct her."

"Just until tonight," said Other Wife. "Then she will be my sister wife, and she will be nothing to you."

"*Aiyee,*" cried Paddle. "If you were not the chief's wife, I would strike you."

As fast as antelopes the five slaves on the bank leaped into the water. It was Breaks Wind While Walking's raised hand that restrained them.

"Go back," she told them. She turned to Buakane. "The proverb goes thusly: gifts are the rolling logs that move large stones."

"I still do not understand," Buakane said.

"Bribes," Other Wife shouted, so loud that a troop of monkeys approaching overhead fled screeching. "To get where you want to go in this world, you must pay, pay, and pay some more."

Withholds Famine pointed to the slaves. "What about them?" she said. "Did they not pay enough *matabisha?*"

"Impertinent child," said Other Wife.

"*Yala,*" said Breaks Wind While Walking. "See how deep the shadows have grown. We must hurry back to the village and get ready for the dance."

"Dance?" said Buakane. "What dance?"

"Not you, little one," said Other Wife irritably. "You are not a proper chief's wife yet. Not until you have felt the thrust of his *lubola.*" She laughed, but none would join in. Perhaps that was because no one liked her, and because her comment was meant to hurt someone young and defenseless.

"Tonight," said Breaks Wind While Walking, "all the wives will perform a special dance to welcome you into the family. Then you will present us each with a small gift in thanks."

"A *gift*?" Buakane turned to her mother. "Why have I not been told of this gift giving?

Paddle smiled. "It has all been taken care of."

"Thank you, *Baba*."

"*Thank you, Mother*," said Other Wife in a mocking voice. "How nice it must be to have a mother."

"Did you not have a mother?" Buakane asked tenderly.

"Of course, child; everyone does. My mother was a queen. Queen of the Bakuba. Then these Bashilele kidnapped me, and I was forced to wed the man whose *lubola* you will share tonight."

"*Kah*," Paddle cried, "for my daughter has yet to have her first bleeding."

"Nor had I," said Other Wife, her eyes flashing in the gathering dusk. "But I guarantee you that there will be bleeding tonight; of that I am sure."

"Do not listen to her," Withholds Famine said. "She is a wicked woman."

Other Wife drew her arm well back above her right shoulder and gave the girl such a wallop that she staggered backward, about the length of a man, before sitting down in the pool.

"You little fool," Other Wife said. "I am a princess, and the wife of a powerful chief. One does not speak to me like this and get away with it."

Withholds Famine was agile and on her feet at once. "If you were captured by a Bashilele raiding party, that means that you are no longer a princess, but a slave."

One could only imagine the laughter this comment provoked. The eunuchs in particular could scarcely contain themselves, and in fact one could not, and he held his belly as he rolled, to and fro, on the spit of sand that bordered the stream. Before passing judgment one should take into account that Other Wife did not have a reputation of being kind to people whose status she perceived as being lower than hers, which included a great many people.

Having been bested by a commoner, and a mere child at that, Other Wife scurried back to the village ahead of everyone and was not seen again until after the women's feast (which followed the men's feast, as was proper). By then Buakane felt as if she had baby frogs jumping about in her stomach. She kept her eyes fixed on no one except for Chief Eagle and her parents, for they were seated with her, on a small platform that had been erected under the men's Tree of Life.

While the chief sat on a leopard skin, as befitting his rank, Buakane and her parents sat on woven palm leaf mats.

Chief Eagle was dressed in his full regalia. It was of his own simple design, but yet befitting a Bashilele chief of such a large village. His hat, although made of palm fiber cloth, was covered in the scarlet tail feathers of the talking parrot and trimmed with a band of cowrie shells. Secured to the right side and extending above the hat about eight inches were three bright purple feathers taken from a plantain eater.

The chief wore no shirt, but across his still well-muscled chest was slung a monkey-skin scabbard containing a short sword with a hand-smelted copper blade. The sword's hilt was wood, but in it were embedded hundreds of slivers of iron, in intricate patterns that included a swastika.

He did not wear pants; instead he wore a sort of skirt made from tightly woven palm fibers that had been gathered into pleats. The edge of the cloth had purposely been left unfinished so that it ended in a fringe. The cloth was held in place by a thong of bongo leather. Because the bongo is a very rare antelope of the deep forest and seldom encountered by the Bashilele, the chief wore a pouch of its cinnamon-and-white hide over his left hip. Strung on the leather thong, and worn over the right hip, were six dried human ears, representing the number of enemies the chief had taken in battle, including his manhood outing. One of the ears was noticeably paler than the others.

At the appropriate time (that is, when enough palm wine had been drunk to bring him happiness) the chief set down his human skull and raised his staff with the colobus-monkey-tail tassel.

"My wives will now dance," he declared. The drums took up, and the chief began to count his wives as their entered the compound. But alas, one woman—wife seven, Born Crouching, was not among their number.

"Where is Born Crouching?" the chief roared.

A female slave was quick to appear from out of nowhere. "My Lord," she said, "her ladyship is yet confined to the house of the women."

"Impossible."

"My Lord, this is truly so."

Chief Eagle struck the female slave so hard with his fist that she was thrown into Bad Odor's lap.

"Do not tell me what is so, when it cannot be. For are you all not on the same cycle?"

"Lord Husband," said Breaks Wind While Walking, "it was but yesterday that Born Crouching gave birth to your son."

"My *son*? What son? I have no son by this good-for-nothing woman—worth not even one goat of her dowry payment—only girl children."

Breaks Wind While Walking did not look away, like a lesser wife might have done. "Yesterday a son was born to you, one so small that he could not bite the breath of life."

"Why was I not told?"

"Lord Husband," said Breaks Wind While Walking, "I did not tell you, because it was you who were responsible for your son's death. You beat Born Crouching so badly that her body could no longer hold on to her child. Therefore, you did not deserve to know of his existence."

Buakane wished more than anything that she could be a child again, perhaps a toddler clinging to her mother's leg while she did her chores. Or she could find contentment in being one of the many bats that were forever swooping overhead. She would be anyone, anything, go anywhere, to just not sit here and listen to the shocked silence, which was surely worse than the battle cries of a thousand men.

Finally the chief spoke, but not to his wife. "Go to the House of Women and bring Born Crouching to me," he said to two of his warriors. "And you," he said to his personal slave, "fetch me my hippopotamus hide whip."

"Lord Husband, I beg you not to do this," said Breaks Wind While Walking.

Chief Eagle stood up and moved in her direction, his hand raised, as if to strike her as well, but in the end he merely stared. And while he stared at her, his lips parted, and the tip of his tongue flickered from side to side in the space where his two front teeth had once grown. At last he beckoned to another pair of warriors.

"Remove this woman to her hut and see that she is not disturbed by *anyone* until tomorrow midday," he said.

Bad Odor leaned close to Buakane, so that only her ears would be the ones to receive his words. "He means to include himself as well."

"*Kah!*"

"He does not wish to beat his number one wife; by then he will have slept off the palm wine."

Buakane was stunned. She was neither feebleminded nor innocent like a child. To the contrary, she prided herself on being a keen observer of others. She had always known that she was a commodity, a thing to be sold to the highest bidder, but then, she had also assumed that her father would mourn her leaving. Apparently, however, the acquisition of twenty goats, and a basenji bitch, plus chickens and pigeons to go with his nightly mush were more important than what happened to his daughter.

There was a slight chance that he was putting on a show of strength for her, but Buakane rather doubted it. After all, there was another occasion when her father put wealth before family. Since it was not something she ever liked to remember, she usually kept it well pushed to a far corner of her mind. That was the time when Mother came down with the "mosquito fever," and her forehead became as hot as coals. Even though Paddle chewed on the bark given to her by the witch doctor (it had worked many times in the past), she grew sicker and sicker, until at last she was writhing in pain. Paddle had shouted many things—some of them curses—but most of them were incoherent.

At the time Bad Odor was aware that there was a clinic at Mushihi Station, which dispensed medicine specifically to combat mosquito fever. However, he would not take Paddle there or allow her to be taken there because he was under the impression that the clinic charged a small fee for the pills. And yes, it was only a small fee; this was something Buakane knew for herself, for she had asked those who had reason to know.

"Buakane! Buakane! Why do you stare at me like a fool?"

Of course Buakane had been staring only at the father in her mind, not the one beside her. Nonetheless, it behooved her to lie. More than that, a plan had begun to form in her mind.

"Father, I ask permission to use the toilet."

"Absolutely not! The dance is about to begin."

"Let her go," Paddle said.

"I said no."

"You were never a bride," Paddle said.

"Then go quickly," Bad Odor said.

"Thank you, Mother," Buakane said. She touched her mother's shoulder lightly and slipped like a stitch into cloth, through the courtiers that surrounded them and into the night.

The plan that had begun to form now took shape with every step. Buakane walked with apparent purpose in the direction of the public toilets. She walked briskly, one hand held to her belly, as befitting a bride with a stomach full of jumping frogs. As she had hoped, no one paid attention to someone in this condition. However, upon reaching the coil of palm thatch that hid the privies, Buakane strode right past them. She marched straight into the shadows of the thick *tshisuku*, the elephant grass that grew along the perimeter of the village.

After three months of rain, the grass grew tall, reaching above her head. The blades were coarse and sharp, leaving welts upon her body, so Buakane made her way forward with her arms crossed in front of her head in order to protect her eyes. She was, however, in more danger from the snakes coiled in the bare spots between the clumps, where they preyed on toads and rodents. But the spirits of the bush were favorable to her, and she was able to make good progress, though she knew not to where.

After having covered a distance equal to that of three round-trips to the stream, Buakane encountered the most curious thing; in fact, it was so startling that she sat down on her heels to take it all in. It was this thing called a "road," which she had heard about many times. But one cannot begin to imagine the magnificence of such a thing, until one has beheld it with one's own eyes.

How could Buakane ever describe it to her best friend, Withholds Famine? It's to a path as a drop of water is to a storm. A road is so wide that one's hut can easily be set right in the middle of it, and there would still be room for the pigeon coop, *and* a plot for gourds. As for the length—surely there was no end. It stretched from sky to sky, and being that the world is round, then the road circles until it meets itself again, like a length of *lukodi* tied around a tree trunk.

In the bright moonlight, the road gleamed silver against the dark, brooding wall of grass behind it. Buakane longed to step out into this strange new thing, to see for herself what it was like to walk, swinging one's arms this way and that, whirling in circles, without having to mind one's step. What a marvelous thing a road was, if only the white men had not been the ones to think of it.

Buakane had heard that these roads were necessary for the movement of the giant iron beasts that the Bula Matadi, their Belgian
rulers, built. Although some said that it was more likely that these
strange beasts were created by magic, and not by the hand of man.

Consider this: the largest of the beasts were even larger than
the largest bull elephants. Instead of legs, the bodies of these bizarre animals were held off the ground by four circles consist-
ing of rubber. Each beast, no matter its size, had a mouth large
enough to swallow a person whole, and every beast had at least
two mouths, and some beasts were said to have as many as four.
Also, the mouths were located on the sides of the animal, behind
the eyes.

It was a fact that a person—even a Mushilele—could enter
a beast and be disgorged by the same beast, unharmed. Clearly,
these creatures were not related to any other living thing—not
even the okapi—therefore one must wisely conclude that they
were the product of magic, and one must treat them with the
utmost suspicion.

Truly, the Bashilele witch doctors were incapable of performing magic that was anywhere near this caliber. Buakane had even
heard her own witch doctor say the same thing, just not directly.
Usually such an omission was voiced as a jealous rant.

Not that it mattered. As much as she had wanted to see the
road, Buakane had no desire to enter the belly of a metal demon
creature. She had heard tales of others who, upon doing so, had
screamed like toddlers denied the breast, and many others who
had vomited, and one supposedly brave warrior even soiled his
loincloth.

Yet nothing terrified the girl more than hyenas, and behold!
Buakane's limbs froze in place, her ears and nose becoming the
totality of her senses. Was that not the sound of some hyenas
crashing toward her, not a stone's throw away? Could she not
smell the carrion on their breath, the stench of flaked blood and
viscera buried in their rough coats?

The witch doctor said that hyenas were possessed, for a hyena's jaws were more powerful than those of a lion. Unlike lions, they were consummate man-eaters, stealing into the village at every opportunity and making off with an unattended child, or even ripping a baby from its mother's arms. Just three years prior, an elderly woman, whose eyes had had grown dim with the years, wandered from her hut into the *tshisuku* in broad daylight, only to be beset upon by the these demonic beasts. The grandmother's screams of agony, as her innards were pulled from her pulsating belly, still haunted the dreams of Buakane.

Buakane now searched frantically for a stick or a branch that she could use to hold the hyenas at bay until she could reach an acacia tree that was climbable. However, the tall clumps of grass grew too dense that close to the road, and the one stick that she did find began to move just as her fingers began to close around it.

Buakane yelped like a kicked puppy and threw herself into the road that the white man had ordered built for his machines. Fast on her heels were eight female hyenas, their jaws snapping even as they sailed through the air.

SIX

"Congo time." That's what missionaries and colonialists sometimes laughingly referred to as the phenomenon of events happening long after they had originally been scheduled. Quite often they
weren't laughing when they said it. Julia had heard about Congo
time being blamed on the steamy weather, the lazy natives, and
the sporadic, but often rather dramatic, interference of the local
fauna (charging elephants, all-consuming driver ants, and so on).
However, not once had she heard about noncommunicative, irre-
sponsible white missionaries being blamed for this phenomenon.
To say the least, to someone who was born in September, that was
most annoying—not that Julia would have publicly admitted to
putting any stock in zodiac signs.

Before he flew off to "who knows where," the disarmingly
handsome Hank had told Julia that Reverend Paul Hayes, the
missionary from Mushihi Station, would be there to pick her up
at eight in the morning. When Julia had protested about the early
hour, Hank had enjoyed a good laugh at her expense. Eight A.M.
was practically midmorning for a missionary, especially during
the rainy season. A proper missionary rose at six, prayed, ate
breakfast, read the Bible and prayed again, and was off to the
chapel for services by seven.

So when the morning hours dragged by, and there was no sign of the promised missionary or his precocious daughter, Julia began to fume. This was supposed to be the real beginning of her African adventure, but the day was just going to waste. Dang it all! What kind of colony were the Belgians running that they couldn't even supply basic necessities like telephones. If she only had a telephone—of course that meant Mushihi Station would have to have one as well, and since they were out in the middle of nowhere, neighbors to a cannibal tribe, that wasn't bloody likely.

You'd think the servants would be more help. The head housekeeper was an insolent man named Protruding Navel. Imagine that! And you'd better be good at imagining, because his amusing name was the only good thing he had going for him. When Julia asked the man if he wouldn't mind running into town (meaning the white section) and inquiring whether anyone had seen Mr. Hayes that day, his response was shockingly rude. Perhaps it sounded all the more so because he delivered it in French.

"I do not understand the language you are speaking, *mademoiselle.*"

"I am speaking Tshiluba."

"*Non, mademoiselle,* I assure you that you are not."

"Yes," Julia said with exaggerated slowness, as if he were a small child, or perhaps someone with a mental disability. "And what I said is that I need you to run an errand for me."

"*Mamu,*" he said, having switched to his native tongue of Tshiluba, "it is possible that I can now understand some of your words. Perhaps I did not understand them before, due to your atrocious accent. Nevertheless, I shall not do as you have requested, because I work for Mamu Jardin, and not for you."

"But you *must* do as I say," Julia said. Be firm with the natives; wasn't that what all the retired missionaries back in America had said?

"*Tch*," said Protruding Navel. "I am not your *slave;* I am the son of a chief, and in addition, I am an educated man. My work here is only of a temporary nature. Soon I will be the lord of this house. Perhaps then you will work for me, white woman."

"*Kah!*"

Julia had not noticed Cripple's presence in the kitchen. Seated on a stool in the corner, between the stove and the pantry door, she was more like a large black doll than a human being. But a large black doll with one corner of her top pulled up, and a mahogany breast completely exposed. There in front of God, and man, sat a half-naked grown woman. Yes, it was only Julia's new maid, but still, she was nursing her baby, as if it were an entirely natural pursuit!

"Cripple!" Julia cried. "What are you doing?"

"I am feeding the future president of the Congo, *Mamu*."

"*Nasha*," said Protruding Navel scornfully. "That woman is a heathen and a Muluba. Our future president will be a Lulua Christian."

"Such foolishness. The Bena Lulua are like children compared to us. Even the Belgians say that the Baluba are the most intelligent tribe."

Protruding Navel actually spat at Cripple, but lucky for him, he missed. "Do you always take what the Belgians say as a compliment?" he shouted. "What if they say: 'Look at that clever little monkey, with her little baby monkey. Let us take it for our pet?' Then what?"

"You have offended me beyond what can be comprehended in this world," Cripple screamed. "I will arrange a curse for you."

"A curse? From where will you get this curse? From that broken-down witch doctor who used to be your husband?"

"*Aiyee*," Cripple screamed again.

"Enough! That applies to both of you," Julia said. "I need to get a message across the river."

"Then take it yourself," the two servants said almost in unison. Even the infant chimed in with a hungry cry, for in her agitation the mother had accidentally swung her breast out of reach of her daughter's mouth.

"But I am new to this place," Julia said. "Why do you treat me like this? I am *not* a Belgian. I have traveled a long way from my home in America, and my parents, to serve *you*. This morning I will be traveling all the way up north to Mushihi Station, to manage a school for little girls who have been married to grown men. Is this not a good thing?"

"*Mamu*," said Protruding Navel, "the people of that region are of the Bashilele tribe, are they not?"

"Yes, that is correct!"

"The Bashilele do not deserve to be called people, *Mamu*. Do you not know that they practice the taking of heads?"

"*E*, but—"

"*Mamu*, did you not know that Cripple is a *Muluba*, and that the Bashilele have taken many of her tribe as slaves? That is the reason that the Bashilele can speak the language in which we are now conversing—even though it is very difficult to understand you, given your terrible accent. Tell me, did you learn our language from the Belgians? It must be the case, for they are likewise impossible to understand. *Mamu*, the next time that you try and learn Tshiluba, you must either learn it from an African or a Portuguese person. The Portuguese are the only white men who can speak our language."

"No, I did not learn Tshiluba from a Belgian, and no, I did not know these things about how the Tshiluba language was spread. But why do the Portuguese people speak your language so well?"

"It is because they marry our women."

"But that is so wrong!"

"On that we agree very much, *Mamu;* you whites are too much our inferiors." Protruding Navel turned his back on Julia.

Meanwhile Cripple tugged on her other breast a couple of times before stuffing it into the mouth of her squalling infant. Immediately the child began to suck, although the sounds she made were disturbingly loud and disgustingly private.

"*Mamu*," Cripple sighed, "pay no attention to this man. You are new here. We should not expect so much from you."

Julia smiled. "Thank you, Cripple."

"*Yala*, I do not wish your gratitude. But you are a child, *Mamu*, like the offspring of a goat. You bound this way and then that. You do not mean to offend, and just as a kid does not know where it will land when it jumps, so does your tongue not know where it will land when you speak. Therefore, I must care for you as a mother cares for her child."

"Then give her your other breast," said Protruding Navel, from behind his back.

That crude remark set the two African employees into hysterics. Julia, however, was flabbergasted by the vulgarity a black man dared to express to a white woman. Even in Ohio, she couldn't imagine such a comment like that being directed at her—although to be perfectly honest, in Ohio she hadn't known any black people. If indeed Oxford had any Negroes, there hadn't been any living on her side of town when she was growing up, and the student body of the small bible college she'd attended had been as white as toothpaste. But what really stunned Julia was the rude behavior on Cripple's part. After all, hadn't the twisted little woman just declared a truce?

"Now it is I who am very much offended," Julia stammered. "I have tried very hard to be patient this morning—knowing that I am especially tired. But you are both unkind. If you were to come to my country, I would not treat you thusly."

"*Bulelela?*" Cripple asked. Truly?

"Truly."

"But, *Mamu*, we have heard otherwise. Is it not true that in your country black people are set upon by dogs?"

"*Kah!* Who told you this? The Communists?"

"What?" Cripple said.

"I asked if it was the Communists who were spreading these rumors, that whites in America were rounding up black people with dogs."

"*Mamu*, I can no longer understand your speech. You accent has indeed gotten very poor," Cripple said. She began to hum to the coconut-size infant at her breast.

Julia strode away in what she hoped was a dignified manner. Clearly, she had her work cut out for her. First, *she* had to understand these childlike people. The next step, which was to have them understand her and then be persuaded to change from their heathen ways, by her Christlike example, was a far bigger job than she'd expected. For some reason she'd expected the natives to be much more passive; she'd thought that they would be eager, perhaps even clamoring, for her to light the way for them to civilization and salvation.

Civilization and salvation—these were the gifts that American Protestant missionaries were so eager to share. All that the Africans had to do in order to receive these gifts was to simply accept them, yet so many of them simply would not—*could* not—bring themselves to do so. *Aiyee*, a thousand times over! Maybe the natives really were just primitive savages, too simpleminded to see a good deal when it was offered.

As the hours passed, and there was still no sign of the Reverend Paul Hayes and Clementine, Julia's agitation grew into desperation. Finally, around midday, she could stand it no longer. She clapped on her helmet, cinched the chin strap, and pulled her kneesocks up to full mast. Then with her eyes half shut, so that she wouldn't see the smirks on the natives' faces, Julia charged back into the kitchen.

"*Yala*," she said, which was a nothing word, meaning anything that you wanted it to. In this case, it was intended solely to announce that she was back, and in fighting form.

The kitchen, however, was empty.

"Cripple? Protruding Navel?"

Then Julia heard what sounded like excited voices over the constant din of the falls. The voices seemed to be coming from the front of the Missionary Rest House, so she dashed out there. Lo and behold, there stood the two Africans, along with the diminutive Clementine, in front of a pickup truck. There was no sign of a Reverend Paul Hayes; instead she found herself staring at Hank!

"Life to you, Julia. Do you think you could shake a leg so that we stand a chance of getting home before dark. Gracie here didn't even want to start up this morning."

Julia continued to stare. Neither what she saw nor what she heard matched up with what was supposed to be. Yet it couldn't be a dream, because the truck was belching noxious fumes, and she'd never had a dream involving odors.

"Gracie is the name of our truck," Clementine said.

Julia smiled her appreciation. "Okay, that's half the riddle solved. But where is your father, dear?"

Clementine giggled as she pointed at Hank. "He's right here, Auntie Julia." Then her face darkened. "But I must ask you never to call me that word again. 'Dear' is what mamas say to their children, and you are *not* my mama."

The child spoke with such force that Julia felt as if she'd been slapped. It felt like everyone was ganging up on her, although of course they weren't. Her only sin just now was to use language she'd heard other grown-ups use on children.

At this point Hank walked over to Clementine and drew her close. "Well, I guess there is no time like the present to confess my little ruse. My given name is Paul Henry Hayes. Reverend is a title I earned by going to school. I was named Paul after my paternal grandfather, who was meaner than a Cape buffalo with a hide full of ticks, and Henry after my maternal grandfather, who could teach that same buffalo to eat out of your hand. So I go by

Henry, but the Mission Board insists on using the name Paul for all their official business, because it's a biblical name."

"But when you picked me up in Leopoldville, to fly me here, you introduced yourself as Hank."

"Yes, but Hank is the nickname for Henry. Surely you know that."

"Still, you were being deceitful!" Julia felt both embarrassed by her naiveté and irritated that she'd been played.

"Oh come on," Henry said. "I was having a little good clean fun."

Julia was gobsmacked. "*Lies* are what passes for fun on the mission field?"

"Papa wasn't lying," Clementine said fiercely. "Auntie Julia, you shouldn't be so judgmental."

"That's enough," Henry said.

Julia could see him draw his daughter even tighter to him, so it wasn't like he was really admonishing her for chiding an adult. And in front of the help, no less. This explained why the little girl was so—so—well, so darn different.

Of course Julia had had to bite her tongue. Being judgmental was something that Julia excelled at; it was her worst fault. It was a good thing that she wasn't one of those poor, misguided Roman Catholics, or she'd be forever going to confession, just like the girl who shared a piglet with her in biology class in high school. Wanda started smoking in the fifth grade and was addicted to smoking by the time she graduated from eighth. Plus, she'd started drinking. Wanda used to joke that she and her priest shared a drink before they ducked into the confession booth, and a cigarette after.

After tousling Clementine's hair (which couldn't have made it any messier), Henry went and got Julia's bags and loaded them on the truck. After adding Cripple's few belongings, he gave her a helping hand as she climbed into the back of the pickup. Next he hoisted Clementine aboard.

"Now me," Julia said.

Henry winked. "You're in luck; you get to sit with me. Up front."

"But I want to ride in back with the others, to feel the wind in my hair. Besides, it will be too hot in the cab."

"Julia," Henry said, "you have just one opportunity to make an impression on the Bashilele people—both at Mushihi Station, and the ones whom we might encounter along the way. You need to appear dignified. They must see you as a woman with position, so that they will take you seriously."

"Wait just a minute," Julia said. "How do I know that this isn't another of your good clean jokes. Cripple," she called, "would you and your baby like to ride in the front of this machine?"

"*Kah!*"

Although Cripple appeared quite distressed by this simple offer, not so little Clementine. "Oh, Auntie Julia," she said, "there is so much I need to teach you concerning local customs. Might I begin now?"

Julia felt her cheeks coloring at a rate that had nothing to do with the tropical sun. "Only if you must, dear—I *mean*, Clementine." she said.

"You see, Auntie Julia, if Cripple rides up front with Papa, then the natives will think that she is his harlot, just like Rahab in the Bible."

"Clemey," said Henry with a twinkle in his eye, "I couldn't have said it better myself." He caught Julia's appraising gaze. "A lot of the Belgian state officials and businessmen—especially the Portuguese—leave their wives back in the comforts of Europe. So out here they take up with harlots who most often ride up front with them."

"And have sexy intercourse," added Clementine.

"If you're going to use grown-up terms," her father said, "at least get them right."

Julia merely cleared her throat, because for once she was at a loss for words.

"But, Papa," Clementine said, "I looked the meaning of 'harlot' up in the dictionary, and I still don't understand what makes it a sin. Didn't you and Mama have sexy intercourse?"

This time Henry colored. Deeply.

"Everyone in the truck," he said, looking expressly at Julia. "Mushihi Station, here we come."

Oh, but if only it were that simple, Julia thought as the trip progressed. Travel in the Belgian Congo was like pulling the handle on a slot machine—one that was rigged so that it never came up with three matching numbers, or pieces of fruit either. The road to Mushihi Station consisted of two parallel dirt tracks, separated by a head-high ribbon of grass, and potholes that in America would be labeled as canyons and designated as national parks.

Wooden bridges spanned streams, but the only way to cross the one true river that they encountered was to board a ferry. This was nothing like the quaint ferries one might still find in rural America; this ferry consisted of four dugout canoes that had been lashed together, over which a platform of wooden planks had been nailed. This contraption was then poled across the water by men with teeth filed to points, men whose ancestors had once been cannibals.

The above conditions might have made for an interesting trip *if* Julia had been allowed to travel in the bed of the pickup. However, the cramped quarters of the metal cab, even with both windows rolled down, made it feel like she was sitting in an oven, while being roasted like a Thanksgiving turkey. Sweat poured from every pore. It streamed into her eyes. It pooled beneath her buttocks. Her blouse stuck to the back of the seat.

The only relief that came was when they entered the swatches of forest that bordered rivers—galley forests, they were called. There the trees rose to dizzying heights, a hundred feet or more, their broad canopies creating dense shade that blocked out the sun to such a degree that the forest floor was open and inviting. Even more inviting was the fact that the temperature inside these vast cathedrals of green was often ten degrees Fahrenheit lower than it had been on the savannah under the broiling sun.

"Henry, please, let's stop. *Please*," Julia said every time they came to a strip of forest.

Of course Henry did. Sometimes he even stopped up on the savannah as well, but usually to fix a flat tire; they had three flat tires and a radiator leak that needed tending to. So what should have been a four-hour drive, at the maximum, took eight hours.

When they were still about twenty kilometers away from Mushihi Station, and the hour was such that the moon and his wife, Venus, were plain to see in the sky, the pickup's headlights shone on a scene that would later give Julia nightmares. In the middle of the road, an African child was desperately trying to fend off a pack of hyenas using nothing but her bare hands. The timing of their arrival was a miracle, there was no arguing that. One minute later, and the poor girl would have been ripped to shreds.

As it was, the largest of the hyenas, a female (the females are larger than the males), sprang at the child, even as the rest of the pack fled from the approaching automobile. The child screamed, and the female bounded away, but not before taking a chunk of the girl's thigh with her. The girl then collapsed into unconsciousness on the dirt.

Henry stomped on the brakes and put the truck into park. "Everyone, stay where you are," he yelled, and then rushed over to the child. After ripping off his shirt, he wrapped it tightly around her thigh as a tourniquet. He carried her gently back in his arms to Julia's side of the truck.

"Open the door," he said. "I want you to hold her. As soon as she starts to come to, let me know."

Julia received the child, but not without wincing. It wasn't the blood; Henry's shirt was doing a good job of handling that. It was just that when she decided to become a missionary, she didn't imagine that one day she'd actually have to hold a mostly naked savage in her lap. Her idea of missionary life was more along the lines of saving souls, which one accomplished by sharing the good news of Christ's redeeming sacrifice. This—she sneaked another look at the child who was missing two front teeth, and whose pubescent breasts pointed straight up like two shiny black eggs— this did not fit her job description.

SEVEN

Nurse Verna Doyer did not undress when she went to bed; she deconstructed, and it was for this reason that she did not take lightly to being disturbed. The first thing she did was remove the hairpins that held the greasy coils of braids atop her skull. With each pin that she removed, Nurse Verna acknowledged a sin that she had committed that day. Those sins could be against either God or man. However, since Nurse Verna seldom wronged another human being, her prayers asking for pardon were usually thought of as sins that she'd committed against God.

Her most common prayer was: "Lord, I should have been more grateful for that ghastly lunch that my houseboy brought for me today."

The second thing that Nurse Verna did was to unwind, and unbraid, her plaits; she recited scripture during that lengthy process. The matrons at the orphanage had drummed it into her that healthy hair had to be brushed one hundred times before one went to bed. Since Nurse Verna was a creature of habit, and ritual gave her comfort, brushing is what she did.

On the other hand, Nurse Verna was quite aware that the excessive brushing contributed to her oily scalp, so she used the brushing time to ask God to remove from her heart the anger that she felt toward the matrons—some of whom had been rather abusive. God never answered Verna's prayers, so she felt quite justified in repeating the same prayers day after day.

When she was finished with her hair, Nurse Verna dismantled her wardrobe for the day. Off came the apron, the dress without buttons, the full slip, the half slip, and the homemade brassiere. On went the cotton T-shirt with the elbow-length sleeves, the night slip, the long flannel nightgown, and *two* fresh pairs of long-legged underpants, for there was always the possibility that while she slept, her nightgown might somehow get bunched around her waist, leaving her vulnerable to violation. Pajama bottoms were simply out of the question, because they resembled men's trousers, and the Bible was very clear on that issue: for a woman to dress like a man was a sin.

The fact that all this clothing made Nurse Verna Doyer unattractive, not to mention practically inaccessible at night to Reverend Arvin Doyer, mattered not one whit. Nurse Verna was closed for business down there—so to speak. The Lord had been good to her, blessing her with late-onset menses, and early-onset menopause. The Doyers had never been cursed with children, and now that all possibility of that curse had been taken from them, it was no longer right that they should lie together as man and wife. God had created that loathsome desire to rub genitals for the sole purpose of procreation—not recreation.

Besides, by the time Nurse Verna was through deconstructing, Arvin was invariably fast asleep for the night. Some nights he fell asleep while still reading his bible, and Nurse Verna would find the holy book perched on her husband's expanding stomach, perilously close to sliding off it and onto the floor. On the plus side, however, Arvin was quick to rouse and didn't seem to require a period of adjustment between sleep and full mental acuity. Verna, on the other hand, could not sleep a wink without the aid of her special friend, a friend whose acquaintance she had made approximately a dozen years earlier following an emergency appendectomy. Because she was a registered nurse, and the only medical caregiver in a large area, the Belgian government had given her a permit to purchase and distribute various medications from a Lebanese-owned pharmacy in Luluabourg.

Thus it was, on the night of Julia's arrival, when Henry pounded on the door with fists the size of lion paws, that it was Arvin—wearing a full set of flannel pajamas, despite the heat—who sprang to see who the visitor was. Meanwhile Verna, who'd gone to sleep with the aid of her friend, struggled to separate dream from fact. Was she a little girl, being spanked for having broken one of Matron's privately owned candy dishes, or was that the Angel of Death pounding at the front door, having come to take her soul?

"Nurse Doyer, wake up," a familiar voice said. The words were repeated again and again, and slowly, fading into consciousness, like someone coming out of anesthesia, Nurse Verna became aware that the speaker was her husband.

"Reverend Doyer?" she asked, to reassure herself.

"Yes, Nurse Doyer. I'm afraid there has been an emergency."

"What time is it?"

"It is not yet nine o'clock."

Nurse Verna struggled vigorously to sit, but fell back.

"In the evening," her husband said.

"Oh."

"Nonetheless," he said, "you must try to rouse yourself. The child has been severely bitten."

"Snake?" she said.

"Hyena," he said.

"That incorrigible Hayes child?"

"No, an African. Probably a runaway."

"Reverend," Nurse Verna said firmly, "thou knowest my position—and my condition. I do not entertain or attend visitors past a certain hour."

"Very well," Arvin said. "I will send them away."

"And please shut the door before you talk to them."

Much to her dismay, Nurse Verna could hear that Arvin forgot to shut the door behind him before delivering her message. Or was it that he simply didn't care enough to follow through with her instructions? The third possibility was that he purposely ignored her. Oh poor Arvin; what must it be like to be just a man? Beyond that, what must it be like to be a man of his ilk?

Nurse Verna was about to give Arvin a small piece of her mind—despite the fact that the misogynistic St. Paul would not have approved—when Arvin returned. Except that Arvin wasn't alone; he was actually trotting after, not leading, the intruder. And she wasn't some little African waif with a deadly hyena bite.

No siree, the intruder was a white woman, one whose looks rivaled those of Queen Esther, winner of the most important beauty contest ever held. This had to be none other than the young woman Henry had gone to fetch from Leopoldville. This had to be Julia Elaine Newton, the new director of the school for child brides. She would be doing what Henry's deceased wife used to do.

Verna's mind cleared like a fog driven by a gust of strong winds. "Reverend, you may put your tongue back in your mouth and leave the room," she said.

"I will not," he said.

"Listen, you two," the intruder said, "there is no time for this. The girl in the truck is in a very bad way. Henry tried to tie a tourniquet, but the blood has seeped through. I'm afraid that she's going to bleed to death."

"By pointing to yourself, show me where the wound is," Nurse Verna said.

"Uh—about here," the young woman said, pointing to her thigh.

"Then it's most probably just a flesh wound; there is nothing to worry about. I'll give you everything—"

The young woman stepped forward, grabbed the sheet and thin cotton blanket, and ripped them off the bed. The motion caused Verna's nightgown to flutter, revealing her pink, untanned calves. Even pinker were her very much suntanned cheeks.

"What—"

"Get out of bed," the intruder barked. "Now! Put on your shoes, get your medical bag—or whatever—and let's go."

What arrogance! This was a brand-new missionary, someone young enough to be Verna's granddaughter, and she was ordering around an "old-timer," as if Nurse Verna were a—a—dolt? A brain-damaged chimpanzee? It was not only unacceptable, but the very first thing on the morrow, Nurse Verna was going to write the home office and demand—not ask—that they nip in the bud Julia Newton's career as a missionary. And believe you me, after reading Nurse Verna's letter and its many accusations, they would. Nurse Verna was far too valuable an employee, despite any small failures one might point to. Miss Newton, however, spelled trouble. With a capital T.

"But can't you see that I'm not dressed? That my hair is down?"

"You're covered, aren't you?" Miss Newton raged at Verna. "And I don't care if you were naked! A little girl is crying out in agony and you want to put on your holy roller clothes? Put on a robe and a hat, for crying out loud."

"W-why, you're j-just a newcomer," Nurse Verna sputtered. "You can't speak to me like this."

"I can," Miss Newton said, "and I *shall*."

Nurse Verna threw her hands up in the air and surrendered, but it was not to the whippersnapper fresh from the States. "Lord, I give it all up to Thee," she cried.

"Amen," Reverend Doyer said, and he likewise threw his hands in the air. "Amen, all praise be to God. Father in Heaven, we just ask Thee—"

"Enough, praying, Reverend Doyer," Nurse Verna snapped. "Now it's time to act. Although we must remember to thank God later that we remembered to leave the generator on, so at least we can see."

"God didn't have anything to do with the generator being on," Henry said. Oh yes, the other reverend had come in unbidden and was cradling the bleeding girl in his arms. "It is our station's policy to leave the generator on until ten o'clock every evening. It's a policy that I insist upon."

Nurse Verna harrumphed. It was a sound that she relished. "Well, don't just stand there, Reverend Hayes; carry the girl into the dining room where the light is the best. The tablecloth is plastic, so you may set her down, if you wish. As for you, Reverend Doyer, run get the Coleman lantern from the pantry, and some bleach." Finally she looked at Miss Newton. "You. Run ahead and light a fire in the stove, and get some water boiling in the big cast-iron kettle. Bring me a *full* kettle of boiling water. And do not bother me again until you have a full kettle of boiling water. Is that clear enough? Because you look like you don't understand English."

"Wood—"

"If the wood box is low, there's more in the shed out back, but you'll have to take the key from the hook by the door. And grab a flashlight and watch for snakes. We've been having a problem with vipers this year. Anything else, girl? "

As she was speaking Nurse Verna had been twisting her hair—her crowning glory—as per the Book of First Corinthians, into a massive bun that could be quickly held in place with oodles of hairpins and then covered snugly with a scarf. She worked quickly, competently, and prayerfully. So focused was she on her task that when Miss Newton piped up, interrupting Verna's train of thought, the nurse started and jabbed the cartilage of her left ear with a hairpin.

"Uh—ma'am," the silly girl said, "what I meant to say is that I don't know how to light a fire in a wood-burning stove. I've never done that before."

"Never lit a stove?"

"No, ma'am."

"I'll show her." It was the Great Distraction: that incorrigible Hayes child. She was forever popping up where she wasn't wanted, where she had no place being, like weeds in a vegetable patch. Children had no place on a mission field. Here they were nothing more than a distraction, siphoning time away from the Lord's work under the best of circumstances, and just plain getting in the way at other times—at times such as this.

"Go back and wait in the truck," Nurse Verna said.

"The truck's all bloody," the child said.

"Then walk home. It's not that far."

"Okay, okay. You needn't work yourself into a slather; Papa says that if you keep it up, you're going to either have a nervous break-in or else you're going to have a heart attack. But before I go, please can't I help her with the fire? She doesn't know *any*thing."

Nurse Verna thought she heard a snicker escape the new missionary, but she couldn't be sure, and since her new resolve was not to judge, she decided to leave well enough alone. For the time being, at least. One's true character could not remain hidden for long.

"All right then," Nurse Verna said to Clementine, "show her how to make a fire in the stove, but be quick about it. The important thing is that I need boiling water to sterilize the needles and instruments."

When the coast was clear, she quickly slipped on the appropriate garments and turned her hands over to the Lord so that they could be the instruments of his bidding.

EIGHT

Julia felt foolish. She felt stupid. She felt cowardly. The wood box next to the stove was empty, and she wasn't afraid to go back outside—she was *terrified*. She was relieved when Clementine grabbed the flashlight on the windowsill by the door, but her knees buckled when she realized that the child was heading out to the woodshed without a weapon.

"You forgot a gun," Julia yelled.

Clementine doubled over with laughter. "We don't have to shoot the wood."

"Of course not," Julia said. "But there are some dangerous animals out there, right? Like snakes and such."

"Except that I can see practically all the way to the woodshed, Auntie Julia, and there's nothing in the path."

They sprinted to the woodshed. Clementine, the experienced African hand, calmly filled the large woven basket that Julia had carried from the house, and then they hurried back—not quite as fast, of course. Then Julia watched closely as Clementine wrapped kindling in pages torn from a Sears, Roebuck and Company catalog. She observed how, when the flames caught, the child added logs in an overlapping pattern, in order to allow air circulation.

Unfortunately, it takes much longer to boil water when one

is starting from scratch on a woodstove than it does to simply turn on the gas, or the electric knob, back in civilization. In the meantime, there was nothing to do in the tidy kitchen but fidget, or talk with Clementine.

Julia was exhausted and wanted nothing more than to go to bed—her *own* bed back home in Oxford, Ohio. She'd been promised a house of her own on Mushihi Station, but there had been no mention of a wood-burning stove. As for the hyenas and snakes, she knew about those things by reading up on Africa, but up until now, they had been only theoretical.

This afternoon they had driven past a party of Bashilele hunters with their little curly-tailed basenji dogs. The hunters wore only loincloths, palm fiber mats slung low around their hips. They carried six-foot bows, quivers of arrows, and machetes. Clementine had called out to them and waved, but the expressions on the hunters' faces remained impassive. Unengaged.

Cripple waited until the truck was at a safe distance, and then she spat over the tailgate. "*Mamu*," she said to Julia, "does not this little white one know that it is not proper to call out greetings to savages?" Of course her criticism was meant not for Julia's ears, but for the little white ears of Clementine.

"*Baba*," said Clementine, sounding a bit piqued, "do you not read your Bible? It says that we are not to judge one another, or else we might get judged."

"No, little *mamu*, I do not read your Bible, for I am not a Christian; I am a heathen woman."

"A savage?"

"*Kah!* I would box your ears if they were the right color. Does your mother know that you speak with such impudence to another's mother?" Cripple nuzzled her whimpering baby.

"I have no mother," Clementine said.

"Truly?"

"*Bulelela.*" Truly, truly.

"Then my heart hurts for you. I wish now to explain why I

called the Bashilele savages. My people, the Baluba, are at war with the Bena Lulua. We are brothers, speaking the same language, yet still we kill each other. At any rate, at the end of last year's rains, my husband took my sister wife, and their seven children together, back to her village, to visit her parents. No one has seen them since the day they left our house on foot. Many people believe that they were killed by Bena Lulua, in revenge for this or that awful deed committed by my tribe upon them. But an equal number of people believe that they were kidnapped by the Bashilele and sold into slavery. My people, the Baluba, are said to be especially desirable as slaves."

Julia had thought such talk was surreal. But there it was, and thinking about it now gave her a headache. If tomorrow she woke up and saw Grandma Newton's corny afghan draped across the footboard of her bed and heard the voices of Miami University upperclassmen, gibbering on their way to classes, she would gladly eat crow for breakfast. Even real crows.

"Auntie Julia, Auntie Julia," Clementine said, patting her arm. "The water is boiling. We can go back now."

Julia had been so deep in thought that in a way she actually was back in Ohio. It took her a minute to get over being annoyed at Clementine for bringing her back to reality.

"I didn't hear the kettle whistle," Julia said foolishly.

"This kind of kettle doesn't whistle. Come on, Auntie Julia, I don't want to miss out on *everything* gooey." That said, the little girl was halfway out the door.

"Wait! Where are the hot pads?"

Clementine slumped back through the swinging door. "Jeepers, Auntie Julia, don't you know anything? Aunt Verna doesn't want the hot water; she just wanted you out of the way, because sewing up that Mushilele girl's leg was going to be icky, and Aunt Nurse Verna didn't know if you were the type to throw up or faint. Either way, she doesn't much like it."

"Like *what*?"

"Having to break in new missionaries—although she's really kind of good at it, because they always leave Mushihi Station broken. Anyway, that's what Papa says."

"Wait a minute! She thought that I might throw up if I was in there watching?"

"Oh yeah, the last missionary who came to work here vomited every time she saw her night watchman, on account of he had elephant eyes—or some disease like that."

"Elephantiasis?"

"Yeah, that's the one. Anyway, come on, or we'll miss out on everything."

Julia found herself chasing after Clementine. The kitchen was semidetached, connected by a short breezeway, as a way of helping to prevent heat buildup in the house. Therefore, the two of them had been quite alone, and quite unaware of the goings-on in the dining room. Fortunately it was Julia's hand on the doorknob first, and she turned it slowly and opened the door cautiously.

What she saw was the African girl still lying on her side on the dining room table, covered with a sheet. All three of the adults were kneeling in front of chairs, so Julia just as slowly closed the door.

"I think she's dead," Julia whispered. Oops, she hadn't meant to say that aloud.

"Who's dead?" Clementine's whisper was just a raspy version of her regular voice.

Julia pulled the child back into the kitchen. "The African girl. I think she's gone to be with the—well, she's passed on."

"Na-unh," Clementine said, not even making an attempt to be quiet. "If that girl was dead, then she wouldn't be lying on Aunt Verna's dining room table anymore. Auntie Julia, the grown-ups are just giving thanks that everything went so well, and beseeching the Almighty Heavenly Father to let her get better, and to quell some uprising in some village somewhere, bring forth a good harvest now that the rains have arrived in due time, lay His Healing Hand on somebody's sick uncle somewhere else, and bless it to the nourishment of our bodies, in Thy Most Holy Name, amen."

Julia tried in vain to keep from laughing. "To the *nourishment of our bodies?*" she asked.

"Or something like that. Prayer meetings are on Wednesday night, and they last an hour—*to the 'dot,'* as Papa says. He calls them Aunt Verna's 'down-on-her-knees time.' I don't have to go on account of we don't baptize until age twelve in our faith, and I'm only ten. But they switch back and forth between houses, and so once I snuck out of bed, and listened to one of them things for as long as I could stand it. It was b-o-r-i-n-g!

"But they prayed about everything you could imagine, and some things that I'd never even heard of, and at one point Papa prayed that I would be a good little girl, and get back to bed, or I was going to get what was best for me, and that it wasn't going to be a box of Jell-O chocolate pudding. That was two years ago, and I've given that a lot of thinking, but I still can't figure out how Papa knew that I was there, crouched down behind the door."

Julia wished to hug the girl, so that's exactly what she did. Much to her surprise Clementine did not pull away.

"Is there a mirror in your room?" Julia asked.

"Yes, ma'am," the girl said. "It's a big old mirror that used to be Mama's. She sat in the back of Papa's truck and kept that mirror safe all the way home from Luluabourg, while Papa drove so slow that moss grew on the wheel rims."

"Well then, that's your answer," Julia said. "Your father saw your reflection in the mirror."

Clementine gasped. "Hey, no fair! Christians aren't supposed to cheat."

"But, Clementine," Julia protested, "that doesn't count as cheating."

"Well, you figured it out before me, and I'm smart, you know. 'Tests ways beyond her years, that one, but her social skills are hopeless.'"

Julia smiled. "I tell you what, Clementine, because I feel that it would be rude to interrupt the praying, what if we play some games until they're through?"

"Goodie! What kind of games. Like I Spy with My Little Eye?"

"That's a good one. Or maybe you try to stump me with a question about something you've learned from your homeschooling, using encyclopedias."

"Yay! I can do that. Okay, here goes: What does the word 'aardvark' mean in the Afrikaans language?"

"Earth pig, and I didn't cheat; I studied up on African animals before coming out here."

"Aw, man! Well, let's see you get this one: who was Anna Akhmatova?"

"Uh—can you please spell the second word?"

"Auntie Julia, we've only barely begun the 'a's. Do you give up?"

"Of course not. You have to give me at least three hints for each question, and it's three stumped questions, and *then* I'm out. Those are the rules, à la Auntie Julia, take 'em, or leave 'em."

Clementine giggled her acceptance. And so they played and played, and of course Julia lost, but not for lack of trying. Julia was constantly amazed at the brilliance displayed by the child who was drowning in her clothes. The kid was a genius, with an IQ that might well have measured off the scale. There was no doubting her mental acuity, but there were hurdles one faced when dealing with a child this bright.

It was so easy to forget that Clementine Hayes was just a nine-("almost ten")-year-old child. Clementine's mouth could spew out facts, it could quote pages of scripture, but her mind could not reason. When Julia forgot the child inside that formidable brain, she could see confusion and hurt in her young friend's eyes. Even worse than that, she saw what looked like accusations of betrayal.

So Julia was careful, and the time passed quickly, even though for much of that time her cheeks burned with embarrassment.

They burned even hotter when they switched to a game of biblical charades, and Julia chose to act out Jacob's ladder. She was
pantomiming, climbing and descending a stairway into heaven,
as the angels did, when she heard a deep male voice speak off to
her right.

"Jonah and the whale."

She turned, mortified. She'd been observed by Henry.

"Jacob and his ladder," she said.

"Looked like a hungry fish to me," Henry said with a wink.

"Papa," Clementine said sternly, "you do know better than
that, don't you? A whale is not a fish."

"You're so right, kiddo," Henry said with an easy laugh. "Hey,
you ready to go?"

"Twenty-three skidoo," she said, and jumped into his arms.
Then, giggling, she buried her tiny face into the sun-browned
skin of his neck. In the process, her ubiquitous cork helmet clat-
tered to the floor.

Julia watched with a pang of envy. Surely she was just missing her own father. After all, she had not come to the mission
field searching for a husband. And certainly not a widower with a
child. On the other hand, if it was the Lord's will—Julia clenched
the fingers on her left hand between the folds of her full-circle
cotton skirt, as if to shut off this unwelcome train of thoughts.

"Well, this is what we've decided," he said. "You're to spend
the night here with the Doyers. It's too late now, and too dark, to
settle into a strange place."

It seemed like Henry had the uncanny ability to see right
through her. Julia breathed a huge sigh of relief. It was probably ridiculously loud, because both Clementine and her father
grinned.

"Okay then. First thing in the morning we'll take you over to
your house and get you settled in. Because it's late, Cripple can
stay here too—but in the kitchen. Believe me when I tell you, I
really had to push for this; it's against the law, you know."

"It *is*?"

"Yup, whites and blacks can't commingle."

"What about the Mushilele girl, Papa?" Clementine asked, tugging on a lock of her father's dark curly hair. "Must we cast her out into the wasteland, a howling wilderness, from whence we plucked her?"

Henry kissed his daughter on the cheek. It was every bit as loud as Julia's sigh of relief had been.

"No, sweetie," he said. "She's not going back to whence she was plucked. She's going to our house—to stay with you, in your room. That way you can translate for her. But only until tomorrow. Then she's going to board in the girls' school that Mama started."

Julia stared in disbelief. "Clementine knows how to speak Bushilele? I thought that missionaries didn't bother learning it, because it was too difficult and—"

"That's right," Henry said. "Everyone speaks Tshiluba as well. But Clemey's only friends are Bashilele children. Although there are some who would never admit it, she is a *great asset* to this mission."

"But a great distraction as well, aren't I, Papa?"

Father and daughter rubbed noses and giggled. That's when Julia knew, without a doubt, that it wasn't just homesickness she felt. It was something strangely akin to envy. But could it be? Could she be envious of the affection that a father showered on his motherless daughter?

If so, didn't that make her disturbed? Or could that possibly mean that she was in love? At the very least, Julia Newton was very confused and had a whole lot of praying to do. She could use some "down-on-her-knees time."

NINE

When Buakane was a little girl, still allowed to suck when thirsty from her mother's breasts, a villager brought in a pangolin that he had captured in a snare meant for a very small antelope. The pangolin can best be described as the offspring of an anteater that has mated with a pineapple. But even that description comes nowhere near the truth. A pangolin is covered with bony plates and has the ability to roll itself into a ball so impenetrable that even a lioness will give up on trying to eat it.

"Do you see that animal?" Paddle had asked her daughter. When Buakane began to shake her head, Paddle pulled the girl from the breast. "Speak with words, child."

"I see no animal, Baba. I see a ball."

"It is an animal, Buakane, and it is alive."

"It is *not* alive, Baba." Buakane grabbed the breast again, for it was a hot day and her thirst had not been abated.

"*Kah!*" Paddle marveled at her daughter's audacity. Surely this was a child for whom fate had much in store. And here was an opportunity to teach Buakane a lesson that might one day save her life. Again she removed her daughter from her shriveling breasts.

"*Baba!*"

"Buakane, this is indeed an animal, and it is pretending to be a rock—or something else very hard like a rock that cannot be eaten. The man who caught this animal—it is called a pangolin—will have to be very clever if he wants it to open up again. For you see, it is the pangolin's wish that the hunter will lose interest in him and return him to the bush. Now listen to my words, carefully, daughter. Someday you too may have to act like the pangolin, in order to save your life."

"Will I have to curl up in a ball, *Baba*? Like this?" At that Buakane sat beside her mother and closed her eyes tightly. Then she brought her knees up, and her head down, to approximate a ball.

"Yes, little one," Paddle said. "But you may also have to lie straight, like my *bidia* stick. The point is, the time might come when you will have to be very, very still, so that whoever has found you will lose interest in you and return you to wherever it is that they have found you. That is what is meant by 'playing dead.'"

"*Baba*, how will I know when it is time to 'play dead'?"

"Do not worry, Beautiful One. When the time comes, the spirits of your ancestors will reveal that path to you. Then it is simply up to you to decide if you will follow their guidance."

Buakane held her head high, for she was very determined for one so young. "Of course I will follow their guidance, *Baba*. How foolish it would be of me if I did not do so."

Thus it was that, although Buakane had been badly wounded by the hyenas, when the white man showed up, riding inside the terrible metal beast, Buakane remembered her promise to Paddle and played dead. Although Buakane did not curl up in a ball, as did the pangolin, she willed herself to ignore the throbbing pain in her thigh, and her body became as lifeless as she could command it.

Buakane was no ordinary girl—a fact that Grasshopper Paddle did not let her forget. Ever since the day of the pangolin, her mother made her daughter practice breath control, in the event that she *was* actually buried alive someday and rescue would not be immediately forthcoming. Paddle also administered to Buakane a variety of subtle but painful punishments, in order to toughen up her daughter and to prevent her from crying out due to pain. After all, the Bashilele were a strong warrior people, and they did not suffer cowards or weaklings—even among their womenfolk.

Although the eyes of the metal beast were blinding with their ferocity, and it roared with the noise of a thousand lions, Buakane forced herself to lie limp upon the white man's road, her own eyes all but closed. Through the slits that remained open, she could see the hideous face of the white man who bent to scoop her up in his arms. In truth, however, his arms were so much like those of any man.

But the smell of such a creature! *Aiyee!* There is no describing the putrid smell of a white man. Even after battling the carrion-eating hyenas, and the acrid metallic odor of so much of her own blood, Buakane was sickened by the stench given off by the man from *mputu*—the faraway place. This man smelled like the bad end of a wet dog, one that has joined you on the sleeping mat, and which you wish to eject.

Buakane was fully conscious when she was placed in the truck. Although she was grateful to have been snatched away from the jaws of the hyenas, she was equally terrified to be in the belly of this monstrous beast, and to discover the presence of two more whites, as well as an African woman not of her tribe.

When they all began conversing in Tshiluba, the local trade language, Buakane nearly cried out in surprise. Surely a white man could not speak an African tongue, even one as backward as Tshiluba. If only Grasshopper Paddle and Bad Odor could hear this for themselves. It was a moment more to be marveled at than had a monkey spoken, for was not a monkey at least from the same forest as a human?

As the evening wore on, the wonders mounted. But through it all—her terror, then her overwhelming awe upon seeing the wonder that was the white man's dwelling, and finally the pain of the sewing implement—Buakane played dead. She'd once watched a man who'd been mauled by a leopardess receive stitches. The witch doctor had used a bone needle and a filament of palm fiber thread. Nonetheless, the wound had gown septic within a day or two, and within three days' time, the man was dead. The man had not cried out in pain during his surgery, but he had shed tears. Buakane was determined not to do the same.

Much to her astonishment, after some mild pricks made adjacent to the wound area, the pain in Buakane's leg subsided remarkably. By the time the white witch doctor (Buakane suspected that it was a woman) was finished with her task, the girl could feel the sensation of tugging, but no real pain. Still, she feigned death.

Perhaps now that the white witch doctor was finished sewing up her wound, she would put Buakane back in the belly of the metal beast. Perhaps if Buakane stirred, to let the white witch doctor know that she yet lived, the white man with the arms of a person would make the beast carry her back into the bush and disgorge her near her village. If the spirits of Buakane's ancestors were kind, she would gladly return to submit to her husband, Chief Eagle.

Any amount of suffering at Chief Eagle's hand was bound to be better than the sort of punishment she had faced thus far this evening for her unspeakably bad behavior. Now if only Baba Grasshopper Paddle and Tatu Bad Odor did not have to likewise pay for her indiscretions.

Thus it was that Buakane's spirits actually lifted a little when the odoriferous white man—yes, he smelled far worse than her father—picked her up and carried her outside. However, instead of returning her to the metal beast, he strode across a compound of short greens and carried her into another, even more splendid place of residence. Tired and wounded though she was, her mind quickened when she was confronted with the glories that were to be found in this white man's home.

The incredible thing was that in each room of the white man's house a miniature sun hovered just below the ceiling. Simply by touching the wall, the white man was able to make this sun rise and set, although it did not change positions in the sky. If either Chief Eagle or his witch doctor could see this magic, they would lay down their bows and arrows and surrender all that they possessed to the white man.

For truly, truly, the conquest of the Congolese had been inevitable. The power of the whites was of a scope so great as to be incalculable. This was the opinion of Buakane, she who married an eagle, but she was just a female, so her ideas mattered not.

Another one of the white man's glories was a sleeping platform upon which were piled clouds—white clouds, such as one sees in a blue sky after a rain. But it was the mat on this platform that was the real wonder. How could Buakane ever hope to describe the experience of lying on such a thing to her mother? It was like—no—but it might be *similar* to the sensation of lying on one of those clouds.

Enough of such foolish thoughts. The smelly adult was gone, leaving her alone with the child. What was the plan? Was this the room where he kept his harem of younger wives? Buakane thought she would retch, not only because of his odor, but because of the peculiar things she had heard about white men while working in the manioc plot alongside her mother.

The whites—this was verified by those who had worked for them—cut off the ends of their sons' penises. Would this not explain the fact that the white man's manhood was always at least half a hand length shorter than that of a Mushilele warrior? One need only ask a Mushilele who had been conscripted into the army; after all, it was an easy task to cut a peephole into the palm-thatch walls of the Belgian officers' bath hut. The peephole also answered the question that had long puzzled many in Mushihi Village. The answer, by the way, was yes; the white man, just like the black man, was of a single color, from head to toe.

Buakane shivered as she eased her stress by trying to imagine just what such a hideous figure might actually look like. Would his *lubola* perhaps be pink? And what about the thatch that grew in the shade?

"*Aiyee!*" she said softly but still audibly. As for her eyes, they were now clamped tightly shut.

"What is it? Do you dream?" The words had been spoken in her own tongue, Bushilele.

Buakane's heart pounded, first in fear and then in great excitement. The only other person in the darkened room was the female child—a white girl, a being incapable of learning the difficult Bushilele language.

"Do not pretend that you cannot speak," the creature said again. "I have been watching you. I have played this game myself before."

Buakane could not help herself. "What game is that?"

"Ah! The game of playing dead. But not too dead, *e*? If you had been truly dead, then we would have eaten you." The white girl made hideous smacking sounds with her mouth and laughed like a troop of juvenile baboons.

"*Kah!*" Buakane attempted to sit, but the movement pulled on her stitches, causing her to lie back with a soft moan. "So it *is* true that the white man eats the flesh of my people?"

"*Tch,*" said the little white. "That is most disgusting. It is only the Bapende tribe—who live next door to you—who have eaten people. I think that now they no longer do, but of this I am not sure."

"Nor am I."

Then without warning the white girl performed the magic of turning on the small sun. The room filled with brightness so suddenly that Buakane was sure that she had gone blind.

"Oh, our mother!" she cried, in the fashion of all distressed women. "Our mother, our mother!"

"You will be fine," the white girl said. "It takes only a little while for your eyes to adjust."

She was correct. It was as if Buakane had suddenly emerged from a very dark forest and stared directly into the sun. Indeed, now she could see just as clearly as if there were daylight streaming through the windows—well, perhaps that was an exaggeration, but only a very small one. At any rate, the white girl was standing next to the wall, and she was smiling. She looked friendly; Buakane could not imagine this girl eating anyone.

"Are you a witch doctor?" Buakane asked.

The girl giggled. "No. But just the same, this is a kind of magic. One that you, too, could learn to perform. Do you wish to try?"

Buakane was but briefly tempted. The stress of the day, the anxiety and agony of the night, all of them had taken their toll. Now she really did wish nothing more than to close her eyes—all the way—and be dead to all thoughts. She wished this even if it meant crossing back to the spirit world.

"Perhaps I could try another time," Buakane said.

"Yes," the girl said. "Perhaps."

However, before she could sleep, Buakane was in need of a favor. "What is your name?" Buakane asked.

"My name is Worthless," the little one said.

Buakane nodded, for she supposed there was a reason for this name that she would discover in due time. Or perhaps not. For the moment, sleep was all that she cared about—and the urge to relieve herself.

"My name is Buakane. Now, if you please, Worthless, show me the way to the privy hut, that I might make water."

Worthless bit her lower lip. "*Aiyee,* Buakane, we do not have a privy hut such as you are used to in the village."

"Then I will use the *tshisuku*. Do you know a place that is safe from hyenas?"

Worthless giggled. "Yes, but it is not outside. Buakane, we make water inside our houses."

"*Ka!* You are joking! Surely—are you not?" Buakane could

tell, however, by the look on Worthless's face that the white girl was not joking.

"We make excrement in our houses as well," the child said.

Buakane was suddenly no longer sleepy. "No! This cannot be!" Although in truth, it did explain the white man's stench.

"Come," the child named Worthless said as she took Buakane's hand. "I will show you how it is done."

Buakane was amazed to discover that the white hand felt just like that of a real person's. It even possessed miniature fingernails.

"Worthless," she said, "are you white people really humans? Or are you animals of some higher kind—like the *tuyeke* that live in caves deep in the forest."

"What are *tuyeke*?" Worthless asked.

"I have never seen one," Buakane confessed, "but those who have say that it is a creature that looks somewhat like a monkey, but mostly like a man. It has a sloping forehead, no chin, but much hair. It cannot talk—only grunts—yet it walks upright like a man."

"I am not a *kayeke*," Worthless said. "Behold, I can speak quite clearly, and my forehead does not slope."

She pulled Buakane into another room and again performed the magic of turning on a little sun. When Buakane received her sight again, she saw that Worthless was standing next to a gleaming white mound of salt—or perhaps something equally as precious. Never had Buakane rested her eyes on something so intensely white. This was whiter even than the whitest eyes, the whitest part of a boiled egg—whiter even than the breast feathers of the pied crow.

"*Kah!*" she said in wonder. "What is it?"

"It is a special variety of night pot, upon which one sits to make their deposit of water or excrement."

Buakane approached, shaking her head in disbelief. "This cannot be."

"But it is. Watch, and I will demonstrate how to use it."

Without saying another word, Worthless pulled her long dress off over her head. Under that dress she had been wearing a pair of white man's shorts—but of softer material—which she removed as well. Now there was absolutely no doubt that at least she was of one color all over her body. And, just as interesting, was the fact that the white girl's parts were in corresponding locations to Buakane's female parts.

Finally, free of her heavy clothing, the girl hopped up onto the tall block of white and smiled. Soon Buakane heard the sound of Worthless releasing water, and a strong stream it was at that. However, not a drop went anywhere, but into the salt block. It was truly a marvel; it was something that she would make sure to relate to Paddle upon returning safely home again.

Then Worthless tore a piece of whiteness, from a roll of whiteness, that hung on the wall. This is what she used to dab the *menya* from her *bisuna*.

"We do not keep leaves inside this house," Worthless said in her tiny voice, "so we use this instead. In the language of the Belgians it is called *papier*. You will learn that word soon enough." She slid off the salt block. "Anyway, now it is your turn."

Buakane shook her head, for she was appalled at the idea that she should place her buttocks where another had so recently placed hers. Besides, she was still not convinced that the white man was fully human. Although Worthless had stated emphatically that she was not a *kayeke*—one of the humanlike creatures who dwelt in caves—perhaps there was more than one kind, and that the *tuyeke* of another region went by another name. Was it not possible that the thing upon which Worthless sat was not a block of salt, but a trap?

"What is the matter?" Worthless asked.

"I will make water outside," Buakane said. "I can walk to the *tshisuku*. I am not afraid of hyenas."

"You are afraid of this *nkumba*," Worthless said, sounding angry. "You do not want to sit on it because I am white."

"*Aiyee!* That is not so."

"Truly, it is so. Bashilele children are naked until their bodies start to change. You do not mind sitting where they have sat. Even under their *madiba* they wear nothing, so do not say—"

"Hello," said Henry in the Bushilele language.

Buakane yelped. She sounded just like a puppy whose foot had been accidentally stepped on, she was sure of that. But never mind, the white man with whom she'd ridden in the metal beast had just entered the room.

"*Kah!*" Worthless said to the man. "How long have you been standing there?"

Unfortunately, the man spoke in his own tongue, which made him sound like he was trying to speak with a mouthful of stones and thistles. Surely, this was proof enough that at least *he* was a *kayeke*. To say nothing of his powerful stench.

"Worthless," Buakane said, summoning her courage and that of her mothers, and her mother's ancestors, "you must take me back to where you found me. Cast me out into the road so that the hyenas may indeed eat me. If not them, then perhaps a leopard, or a lion, will devour me. In any case, I will be happy. And in any case, our husband will not lie with me, nor will I sit upon your trap. I swear this oath upon the life of my mother—who yet lives!"

Worthless put her hand over mouth, but behind it she was laughing. She said something to the *kayeke*, who laughed as well.

Then Worthless spoke rapidly, while spitting laughter with each word. "He is *not* my husband! This man is my father. And he is *not* your husband either!"

"*Kah!*" Buakane said.

Again the whites exchanged gibberish.

"Buakane," Worthless said, "my father says that you should not be afraid. That we wish only to help you."

Buakane could but stare helplessly. Her chief fault, her own father always said, was coming to judgment without carefully considering all the facts. In this case, she should have given more importance to the behavior that the man had exhibited earlier toward Worthless. *Bulelela.* He had been tender with her.

Paddle had once remarked that only men who preferred other men could show the trait of tenderness. Gentleness as well. Oh, if only Paddle were here! Buakane commenced blinking back tears. Hot, salty, unbidden tears.

"Please do not cry," Worthless said.

"*Tch*," Buakane said and turned away. "I do not cry; it is only that my eyes water from too many suns."

There was even more of the strange talk, after which Worthless spoke, pointing frequently to her father. "He has a white man's gun. We will go with you to the edge of the *tshisuku,* and he will stand guard against dangerous animals. Meanwhile, I will guard your modesty. When you are finished with your business, you will return here and spend the night. Tomorrow, we will take you to a school where all the students are Bashilele. They are all girls who have run away from very old men—some of these men are even older than my father."

Buakane shook with emotion. How could such words be true? She had done a very bad thing by running away from Chief Eagle. The man had paid her parents a very handsome dowry. Now they would have to repay him. And what of their reputation? Would Paddle and Bad Odor now become outcasts in the village of their birth?

What were the chances that Buakane should just happen to stumble upon a school that sheltered Bashilele girls who'd run away from arranged marriages with elderly husbands? Such a thing was not possible, unless the witch doctor had cast a spell on her—or the missionaries—and one or the other of them was in a trance and no longer in touch with reality.

Who should Buakane trust? The whites and the kindness they had shown to her? Or should she listen to the voice inside her, the one that called for her to run as soon as she reached the *tshisuku*?

If this was a trick, would the white *mamu* have bothered to sew her wound closed? On the other hand, perhaps whites enjoyed playing with their catch, such as a cat does.

Buakane, daughter of Bad Odor and Grasshopper Paddle, decided that she would keep her options open until she reached the edge of the *tshisuku*. Only then would she decide. At that time, her deceased ancestors would whisper through the tall grass blades, and she would listen. For they lived in the past, which is also the present, as well as the future. It is our ancestors to whom we must turn, and so for now they would be her guides.

TEN

While the dew was still heavy on the ground, and the sun not yet above the *tshisuku*, Nurse Verna Doyer took her daily walk with God. To be sure, by then she had clad her body in its full physical armor and had conducted her private devotions by lamplight, but neither food nor drink had passed her parched and shriveled lips. For verily, Nurse Verna was a mouth breather. At any rate, Verna's favorite hymn verse, from "In the Garden," had always been "I come to the garden alone / While the dew is still on the roses." There were no roses on Mushihi Station, but there were dog-faced baboons.

These large monkeys came out of the canyon in the early morning hours to catch the grasshoppers that were so weighed down by the heavy dew that they couldn't jump properly, much less fly. When the baboons and the missionary first came face-to-face, there were a few uncomfortable moments. When the dominant male reared on his hind feet, he stood nose to snout with the implacable little woman. When he bared his dripping fangs and barked, he looked every bit as vicious as the rottweiler that had lived in the junkyard across the street from the orphanage in St. Louis where Nurse Verna grew up.

One day little Verna took baby Jackie, another orphan, over to pet the "nice doggie." Despite the heavy chain-link fence between them, the ugly rottweiler managed to nick baby Jackie with its hideous yellow teeth. For her kindness, little Verna received the whipping of a lifetime.

Verna, who was eleven at the time and had a library card, did a little research. While the other orphans were attending a compulsory church service the following Sunday morning, little Verna, who was supposed to be in bed sick, took a bowl of antifreeze soup over for the "nice doggie." Thereafter, her only regret was that she had taken the life of one of the Lord's creatures on the Sabbath instead of on a weekday.

Nurse Verna was quite unprepared for her encounter with the baboons. The troop could have torn her limb from limb and dined on her for breakfast, instead of on grasshoppers. She had no weapons at her disposal—none at all, except for the two-edged sword that was her tongue, which was also the bane of her existence. Of course there was the Lord, and the power of prayer. If God could send an angel to shut the mouths of lions on behalf of Daniel, after he'd been cast into the lions' den, then surely God could intervene now. After all, was not Nurse Verna in this very place, Mushihi Station, to win heathen souls over to the Kingdom of Christ?

So Nurse Verna prayed that the Lord would shut the baboon's mouth, and that the troop would leave her alone. Despite her faith in her God, Nurse Verna didn't want to have her eyes open at the moment of her death, so she closed them and prayed silently. Besides, one is *always* supposed to pray with closed eyes.

That being said, when Nurse Verna was finished and dared to open her eyes again, the baboon troop was calmly grazing for grasshoppers all around her. The dominant male was now about ten yards away, on his haunches, and doing nasty things with a young female. The totality of that miracle was that not only had she been spared, but that from that day on, the troop accepted her almost as if she were one of their own.

Verna's early morning walks with God, which sometimes led her among the baboon troop, were not always dominated by prayer. Often she talked to herself. Aloud. And in English. Nurse Verna enjoyed the sound of her own voice. Arvin was not a conversationalist, and when she attempted to converse with Henry, they were invariably interrupted by the Great Distraction. Did not that man understand that children were to be seen and *not* heard? If Nurse Verna had butted into adult conversations the way that this child habitually did, she would not have been able to sit down—ever!

Anyone who believes in the literal truth of God's holy writ, and who is a parent, should read Proverbs 29:15. It explicitly advocates putting the rod to the bottoms of impudent children. And speaking of impudent, the Great Distraction and all that she represented were a cross so heavy that Nurse Verna could hardly bear them. Even with the Lord's help, Nurse Verna staggered.

The Great Distraction and her family were the cause of Verna's one great sin. It was the one thing that she could never tell—not even whisper—to Arvin during their shared prayer time. She surely couldn't bring it up to Henry, not even under the guise of a confession. Only the Lord and the baboons were privy to the awful burden that Nurse Verna had to carry around in her heart, and all because of that awful Great Distraction. Of course and her mother. Her *dead* mother.

That was the crux of the problem, wasn't it? The Hayes woman had selfishly gone ahead and died on Nurse Verna, even though she didn't really have to do so. There was no reason for her to; a Mushilele woman would not have died so easily. Nurse Verna had not even intended for the fetus to die—fetus, wasn't that how they referred to them in nursing school? Nevertheless, if the Hayes woman hadn't so foolishly attempted to birth a seemingly endless string of fetuses—so very many distractions from the Lord's service—she might *not* have bled out so easily that day. Truly, she might not have. *Bulelele.*

This morning, as on every other morning, Nurse Verna gave the little white cemetery a wide berth. Actually it couldn't properly be called a cemetery; strictly speaking, it was a medical waste disposal area for all the miscarriages that Mrs. Hayes had needlessly experienced. Four in all—even if you didn't count the last one. That was the sum of her vanity. Not one of them was bigger than a walnut, except for the last one, which was going on six months. A baby boy—*no*, it was a male fetus! And it was the Lord God himself who took the life of Elizabeth Hayes. It is God, and only God, who has the power to give and to take life.

"You must remember that, Nurse Verna," she said speaking quite loudly to herself. "It was that woman's job to save souls. That woman had no business breeding like a rabbit. No Christian does. We are living in the Last Days. All around us heathens are dying in sin. We can't afford to waste—"

Nurse Verna stopped in midsentence because she'd had a "speaking of the devil" moment. It was an expression that she hated, but one that was too often most appropriate. Like then. To think that she'd just been talking aloud about heathens, when out of the wet elephant grass, in the diminishing fog, stepped an African. More accurately, it was an African woman: the same bent and crippled woman who had accompanied Henry and Julia from Belle Vue the night before. Oh yes, and the infant. The infant was so tiny that Nurse Verna had an impulse to snatch it from its mother's arms and run it over to the clinic, where she might feed it some formula. Instead, she remembered her place in life and nodded brusquely.

"Life to you," she told the mother.

"Good morning," the mother replied. In *English*!

"How—are—you?" Nurse Verna said with much exaggerated slowness. Occasionally an African would learn that phrase by rote—perhaps from a missionary child—but that was always the extent of the native's English. The Mission Board had a policy prohibiting the teaching of English to blacks. After all, how else were the missionaries supposed to be able to communicate among themselves in private?

"I am quite tired after my trip," the African said. "Thank you for asking. Now please, allow me to inquire of you; how are you today? Did you sleep well?"

"Yes, yes, of course!" Nurse Verna said. "No, no, this will not do."

"Excuse me, *Mamu,* but you speak from both sides of your mouth. What is it that will not do?"

"Your manner of speaking. You cannot speak in English."

The little woman with the twisted body stepped back and cocked her head. "Please believe me when I say that I did not wish to offend. I did not know that you were Belgian, and that English was not your native tongue. By your unattractive way of dressing, you appeared to be a Protestant missionary."

Nurse Verna was stunned. She was appalled at the woman's cheek. At the same time, she was delighted.

"Tell me about yourself, *Baba.* What is your name? Who are your people?"

Just then the infant began to fuss, so the African matter-of-factly lifted her blouse to expose a breast, stuffed it into the child's mouth, and calmly began to answer. The infant, however, continued to fuss.

"My name is Cripple," the native said, "and I am a Muluba. Do you speak Tshiluba?"

"Yes, Cripple, I do. Do you prefer that we continue in your language?"

"Indeed, *Mamu,* for I find the sounds of your language very unpleasant."

"Is that so?" Nurse Verna said, feeling justifiably irritated by this rude and judgmental remark.

"Oh yes, they are much like grating a tuber of manioc with a dull knife."

"*Kah!*"

"There you see? *Mamu*, is that not better than saying 'what'?"

Nurse Verna couldn't help but laugh. My goodness, when was the last time she had done that? To be honest, she couldn't remember. Perhaps she hadn't even laughed since that happy day she'd received the letter informing her that she had been accepted as a missionary to the Belgian Congo. Oh what a joyous day that had been! And let her not forget; Nurse Verna had been saved from the eternal fires of hell. Nurse Verna had a right to be happy.

The woman Cripple shifted her fussing infant to her other breast. "*Mamu*," she said, "what is your name?"

"What do you wish to call me?"

"*Kah!* That is a nonsense question. Surely a woman as ancient as yourself is in possession of a name."

Nurse Verna laughed again. "Me? Ancient? Yes, I suppose that I am ancient by Congolese standards. I possess a Bushilele name, but not one in Tshiluba. I do not like my Bushilele name, so perhaps you could give me a new name in Tshiluba."

Cripple shook her head. To do so, she had to move her entire body. On the plus side, that was the only thing that made her baby shut up.

"A name does not fall from the sky like bird droppings. Or hailstones. It settles on the soul softly like this mist."

"*Tch*," Nurse Verna said, "when it has settled on my soul, let me know what it is. In the meantime, let me see your baby."

"*Aiyee!*" Cripple said.

"*Baba*, are you a Christian?"

"No," the African said with shocking vehemence. "Most certainly not; I am a heathen."

"But have you not heard of heaven with all its wonders?" Nurse Verna asked.

"Indeed, I have," Cripple said. "But now I put to you a question, for which I desire an honest answer."

"*E?*" Nurse Verna said.

"Will there be white people in heaven?" Cripple asked.

"Of course!" Nurse Verna said.

"Then I have no desire to go," Cripple said.

"*Kah!*" Nurse Verna had never been so insulted in all her life.

"Oh, do not be offended, *Mamu*," Cripple said. "My desires have nothing to do with you, but with all whites. For is not this heaven, of which you speak fondly, is it not a place of days without end?"

"*E*," Nurse Verna said. "What of it?"

"You whites crossed the Great Waters, took countless of our people back to your side as slaves, killed just as many of them here, and forced others to harvest rubber sap in the forest. If our men could not meet their sap quotas, you chopped off their hands.

"Here we are not allowed to live in your white villages—but we may work in them. We cannot not sit with you or eat with you. We are forbidden to marry you—although not one of us would want to do such a disgusting thing. This I assure you. Yet now you ask if I would like to spend the period known as the 'days without end' with you? *Mamu*, it is you who have offended me with such a question."

"*Aiyee!*" cried Nurse Verna, who was quite taken aback. "Would you not even consider heaven for the promise of a house that was nicer than mine?"

"*Mamu*, would you consider such an offer if it meant living in a house filled with thousands of snakes? Snakes even in your bed?"

"Do not be ridiculous," snapped Nurse Verna, whose Bushilele name was Mamu Snake. "If there were snakes in your house, then it would not be in heaven."

"Exactly, *Mamu*," Cripple said, and gave her crooked chin an irritating and triumphant tilt.

"You are a wretched heathen," Nurse Verna growled. "Now hand over your baby."

"I will do no such thing!"

"You child is very ill, *Baba*. Surely you can see that. Behold, she lacks the strength to latch on to your breast."

"No, *Mamu*, my daughter is no longer hungry."

"Allow me to feel her for fire."

Then, against all odds, Cripple actually held her infant out so that Nurse Verna might touch her. Nurse Verna didn't believe in instinct—that was too Darwinian—but she did believe in the power of the Holy Spirit to move and direct people, both spiritually and physically. She wasn't sure just how the latter worked; maybe with the help of unseen angels. At any rate, Nurse Verna did not believe there was any such thing as coincidence.

"*Baba*," Nurse Verna said, "your child has the fire burning inside her. How long has she been this way?"

Cripple closed her eyes and swayed with remorse. Or was that the way her deformed body reacted to standing still for that long?

"*Une semaine*," she said in French. One week.

Nurse Verna took care to corral the smile that had begun twitching the corners of her mouth. She knew only too well how switching to another language helped to mask the shame of that which must at last be spoken aloud.

"Come," she said. "Follow me. I am a *mulami* of the white man's medicine. I can help your daughter."

"Truly?"

"Truly, truly."

"*E*, but is there also a witch doctor in this place? A Muluba witch doctor—or, if we must not be choosy, it can even be a Lulua man."

Nurse Verna was neither surprised by the question nor incensed. When she was a new missionary, she had experienced both those feelings in a very similar case. She'd gone on for days about the patient's gall in wanting a witch doctor in attendance when she had just offered to save his life—in that case it was amputating a horribly infected finger. But my, what a difference thirty years' experience in the Congo made—twenty years at Ditu Dinene Station, and ten years here at Mushihi Station.

"*Baba*," Nurse Verna said, "I am sorry, but we no longer have a witch doctor in this place. We used to have a great one. Perhaps you heard of him: He Who Was Born with His Fingers Crossed?"

"No, *Mamu*," Cripple said.

"Are you sure?"

"*Mamu*, I would remember a name so unusual as that."

"Yes, of course. At any rate, he got to be a terrible nuisance—too much competition for me, really, so I put a curse on him, one that turned him into a goat."

"*Kah!*"

"Oh, I tell you, it was very hard on me. Look at me, Cripple, do you see my white hair and these many lines on my face? They are result of the power leaving my body and going into that curse." Nurse Verna could see that Cripple's eyes were wide with fear, so it was no time to stop. "So what do you think I did with this goat, Cripple?"

"You ate him?"

"*Nasha!* I did not eat him. That is a foolish answer. Remember, the witch doctor was a nuisance, but his magic was no match for mine. Instead of eating him, I put another curse on him, and made him run into that canyon yonder, and over the steepest cliff. Later that day the buzzards ate him. And that night a leopardess took her turn."

Cripple was not considerate enough to control her smile. "You tell bold lies for a missionary. Usually missionaries restrict their lies to what is written in their Book of God. Frankly, it is most refreshing to hear a new story, one in which you became an evil spirit capable of performing magic."

"*Kah! Baba*, I did not claim to be an evil spirit! I said that I was a witch doctor. Besides, this story was not meant to be believed."

"You lie again, *Mamu*. Only an evil spirit would be so *stupid* as to turn a man into a goat and then drive it over a cliff."

By now the sun had burned off the fog, and Nurse Verna was getting hot under the collar in more ways than one. *Lord, help me,* she prayed to herself, *help me to keep my cool.* Ha-ha. Well, it was funny the way the Lord kept popping those puns into her mind, just when she needed a diversion the most. Just not that Great Diversion. She detested the Great Diversion. Oh Lord, *anything* but her.

"*Mamu,*" Cripple said, "I did not mean to offend. I will go with you now to your place of healing, *e*?"

"*E,*" Nurse Verna said.

ELEVEN

Buakane awoke to sunshine streaming through a fly-splattered screen. It was a screen, something that she had never seen before, and the sight of it made her sit up, her back as straight as an arrow. The soft cover that someone had spread over her during the night puddled around her waist. She glanced to her left and saw that there was indeed a white girl lying in an adjacent bed. She could hear the white girl snoring now, not loud, sounding more like a puppy or a human child—a *Mushilele* child, that is.

So there had been truth mixed in with some of Buakane's nightmares. The whites, the monster with the blinding eyes, the hyenas—Buakane gently fingered her leg through the cover and then threw it back.

She gasped. It was an enormous wound, but it was sewn shut! Sewn! Like one might sew a rip in a loincloth, but instead of using a very fine thread of tightly braided palm fiber, this thread was stiff and black—even darker than her skin.

Her wound was tender, and it throbbed, but by rights it should have made her grasp her belly with both hands and cry aloud for Grasshopper Paddle, and all the mothers who came before her. What sort of magic had the white witch doctor performed on her thigh to hasten its journey of healing?

Buakane shivered and drew the covers back up around her shoulders. *Muena tshihaha mukashi mutoke.* A white woman who was also a witch doctor. Buakane had heard of this thing! For surely it could not be a real person, not like the child still asleep in the bed next to her. This thing had come into Chief Eagle's territory along with some other whites, claiming that they had permission from the Bula Matadi—the Belgians—to settle in the tribe's traditional hunting lands.

These whites did not request Chief Eagle's permission; instead they gave him permission to send his children, and the children of his village, to a school that they were building. In addition, one of the white women claimed to be a very powerful witch doctor, one who could heal the swollen bellies of the little children with red hair, such as were sometimes seen in Mushihi Village.

The white witch doctor could do many other marvelous things as well—one need only come and ask. But there was a catch; if you were a child, and you survived the white witch doctor's treatment, then you had to attend the school. And if you were an adult, what then? Adults who survived the *mamu*'s treatment had to bring her their idols—all of them—and she would burn them. Imagine that! This white, foreign ghost-thing—this *tshintu tshitoke*—would demand that you destroy the images that represented the unseen spirits that had shaped the destinies of your ancestors since *before the before*. Then she would try to convince you to worship an unseen spirit from her foreign land. This land supposedly lay across a lake so wide that no dugout canoe, no matter how large and stocked with provisions, could be paddled to the other side.

But what this foolish woman, and others like her, did not understand was that the idols themselves were just symbols, objects standing in for that which was spiritual and unseen. Christian missionaries had their symbols as well. For Protestants it was two very plain, crossed sticks of wood that hung in the back of their

churches. The Roman Catholics, at their mission up near Basongo, possessed a much nicer symbol. Somehow they managed
to do a perfect job of mummifying a Belgian dwarf, which they
hung on crossed sticks of wood. When the Bashilele heard about
the white dwarf mounted on crossed sticks, they came from villages as far away as twenty-four kilometers.

Yet even though the Bashilele knew just how stupid the white
man was when it came to matters of theology, they were a pragmatic people, and little by little they began to wander onto the
mission grounds in search of help for sickness and wounds that
would not heal. Well, Buakane had brought no idols with her. She
looked around the bed—*aiyee!* Even her bloodstained *didiba* was
gone. Now there remained to her not a single possession. *I am like
a newly born infant,* she thought to herself, *but even less that that.
At least an infant is wrapped in a blanket of innocence, but I have been
stripped of everything.*

"You need not worry," the white girl whose name was Worthless said. "I will give you one of my mother's dresses to wear."

The unexpectedness of the girl's soft voice was startling, but
her accent was entirely perfect, and thus both comforting and
alarming. It was as though a pet monkey had spoken.

"What?"

"Just a minute," said the white girl. She jumped out from beneath her covers and scurried away like a large rat into the *tshisuku.*
Soon she returned, her small arms weighed down by a pile of colorful cloth, which she carelessly threw on the bed. Then selecting
one long piece of cloth, she held it up to her chin. The other end,
however, touched the floor.

"This was my mother's dress," she said. "You are to wear it
today when you go to the school for runaway brides."

"*Yala!* I cannot wear your mother's dress, Worthless. She will
get angry with me and beat me with the stick that she uses to stir
the mush. *Aiyee!*"

Worthless did not laugh as Buakane had hoped that she

would. Instead she turned to her and looked down, as if she had spotted something important on the floor beside her. Perhaps she had seen a spider, or perhaps not.

"My mother is dead," Worthless said. "She will not mind."

What was Buakane to do now? She could not risk offending Worthless, for this white girl was her only hope for the future. But neither could she wear the dress of a dead woman. How was she to explain this?

Worthless solved the problem for her by pointing a tiny finger straight at Buakane, going so far as to poke her in the chest. "You need not worry about her spirit entering your body. My mother was a Protestant, and Protestant spirits cannot enter bodies of heathens such as yourself. When Protestants die, their spirits go straight up to a place called *diulu*, which is above the clouds, and because it is such a wonderful place, they stay there forever. Believe me when I tell you this, Buakane, not one Protestant has ever come back to haunt his village."

Buakane reached out to finger the material. Two of the dresses were the color known as *the color of manioc leaves*, and thus very pretty. This one, however, was special. It was the color known as *black*, which could have many meanings, although in this case it meant the color of sky on a day without clouds.

"Then I will wear this one," she said. "But you must tell me what happens to those whites who call themselves Roman Catholics when they die. We have heard about the little Belgian dwarf they keep nailed to their sticks. It is my wish to see this creature someday."

Worthless shook her head. "It is not a Belgian dwarf, Buakane; it is an idol. In fact, it is an idol that they actually worship. It is because of this idol worship that the spirits of the Roman Catholics will go straight down, deep into the earth when they die. Deeper even than the deepest cave. There it is even hotter than the giant fires that your hunters set in the *tshisuku* at the end of the dry season."

Such foolishness, Buakane thought, but again, she decided it was best to refrain from putting her thoughts into words. In many ways the whites were like little children who played in the dirt. They imagined various actions with bits of fluff or sticks wrapped with twine. This was an infant, the little girls would say, but in reality, anyone with eyes could see it was a stick wrapped in a corn husk.

Anyway, Worthless was in a great hurry. "It is my duty," she said, "to see that you are fed. Real food—*bidia bwa bene Kasai.* In order to do that, we must stop in at the girls' compound on the way to school."

Buakane was taken aback. "What sort of food do you eat, Worthless? Is it not real?"

"*Eyo,* it is real—but it is not as satisfying as cassava mush. On that account we whites must eat three times a day, instead of just two, and as you can see just by looking at us, we are neither as strong nor as handsome as the Bashilele."

Buakane nodded. Her new friend was capable of admitting the truth, even when it did not flatter her, which meant that quite possibly, here was a base upon which trust could be built. Who could have imagined, just one moon cycle ago, that a Mushilele girl—one of the nobility on her mother's side—could one day be friends with something so hideous as a girl with white skin?

"Please," Worthless said, "you must put a fire under your feet; this is no time to savor compliments."

Again, the truth. Therefore, after putting on the sky-colored dress—with some help from Worthless—Buakane allowed herself to be pulled into another room where there was a very large mirror.

Now, Buakane had once caught a glimpse of her face in a mirror smaller than the palm of her hand. This was the year that old Diamba had an extraordinarily successful Indian hemp crop, more than he and all the men in the village could ever smoke and still do any hunting. So the old man dried and bundled part of his crop and toted it to the nearest Portuguese-owned trading post. In exchange for the plants (which were widely known to bring peace and euphoria), Diamba was given a gray blanket, a speckled gray enameled basin, two axe heads, six bars of blue-and-white lye soap, each the length of his forearm, nine cans of sardines packed in olive oil, and a kilo of brightly colored beads. Plus one small mirror, with glass on one side and a portrait of King Baudouin of Belgium on the other.

Everyone of rank in the village was allowed to glimpse themselves at least once in the tiny mirror. Each person, upon beholding their visage, could not help but yelp with astonishment—no matter how clearly they might have seen their faces reflected in water at some earlier time. But then a terrible thing happened; almost everyone who had seen their reflection thus desired a little mirror of their own. When the next planting season rolled around, no one planted manioc—only hemp, so that the village would have faced starvation for the first time had not something happened.

That something was Chief Eagle. In a rage, Chief Eagle—for he really did care about the welfare of his people in general— seized the mirror from Diamba and ground the reflecting glass into powder. He then ordered his people—with the exception of Diamba—to replant their gardens, each one to grow only manioc and corn. Old man Diamba died the following year, but his oldest son was allowed to take over the tradition of growing hemp—but only enough to fill the village's needs.

Buakane had never encountered another mirror until now, and to think that the little one with the king's face on the back and this one that stood on the floor were the same thing was to remember that the shrew and elephant were both animals. But that was later. Her first reaction was to jump to the conclusion that she was witnessing a form of serious magic. Or was she gazing upon her spirit body in that other world, the real world? How was Buakane to know if she was alive now? Or dead?

She pointed to the image she saw standing before her. "Can you tell me the place where I used to hide when my mother sought me out to do work."

The image mocked her, saying the same words, and in the same way. It too pointed a finger.

Buakane's anger gave the her courage to step closer. This time she held her hand out, with the fingers open, and the palm pointing up.

"If you are from the true world," she said, "and I am but the illusion, then please take my hand and guide me back to your world, so that the thought of a thing and the thing itself can again be one. Only then will I finally be at peace."

Clap, clap, clap. Somebody—in this, the world of illusions, the existence of sorrow and pain—someone here had been watching and listening, and now the person spoke. Make no mistake, that person was not Worthless; Worthless had been watching Buakane, where Buakane could see her. The little girl's mouth was open in astonishment.

"You will never find peace," the someone said in Tshiluba, "unless you believe that Jesus died for the bad things that you have done, and then you ask him to forgive you."

Buakane could see now that the mirror revealed the image of the same white man she had seen the night before in the house where her wound had been treated. From this information she understood that she was not being given a glimpse of the real world.

The white man spoke again. "Child," he said, "have you heard of Jesus?"

Buakane looked to Worthless for help, but found none forthcoming. Instead, Worthless giggled.

"Quit the noise!" the man barked.

Worthless jumped forward and grabbed Buakane's hand with both her tiny hands. "Come! We must get you some *bidia* to eat before school begins."

"*Nasha*," the man said. No! "It is too late; that is why I am here. The savage has overslept, and already she has missed prayers in the house of our one true God. Now she must go straight to school."

Worthless dropped Buakane's hand and spoke what sounded like words of pleading, but in her own tongue, to the stern white man. Meanwhile, he shook his head vigorously. Finally, they both grew so agitated that the old man struck Worthless across the face, sending her reeling into a wall. There she crumpled to the ground, like a wilted manioc bush that has had a machete laid to its stem.

The man then grabbed Buakane's wrist. To be sure, he did not touch her hand, for that would have been an intimate gesture.

"You can eat this evening in the girls' compound," he said, "assuming that you behave the rest of the day. And do not ever speak of what you have seen or heard this morning. Is that clear?"

"*Eyo*," Buakane said.

"Do not think about it either. Instead, think about all the wicked things that you have done in your life, so that you may ask the one true God to forgive you. Otherwise you will be punished severely."

"Master," she said, "what is this punishment?"

"You will burn forever in a lake of fire."

Buakane stumbled, for such a harsh punishment came to her as a great shock.

"Up, child," the white man ordered. "We must hurry. Classes will have started."

"But truly, master? I will burn forever?"

"*E.* That is why we have come all the way to this terrible place to tell you—to warn you before it is too late."

"*Aiyee!* Surely, I have no wish to burn, master; I have a terrible fear of fire. My mother's sister fell asleep while tending a fire, and she fell face forward into it. Master, her face is now as white as yours."

The white man jerked her off her feet for a step. "You are a rude child!"

"Master, I did not wish to offend you, only to express my deep concern."

"About the color of my face?"

"*Nasha*. Master, it is true that I am very much afraid of fires. However, I can think of no great wickedness that I have committed. Since that is the case, why must I ask your one true God to forgive me?"

It was Buakane's turn to be thrown to the ground. As they were now outside, she landed on some coarse grass.

"You are a whore," the white man shouted. "I have changed my mind. You will have nothing to eat until you confess your sins before my God. Do you hear me?"

Buakane said nothing aloud, which only made the man angrier. But inside, she said to herself: *You are shit! You are nothing but dog shit.*

TWELVE

Julia felt as if she were going to explode. In front of her was half a moldy grapefruit, a large bowl of oatmeal (which was congealing like concrete in the sun), and a plate bravely bearing two slices of incinerated toast—yet none of the breakfast was available to her. That is, none of it would be available until Reverend Arvin and Nurse Doyer were finished with their interminable prayers. Julia was all for thanking God for one's food before tucking into it, but she had never seen anything like this before.

The prebreakfast ritual had started harmlessly enough. Reverend Arvin began by reading aloud a page from a booklet titled *The Upper Room*. Julia's family also read from that book every morning. But then Reverend Arvin asked Julia to lead them in a "word of prayer." Her prayer was actually nine words long—but they were very intense, heartfelt words, so they should have been quite sufficient.

Oh, if only that were the case! Julia was reaching for her spoon when Nurse Verna began praying in a voice loud enough to call Lazarus forth from the grave. For twenty minutes Nurse Verna laid the problems of Mushihi Station before the Lord—illness, shortages of supplies, infidelities among African teachers, encroachment of Roman Catholic missionaries—but not once did she thank God for the food. She did, however, use the word *just* seventeen times.

Reverend Doyer was a bit more formal, He said "thee" and "thou" and "thine" like he'd gotten a bargain deal on them at the five-and-ten store, but when it came to the word *just*, he trumped his wife by using it eighteen times.

Julia couldn't help but roll her eyes. She considered herself to be a good Christian—a real Christian—but she couldn't for the life of her understand why some folks had to come out with sentences along the likes of " . . . we *just* ask that you bless this food to the nourishment of our bodies . . ." What the heck was that supposed to mean, when that same person had already "*just* asked" the Good Lord for a million other favors?

"I saw you roll your eyes, girl," Nurse Verna said.

Julia stole a look from beneath her right eyelid, which was the only eye she could open independently. How could that grouchy old woman have seen her when the old woman's eyes were pressed tightly shut. *Or* had they been? They said that the best defense is a good offense, didn't they? Okay, so maybe that applied to sports, and not to garrulous, crabby missionaries, but Julia Elaine Newton did not react well to being bossed around.

She flicked her tongue at her hostess. It was lightning quick, like a lizard catching a fly. Was it an immature thing to do? Absolutely! Was it provocative? No—not *if* Nurse Verna, her sourpuss hostess, had *her* eyes closed as *she* was supposed to. Then it was akin to the proverbial tree falling in the forest when there was no one around; it made no sound. Except that in this case, no one should have seen it.

"Why, you little heathen!" Nurse Verna screeched.

Meanwhile her husband, Reverend Arvin Doyer, droned on for yet another "just." This one was for the true salvation of the new Roman Catholic priest up Basongo way. But as soon as that petition had cleared both his mind and his thin gray lips, the reverend's eyes flew open, and pushing back his chair, he jumped to his feet.

"What is the meaning of this, wife? Didst thou hear me say 'amen'?"

Nurse Verna's face turned whiter than the steer skull that Julia's brother had hanging on his bedroom wall back in Oxford, Ohio. Her lashless eyelids blinked rapidly, a sure sign that she was struggling to hold back tears. Oh boy, was Julia ever in for it now, and all because she'd been stupid and juvenile.

"Amen!" a hearty male voice boomed from the kitchen door.

Julia turned, her heart pounding with excitement and relief. "Henry!"

"You should address him as Reverend Hayes," Nurse Verna snapped.

"Or perhaps Uncle Henry," Reverend Arvin Doyer said. "After all, you are barely more than a child."

Henry stepped through the doorway and squared his shoulders. "She is a full-fledged adult, and a college graduate to boot. I insist that she calls me Henry—or even Hank. Would either of you prefer to call me Hank as well?"

"Most certainly not," Reverend Doyer and his wife said in unison.

"Well, then," Henry said, smiling as usual, "now that you are through with your morning devotions, you don't mind if I steal the young one, do you? I want to get her settled in her accommodations before she begins this auspicious day."

"There is nothing suspicious about today," Reverend Doyer said, "except perhaps the idea of you, a handsome widower, and a not unattractive young maiden paying a visit, without a chaperone, to a house on the other side of the station. Besides, she has not eaten her breakfast."

Julia thought she saw Henry wink. "Miss Newton," he said, in the most fatherly of tones, "if you're anything like I was when I was your age, you're probably too excited to eat. Am I right?"

Although she thought that she knew where he was coming from, Julia was furious at Henry. Couldn't he have simply ordered her to accompany him, rather than emphasize their age difference? She'd been led to understand that once a person reached the age of majority, age was no longer an issue. Her mother, for instance, had friends from many different age groups. The way that Henry had just put things made it sound like he was a grown-up and she was a child. Dang him! Dang him all to pieces!

But Julia was nothing if not pragmatic. "You're absolutely right," she said, bounding to her feet.

"Nurse Verna has patient rounds to make," Reverend Doyer said, "so I will accompany the two of you."

"No," Henry said. "We will be fine; I know the way." He chuckled perfunctorily. "I built that house. Remember?"

"You are tempting the devil," Reverend Doyer said. Meanwhile, unconsciously to be sure, the tip of Nurse Verna's tongue flickered from side to side in the space between her teeth, reminding Julia of a snake she'd once seen in the biology department's terrarium.

"Thanks for breakfast," Julia blurted, and then fled from the room—as well as the house—as though she were running from the plague. Oh, what a liar she'd been. Thanks for the breakfast, indeed! Why, she hadn't even taken a bite.

Outside, when she dared to stop running, she turned and saw Henry slapping his thighs and guffawing. "Young lady," he said, as he straightened his broad shoulders and assumed a serious preacher's voice, "you do know where you're going now, don't you?"

Julia was at a loss for words. Was he kidding? Was he serious? Was Henry about to consign her to hell? Surely not! She couldn't possibly have misjudged him that badly. But if he was going to be that narrow-minded, then she was out of there. Call her a chicken, a coward, whatever you wish; Julia was not cut out to be the sole defendant of reason, plunked down on some far-flung bastion of fossilized thinkers. This was not her idea of missionary life.

"How about you tell *me* where I'm going," she finally said.

"To see your new house, of course. Where else did you think?"

"Uh—well, the way that my morning has been going so far, I thought maybe you were going to consign me to that other place that starts with H."

"Ah, that place!" Then he began singing a ditty that Julia had learned in grade school, but one that her pastor had actually made a point of condemning from the pulpit as being sacrilegious.

> He told her he loved her, oh how he lied,
> Oh, how he lied, oh, how he lied,
> They were to be married, he up and died,
> He up and died, he up and died,
> He went down below her, sizzle he fried,
> Sizzle he fried, sizzle he fried,
> She went up above him, flip-flop she flied,
> Flip-flop she flied, flip-flop she flied,
> Now this is the moral, don't ever lie,
> Don't ever lie, don't ever lie,
> Now this is the moral, don't ever lie,
> *Don't* ever lie!

Julia couldn't help herself; she just had to join in. In fact, it was so much fun that they sang the song twice, the second time in harmony. Julia, who had some musical training, was a competent soprano. Henry, on the other hand, would later claim to never having had a lesson, but he was a natural at singing parts. His tenor voice so enthralled Julia that she couldn't wait to hear him sing hymns. She was about to asked him to sing her favorite hymn—"The Old Rugged Cross"—when he stopped abruptly and pointed to the short lawn grass on the right.

"Look," he whispered. "There. And there!"

At first Julia didn't know what to look for. Was it snakes she should be watching for? A bunch of snakes, heaven forfend! *What?* But then with a sigh of relief and a sense of awe and wonder, she realized that Henry wanted her to appreciate the strange little bird that was flying only a few feet above the ground.

Perhaps flying wasn't quite the right word. This little black, brown, and white bird appeared to jerk from location to location, hampered as it was by a tail that was nearly twice the length of its body.

"That's a male pin-tailed whydah," Henry said. "It grows that tail only during mating season. When Clementine was about four—maybe five, I told her that if she could sprinkle salt on the tail of one of those birds, then she could catch it. For days she ran all over the yard with our saltshaker. Tuckered her out so much that she always slept like a log."

"How do logs sleep?" Julia asked.

Henry chuckled. "Lying down."

"Good one!"

"Listen," he said, his voice suddenly grave, "feel free to run all over the grass, but always keep a watchful eye out when you're on the path. Snakes like to sun themselves out in the open—on second thought, be careful when you're on the grass as well. That's where the snakes hide when they're not sunning themselves. And bathrooms; toads will always manage to get inside your bathroom, and the pit vipers will follow."

"Pit vipers?" Julia was trying desperately to walk in Henry's exact footsteps, the better to avoid stepping on anything that might be skilled at blending into the path.

"A pit viper—in this case a Gaboon viper—is related to a rattlesnake, except that it is more deadly. Plus, we don't have any antivenom."

"Oh, Cracker Jacks!" Julia said.

"You'll be all right," Henry said. "I've put a kerosene lamp in your bathroom and another one by your bed. Turn the wicks down before you go to sleep, but don't let them go out. If you get up during the night, either carry the lamp with you or use a flashlight. Also, I built a wardrobe for you in the bedroom and put a machete inside it, just in case something four-legged finds its way inside your house."

"Jiminy Cricket!" Julia cried, and lunged at Henry, grabbing his shirt with both hands. It was a wonder that they didn't both fall.

"You don't have to get so dramatic," Henry said calmly. "I was just trying to prepare you for every possible scenario, given that your house is on the far end of the station. Kind of isolated, so to speak. Every missionary family owns a machete. At the very least, they are good for cracking open coconuts."

It was, of course, too late for Julia to turn back now, but she realized that she had bitten off more than she could comfortably chew. She was mildly afraid of the dark—and that was under conditions in which there was a constant supply of electricity and a working light switch. But slaying poisonous snakes in the bathroom by lantern light? Now that was straying into the territory of nervous breakdowns and rubber-padded rooms.

They walked in silence while the long-tailed whydahs twittered and the cheerful sun shone deceptively down on Julia's arms and hair. Had she not been expected to spend the night alone in an "isolated" house, with headhunters and hyenas as neighbors, and possibly vipers as roommates, Julia would have viewed this as an adventure, one with a very handsome man leading the way. Oh, hush that thought! She wasn't supposed to have thoughts like that about a fellow missionary—especially not about one who was so recently widowed.

"A penny for your thoughts," Henry said, just when she'd allowed the devil to lead her thoughts as far astray as one can possibly imagine.

"They're not worth even that much," Julia said. "Trust me on that score. But I do have a question."

"Shoot."

"The Doyers don't have running water—well, not really. They have a couple of barrels outside up on a platform, which two native women keep filled. The women carry water up from a spring in the canyon below. Nurse Verna said that they carry it in large gourds placed in six-foot-long baskets, which the women balance on their heads. She said it puts a terrible strain on their necks. Anyway, the water in the bathroom sink comes from those barrels, and then it is caught in a slop bucket, which is then used to flush the toilet. Is that how it will be in my house?"

Henry stopped, causing Julia to run smack-dab into him. "Whoa," he said as he gently pushed her away from his chest and made sure she was standing on her own two feet before letting go. "Are you all right?"

"As right as Seattle rain," she said.

"Seattle? Why Seattle?"

"I don't know; isn't it supposed to rain there a lot?"

"Hmm," he said. "I wouldn't know. But back to your water. You can brush your teeth and wash with your bathroom water, but don't drink it. Your kitchen is a separate building altogether, connected by a breezeway. There is a smaller, galvanized barrel in there, which is covered with a white cloth. The ladies will keep that barrel filled with water as well. You must see to it that Cripple, or whomever else you hire, takes only that water and gets it boiling. It must be boiled for no less than five minutes, and then strained again into the three galvanized buckets that I put inside the kitchen. Only then will you have water that is safe to cook with, or to drink."

Julia thought her head was going to burst with the responsibility of keeping track of all these lifesaving instructions. "Cripple? Uh—where will she live?"

Henry caught Julia's wrists, which wasn't easy, given that her arms were flailing around like a seal's flippers. That is, if that seal were ever to conduct an orchestra.

"Hey," he said, "like I told you, everything's going to be fine. The kitchen building has an attached room for servants. All missionary homes are built with accommodations for servants. Even if the rooms are not used for that, they can always be used for storage."

"You mean I won't be living out there defenseless, and all *alone*?"

"That's right, and neither will Cripple, because she'll be getting her own machete."

"Fabulous. You're putting a lethal weapon in the hands of a woman who hates me?"

Henry, who was holding both her hands now, let them drop. "She doesn't hate you; she just doesn't know what to make of you yet. Cripple is a Muluba, and to her, the Bashilele are every bit as enigmatic and heathen as they are to you. I guess the one big difference is that you see them as worthy of redemption. Cripple does not."

"But she's a native—like them! And she's a heathen! It's not the same thing."

"Forgive me, Julia, but now you're starting to sound like your run-of-the-mill colonialist. Tell me, honestly, if I could peer into your innermost heart, would I see the heart of a racist?"

"*What?*" Julia was furious. What a horrible question to have asked her. Reverend Paul Henry Hayes (aka His Holiness, from now on) obviously thought that she was a racist or else he wouldn't have brought up such a sensitive question—not now, not with what was happening back home in the States. What His Holiness didn't know was that Julia had marched shoulder to shoulder with her Negro coeds to protest the "all white after dark rule" of many small towns surrounding Oxford.

Take Trenton, Ohio, just twenty minutes from Oxford, where

Julia grew up. It was a bedroom community right across the Miami River from Middletown. While a sizable number of Negroes lived in Middletown and worked in at Armco Steel Mill, there was not a single Negro living in Trenton. That's because Trenton, like many other small towns in the northern states, abided by the "all white after dark rule." Oh, this was an unwritten rule, to be sure. And Negroes were quite welcome to drive over to Trenton during daylight hours to work as domestic servants—although because the town was solidly middle class, there were few who could afford such a luxury.

At any rate, Julia was most certainly *not* a racist. She had even stayed up all night once, arguing with her roommate over the issue of receiving a blood transfusion from a Negro donor. When she couldn't persuade her roommate, Claire, to change her mind and accept the fact that human blood was just that: human blood, Julia put in for a transfer of rooms.

So there, Reverend Know-It-All Hayes, Julia thought. *Stick that in your pipe and smoke it!* Of course, Julia being who she was—at least she realized this—the polish had been taken off the rest of the day. No matter what she did or no matter whom she saw, no matter what happened, it just wouldn't be the same now. And it was all because Henry had jumped to conclusions about her character. Her *character,* for crying out loud.

"Julia," the guilty man said, "we need to take it down a notch; we have an audience." He pointed with his chin to where a group of children—maybe seven or eight—were literally rolling on the ground while pointing at her and laughing. She was obviously being mocked, and for what reason? For being a stranger? Now this really took the cake!

The children were only about thirty yards away. Where had they come from? As angry as she was, she posed this question to Henry.

"From there," he said, pointing to the elephant grass at the edge of the Mushihi Station. "From the *tshisuku.* Those are some of *your* girls on their way to chapel. The rest should be following shortly."

"I don't understand," Julia said. "Those are little children."

"Surely you knew that. I mean, the child bride thing was explained to you—right?"

"Yes, yes, of course. It's just that they seem so young when one actually sees them."

"They're between the ages of nine and fourteen—give or take. No one in the Congo knows their exact age. Chronological age is a white man's obsession. Would you like to meet the girls?"

Julia's heart was pounding with anxiety, but she wasn't about to let Henry know. "Sure," she said.

"*Nuenu, bika ne lua!*" Henry said, clapping his hands.

The girls immediately jumped up and began marching toward them. They held long arms ramrod straight down their sides, and their backs and necks they carried straight as well. They were no longer laughing, but stone-faced. They had bitten the hand that was supposed to shelter and feed them for at least the next several months until independence. If the new *mamu* so desired, they knew, each girl could be sent back to her village, and the husband to whom she had been sold.

And when you thought about it, why should these poor little Bashilele girls believe that these strange, white-skinned missionaries would act any differently than their own parents whom they had grown up loving? For was not the Old Testament, which the missionaries made them read in school, full of stories of betrayal and revenge?

Well, Julia certainly couldn't blame these girls if they were as anxious as she was. She had grown up in a good Christian home, and she still couldn't see how Abraham got away with forcing his concubine Hagar and her son Ishmael out into the desert to die of thirst!

Julia would make these exquisite children trust her. And oh, yes, they *were* exquisite—there was no other word to describe them. It certainly wasn't their clothes, that was for sure; their clothes were on the hideous side. They wore identical dresses of simple design. The flimsy frocks had been sewn from the same bolt of cloth, featuring a geometrical "African" print in red, orange, hot pink, melon, and yellow—hot colors for a hot climate.

On the plus side, to a girl, they had high prominent cheekbones, large almond-shaped eyes that were thickly lashed, and on closer inspection, necks as graceful as those of gazelles. To see so much beauty, so concentrated in one place, was truly humbling. In any case, what Julia had heard about the Bashilele being a handsome people was certainly true, if one was to judge by these girls, for in a world where fairness counted, every single one of them could have gone on to be a model.

"Would you like them to give you a Tshiluba name?" Henry whispered.

"I already have one," Julia whispered in return.

The girls arrived, but much to Julia's relief they remained about as far from her as one might expect an American girl to stand. The only difference is that these girls were without guile, which is to say that they stared quite openly. One would say something in Bushilele, and then the rest would crane their long beautiful necks, in order to get a better view of whichever part of Julia was being discussed. Julia wondered if this was how a chimpanzee or other great ape might feel in a zoo setting.

"Do you understand anything that they are saying?" she said aloud to Henry.

"A little," he said. "Something about you having ugly eyes and hair. They think that your hair looks like dried grass."

"Because it's blond?".

"You asked."

Julia grabbed a hank of her hair and stepped toward the girls. "Do you think that this hair is ugly?" she asked in Tshiluba, the local trade language, which was the language she'd learned in America, and the language in which the girls did their lessons.

"Yes, *Mamu*," two girls chimed in at once.

"It is very ugly," a third girl said. "It looks like dead *tshisuku*, at the end of the long dry season. Does it burn easily?"

"*Ka!*" said Julia. "What kind of question is that?"

"May I touch it?" asked yet another. Then without waiting for an answer she stepped into Julia's personal space and began to finger her hair. "Very bad, very bad," she pronounced.

Soon virtually all the girls were tugging at Julia's hair. "*Tshianana beh*," they said over and over again. They said it about her eyes. They even said it about her skin color, which they claimed reminded them of poisonous mushroom stems. Julia had been warned that this would happen, so she wasn't traumatized. But when one girl grabbed the neckline of her blouse and tried to peer down at her breasts, she'd had enough.

"Stop it!" she said angrily, and even though it hurt like the dickens, she yanked her head loose from the hands of those who claimed to loathe her hair—a claim she still couldn't quite believe!

Henry, of course, was no help at all. "She was just trying to see if you were white all over. You know, like a poisonous mushroom stem." He roared with laughter.

Julia couldn't stand it when folks laughed at their own jokes, especially if she was the butt of their humor. She glared at Henry, who didn't even seem to notice.

"When I was growing up," he said, "my native friends were always trying to sneak peeks. Clementine's friends still do. It's a hard concept for these kids to swallow, that our entire bodies should be so hideous."

Julia couldn't help herself. "But that's just stupid. Have they ever seen a native who was black with white privates? Whoever put such a crazy notion in their heads?"

"We did," Henry said.

"We *who*?"

"We, the white man," Henry said. "We insist on keeping our erogenous zones covered. Ergo, the natives have come to the conclusion—and quite logically, I might add—that there is something there that we are trying to hide."

"Well, you are darn tootin'," Julia said, "but it isn't because we're ashamed. It's because we are no longer heathens."

"Oh, is that it?" Henry said. "Adam and Eve weren't heathens either, and they walked around the Garden of Eden without a stitch of clothing on."

"Let me remind you, *Reverend*, that the nudity in the Garden of Eden garden predated Adam and Eve tasting the forbidden fruit. Once they ate that fruit and their eyes were opened, they became just as evil as the rest of us."

"My, how you do like to carry on," Henry said. "It looks to me like you're about to lose your audience as you stand here arguing with me. Do you want me to ask them about a Tshiluba name, or are you afraid that they might name you something mean, like Grass Head, or Toadstool?"

"I already said," Julia hissed, "that I have a Tshiluba name. Cripple gave it to me back at Bell Vue."

Henry smiled. "What is it?"

Julia turned to the girls, who were indeed beginning to drift away. In passably accented Tshiluba, she called out to them. "My name is *Mamu Mukashiana*."

The girls stared at her. Henry did as well. After a few very long agonizing seconds, Henry said, "Julia, please, tell us the end of your joke. This is beginning to feel uncomfortable."

"You feel uncomfortable?" Julia said. "What about me?"

Henry waved the girls away, telling them that he would be at chapel momentarily, and that they should behave for Reverend Doyer—or *else*! He punctuated his words by pounding his fist into the palm of his hand.

The girls fled, but as they did so they also pushed at each other and laughed. Julia got the impression that the girls weren't really scared of Henry, but they were more than a little amused by her African name. It was then that it dawned on her that she didn't quite understand the translation of her new name: *Mukashiana*.

The first half of this name meant woman, but the ending was unfamiliar to Julia. Still—"*iana*" was such a pleasant suffix, how bad could that be? Julia had a Tshiluba dictionary, but she had been saving the "discovery" of the meaning as a special treat. Anyway, until that moment, she really had not had time to do anything but live in the present. Well, now was the time to find out.

"Henry, what does my name mean?"

He'd resumed walking, and at a brisk rate, but he stopped and turned. "You honestly don't know?"

"Obviously, I don't," Julia said. She was close to tears. It was a beautiful day, and she was just beginning what promised to be an exciting adventure, but how could she navigate this course without all the cues? It was frustration that drove her to this point, not fear, mind you. Julia never cried when she was afraid, and she never, ever cried from physical pain. It was only anger and frustration that ever filled her baby blues with salt water. Henry could ask her mother if he didn't believe that.

"Hey, kid, take it easy," he said, then bit his lip. "Oh, shoot. I didn't mean it—that 'kid' part. That's not how I see you. That just sort of slipped out because I'm so used to talking to Clementine. Honest. You're just like any other missionary; why, you're exactly like Nurse Verna!"

Julia smiled, despite herself. "With a mouth as slippery as yours, you should have no trouble extracting your foot. Therefore, I shan't concern myself about the possible need for mouth-to-mouth resuscitation."

Henry's tanned face darkened considerably. "Now *that* was an inappropriate remark. Nurse Verna would never have said that."

"You are absolutely right on that account," Julia said. "However, she might have thought such a thing. Face it, undoubtedly there are some people who think that you are a very handsome man, and who knows, she could be one of them. As the old saying goes, 'still waters run deep.' Anyway, my reference to the afore-mentioned procedure was strictly clinical, I assure you. I was a lifeguard at camp, and I've had considerable training on dummies. Oops—and I didn't mean to call you a dummy, either!"

Henry turned again, and continued his brisk pace, but not before calling one last remark over his shoulder. "Your name means: She Whose Name One Can't Be Bothered to Remember. However, Julia, I am certain that I will never forget yours."

THIRTEEN

If there were no true emergencies—deep lacerations to sew up, uteruses to push back inside—Nurse Verna would try her level best to attend morning chapel. She would pull down the rolling metal window through which drugs were dispensed and slip the Yale lock through the heavy-duty hasp on the reinforced wooden door. Of course she always took Many Boils with her to the brief service. It was, after all, primarily for the sake of Many Boils's salvation that she kept so many patients waiting in the broiling sun.

The schoolchildren sat up front with their teachers, boys on the right, girls on the left. In the Tshiluba language the word for "right hand" was "boy's hand," and the word for "left hand" was "girl's hand." This was as it should be, Nurse Verna though, since boys were usually stronger and more dominant. Nurse Verna was very fond of the Tshiluba language; it made a lot more sense than English, which was a tongue that had been cobbled together from French, German, Latin, Danish, Greek—you name it.

Besides the students, at chapel there were always a few of what Nurse Verna privately referred to as "petitioners." These were mainly the elderly or very sick people who had come to church to beg God for healing or to be put out of their misery. Occasionally, one saw a "fat cat." These were always men—

some were literally fat—who were there to pray for wealth or give thanks for favors received in hopes of receiving more wealth.

"Ask and ye shall receive" was the most popular prayer among the fat-cat set. Nurse Verna abhorred the fat cats with righteous indignation pulled straight from the holy scriptures. Of course the fat cats sat on the right side of the church—on the male side. But unbeknownst to them, Nurse Verna prayed that her God, the God who loved justice, would shrivel the testes of the fat cats, rendering them sterile.

The people with whom she had no problem—but they were sure to upset that Marilyn Monroe look-alike, that dilettante missionary fresh from the States—were the beggars, lepers, and nursing mothers who sat on the women's side directly in front of Nurse Verna. Actually, there weren't beggars in the group, as the Bashilele were too proud for that, but there was a leper, and a woman with a goiter the size of a grapefruit, and tons of nursing mothers. Blouses weren't required in the back of the church, and it was common to see children as old as three standing while nursing. Most often the children's eyes would be fixed on Nurse Verna while they stretched their poor mothers' breasts out flat, like hot water bottles filled with milk.

On this particular day, Nurse Verna was a trifle late taking her seat on the bench reserved for the buttocks of white people, which was located at the far rear of the church. She arrived just as the children from the girls' school marched into the building. As usual, they processed behind their native headmaster. Miss Julia Newton brought up the rear, looking grim, stiff, and totally out of place. However, few people managed to get under Nurse Verna's thick, sun-mottled skin as did the native headmaster.

Ever since the unfortunate death of Mrs. Hayes, the mother of the Great Distraction, the girls' school had had to resort to having a native headmaster. This being the Belgian Congo, that native had to be a man. Virtually all the teachers in the Belgian

Congo were male, and certainly all the principals. No student was going to take instructions from a black woman seriously—a white woman, yes, but not from a native woman.

This temporary headmaster was an impressive fellow, one who had a secondary-school education that he'd received at Djoka Punda. Plus, he was married, and since he and his wife were both middle-aged, they could serve as houseparents to the girls and live with them in their compound. The only negative quality that Born Without a Neck had was that he was a pompous fool.

Whereas even the missionary men wore their neckties only on Sunday mornings, Born Without a Neck wore one *every* day. It was one that had been discarded by a missionary when it became too frayed, but this didn't seem to bother its new owner. Neither did the fact that, without the semblance of a proper neck (he had one, but his vertebrae were fused), the tie cupped his chin, rendering him ridiculous in the eyes of his white beholders.

However, this tie, and the fact that he was meticulous about laundering and ironing his two shirts, very much impressed the Bashilele. Not long after he took over the girls' school, some of the older male students began referring to him as the "little white man." Instead of finding this offensive, Born Without a Neck was actually flattered.

One might say that Nurse Verna's simmering dislike of this pompous little twit reached the boiling point when she saw him strutting down the aisle with his protégées in tow, including that poor wounded Mushilele girl she'd sewn up the night before. That did it; that was the bamboo pole that broke the camel's back! May the good Lord forgive Nurse Verna for the scene that she was about to make in his house.

Nurse Verna was on her feet just as fast as if she'd been bitten by driver ants. "Stop," she cried, in a loud and what sounded to her like a terrifying, prophetic voice. "In the name of *Yehowa Nzambi*, I command thee to stop, *Directeur* Born Without a Neck!"

Now, a weekday congregation such as this was neatly drawn along two lines: those who were dedicated believers, but who were young and in need of a good laugh; and those who were old, and who were in attendance primarily to seek favors, and in need of a good laugh. The result was that everyone laughed hysterically—that is, everyone except for *Directeur* Born Without a Neck, and, of course, both Reverend Doyer and Nurse Verna. Even that irascible, motherless cub, the Great Distraction, howled with unbecoming glee.

That was to be expected. *However,* for that new girl, Miss Julia Newton, to show disrespect to a fellow missionary in front of all the natives—well, even Jesus might have tapped his sandal-shod toes a few times before forgiving that egregious sin. The natives were restless—on the verge of rioting, one might say—and the only way for the white community to survive was to appear unified at all times.

Fortunately for everyone, Born Without a Neck did stop, causing his girls to pile into each other. "*Mamu,*" he said, "what is it that the Lord God Jehovah wants of me?"

"You fool," Nurse Verna snapped. "He does not want you! He wants that girl—the one with the bandage on her leg."

"*Aiyee,*" said Born Without a Neck. Strange as it might seem, he could shake his head vigorously from side to side, even through it sat directly atop his body. "God could not possibly want anything with a girl—and certainly *not* with a Mushilele girl."

Nurse Doyer would be the first to admit that one's husband should be the head of the house, just as God intended. And, when it came to preaching, a woman should sit back and do the listening. These things were all written down in the Bible and carved into stone by that bitter little man, the Apostle Paul. But when it came down to the sort of racist bigotry purported by the pigeon-chested little headmaster and his vocal disparagement of the female gender—well, Nurse Doyer's dander had now been officially raised.

"*Yala*," she said, "you are a wonder to behold!"

"I am?" said the clueless headmaster while beaming.

"Surely," Nurse Doyer said. "Never before have I seen a small stone, such as your head, turn so easily upon a larger stone, such as your body, without there first being an application of thick grease. Tell us, if you will, Headmaster, how such a dense and heavy stone can swivel back and forth so easily? What grease did you first smear on that slab of rock beneath it? Please, if you will, bend forward as if to tie your shoes. We wish to see if the small stone slides off."

Oh yes, the congregation enjoyed that very much, although Nurse Verna was quite sure that the Lord Jesus did not approve of her mean streak. But it did generate some much needed results. As soon as she'd finished her vicious and very unchristian-like attack on Born Without a Neck, the so-called Reverend Paul Henry Hayes, the father of the Great Distraction, was at her side.

"Nurse Verna," Henry said in English, "what is it?"

Nurse Verna swallowed hard. She swallowed three times—one for each person of the Trinity. It was her version of counting to ten before answering.

"You were there last night. You saw this child's open gash. She has to stay off her leg or she is going to open up the stitches. If that happens, then there is a good chance of her wound going septic, and then—well, you know what comes next. So you tell me!"

Henry sighed, just as Nurse Verna knew that he would. The man had a heart as soft as Limburger cheese.

"Death," he whispered, so that the Great Distraction wouldn't hear, but she did anyway.

"Oh, Papa," the urchin practically wailed. Then she ran to him and fell into his arms with a great show of generated drama. That was her specialty, and of course the natives thrived on it. "Are you saying that Buakane might die if she doesn't stay off her leg?" The

Great Distraction had the annoying habit of speaking loudly, and in perfectly accented Tshiluba.

Upon hearing such an extreme, although medically sound, prognosis, Buakane collapsed on the dirt floor of the church and commenced keening at death's door. There she implored the Grim Reaper to grant her immediate access. But if that was not to be the case, then would her ancestors intercede on her behalf, so that she might be spared all the pain and suffering that normally accompanies gangrene and amputation.

Clearly the child named Buakane had witnessed much in her young life, but that didn't make it all right for the Great Distraction to spill the beans. If that spoiled brat Clementine was Nurse Verna's child, she'd soon be the recipient of a spanking that would make it all but impossible to sit on her gluteus maximus for a few days.

The only redeeming quality the Hayes girl possessed was one that Nurse Verna shamefully coveted; Clementine had the ability to actually sound like a native when she spoke Tshiluba—not to mention that she had mastered the much more difficult tongue of Bushilele. Okay, to be honest—and Nurse Verna was *always* honest with herself, unlike *some*—the child did possess an uncanny ability to think fast on her feet. In that regard, she was sometimes way ahead of the adults.

Like the very next moment. This pint-size person, who was practically drowning in her mother's clothes and oversized pith helmet, suddenly released herself from her father's embrace and just took over.

"*Muyishi*," Clementine said, addressing the headmaster as "teacher" and thus demoting him on the spot, although she had no authority to do so. The congregation certainly found the disrespectful twerp funny—of course, natives laughed at just about anything.

"Teacher," Clementine Hayes said again, and again it was in

Tshiluba, "you must send one of your girls to where my father is building the new bookshop. There she will find a wheelbarrow. Have her bring it here, and then you will ask Mamu Snake to assist you in putting Buakane in it, and after that, you will take her back to the girls' compound. There she will stay and rest— sitting or lying down, as Mamu Snake instructs you. Listen to me, you Teacher of Girls, your wife may not use Buakane as a servant. Neither you nor your wife may press her into any sort of work that involves standing or walking. Is that clear? Do you hear my words?"

"*E*," Born Without a Neck said.

"Why, I'll be a monkey's uncle," Nurse Verna said aloud.

To be sure the congregation was practically rolling in the aisles, and there was even a smattering of applause, but clearly, the child's words had been quite effective. Oh, what a bitter pill to swallow; the Lord of Hosts using the Great Distraction to ac- complish something that was beyond Nurse Verna's capabilities.

But that didn't necessarily make it right. A child ought not to speak to an adult that way—even if the adult was a native. On the other hand, the Bible did say that "a little child shall lead them." Isaiah 11:6. Yes, well, it wasn't natural for a child of not quite ten to talk like that. What's more, given the political climate, it was downright dangerous. Now that Born Without a Neck had been shamed in front of a congregation composed mostly of children, fat cats, and old women, he was sure to take revenge.

Born Without a Neck claimed to be the younger son of a Muluba chief. It was even possible that he was the *eldest* son but had been passed over in the line of succession because of his defor- mity. Whatever the case might have been, Nurse Verna believed that Born Without a Neck was a person to be reckoned with. From now on she would keep a better eye on the disgusting little man to see that he treated his girls right. Miss Julia Newton was going to need all the help she could get, to put the girls' school back in shape, whether she wanted it or not. By the grace of God, Nurse Verna was there to give her just what she needed. That's what older, more experienced missionaries were for.

In the meantime, she was happy to take over entirely. "Born Without a Neck, a wheelbarrow! Send one of your girls!"

"Yes, Mamu Snake," the headmaster said, bowing with his entire torso, although his eyes burned with rage. He swiveled to face his girls. "You, you who are called Born After Much Medicine, go fetch the wheelbarrow. Do not return without it. And take She Whose Eyes Are Vacant with you. I do not want to discover that you have taken the morning off to pick mushrooms or to nap under a mango tree. I want the wheelbarrow now. *Buasha, buasha.*"

No one laughed. One girl looked terrified, the other stared blankly, then off they ran. After that Henry led Buakane to the nearest bench in the native section, and Born Without a Neck continued his strut down to the front with his conga line of very young and very attractive Bashilele girls.

As soon as everyone was seated, Reverend Doyer, who'd been seated up front on a metal folding chair, took his place behind the pulpit. He smiled as if nothing untoward had happened, and he held up a pocket-size blue hymnbook.

"Let us praise God by singing 'What a Friend We Have in Jesus,'" he said.

Immediately the boys' headmaster, *Directeur* Ends Famine, took his place at the front of the church and began waving his arms. The congregation burst into song with great gusto and full voice, but no one paid attention to poor Ends Famine. With the exception of some of the heathen women at the back of the church, virtually everyone, fat cats included, knew both words and tune to this simple song by now. However, no two people could be bothered to sing quite the same tune as anyone else, or at quite the same speed.

"Mulunda, mulunda muimpe, Yesu udi mulunda!"

Perhaps the worst offender of anyone was Henry Hayes. His normally beautiful tenor voice seemed to try to unite their voices by wandering all over the map with them. Nurse Verna could only sit through the first stanza, then she *had* to flee. May God forgive her, she really had to.

FOURTEEN

Buakane did not let on how terrified she was to be lifted into a shallow metal box that was mounted over a single wheel, and to which were attached two long wooden handles. When the girl's headmaster Born Without a Neck began to push it, she did not scream. When twice he lost control of it to the point that the device tipped entirely over, spilling Buakane—once onto dirt, and once into a clump of head-high, bug-infested *tshisuku*—she forbade her throat from making the slightest noise. She was, after all, the highborn daughter of Grasshopper Paddle, of the Leopard Slayers clan, and the twenty-third wife of Chief Eagle of the Snake Eaters clan.

Although she was in great pain, especially following the second fall, Buakane eventually learned how to compensate for the movement. Toward the end of the trip she was almost enjoying herself. But as with most good things, that too came to an abrupt ending. One moment the stout, panting headmaster was pushing her through the *tshisuku* on a footpath, and the next moment they were in a large clearing, surrounded by a stockade of sharpened bamboo stakes, each twice as tall as your average Mushilele man (almost four meters in height as a Belgian measures).

Inside the stockade were ten tidy palm-thatch huts. In the

center of the huts stood a palm-thatch house with mud walls. The mud walls gave the large house a more permanent nature, so that in addition to its size, one knew instinctively that this was where the headman lived. There were a few smaller structures within the stockade wall—sheds of sorts, chicken houses, and the like, but nothing intended for human habitation.

At this hour of the day there was no activity at the girls' compound except for the antics of a buff-colored hen with an orange-brown and black neck ruff. She'd managed to overturn a large piece of rotten wood that was riddled with termites and was calling frantically to all twelve of her chicks. In the meantime, a leathery old hen about half her size, but with twice the temperament, was trying to scare mother and brood away with a series of vicious attacks.

"The old one will be our supper," Born Without a Neck said.

Buakane shrugged. After all, she was not supposed to know Tshiluba, which was the headmaster's language.

A woman emerged from the mud house with an infant tied to her back, a toddler on her hip, and a slightly older child gripping her wrap cloth. She looked hopefully at the approaching wheelbarrow, but when the headmaster shook his head, the woman stepped immediately back inside.

"My wife," the headmaster said, almost ruefully, "and three of my children. I have eight altogether. Look, I am putting you in the far hut for today. No work for you; if you lose your leg, then I will lose my job. Do you understand? Have you eaten today?"

She shrugged again. Strictly speaking that was a lie. She had eaten a piece of something called toast that morning, but it had been like eating a flake of white ash after the hottest of fires.

"*Tch.* Unfortunately, now you must wait until the evening meal. But as I said, then we will all share that mischievous black hen, cooked up with chilies and palm oil, cassava greens, and a big ball of cassava mush. I will put all forty of the girls to work on this night's dinner so that we can all eat until our bellies groan.

That way, tomorrow when you've been asked about your treatment, you can put in a good report. Yes?"

Buakane's head hurt along with her leg. The thing about foreigners—white ones and black ones—is that you could never tell when they were joking. Often, she thought, it was just simpler to ask.

"How can just *one* chicken serve *fifty* people?" she asked.

The headmaster stopped the wheelbarrow so quickly that he neatly sent Buakane pitching face forward over the front. Although she was able to grab hold of the sides in time to prevent a spill, her right elbow jammed into her thigh, causing a blinding shot of pain that would have made her cry out at any other time—except for this one. She would never give this fool the satisfaction of having contributed to her misery.

"You speak Tshiluba!" he cried. "You speak the language of Kasai! The language of civilized peoples!"

"*Tch,*" she said, pretending to herself that she was an old woman, instead of a small girl, so that she might have the courage that she needed. "Tshiluba is an easy language. That is why it is a trade language for all of Kasai Province, where there are many languages spoken. Before yesterday, I knew that even a baby could speak your tongue. Then yesterday, I learned that the white man can speak your tongue. The *white* man!"

"*Wewe wakuhende meme,*" he said ominously. You have offended me.

"*Nasha,*" Buakane said. "I was merely making an observation. If I offended anyone, it was the white man. Yes, that was my intent: they are so stupid that the only language that they are capable of learning is Tshiluba."

Unable to cock his head, Born Without a Neck tilted his body this way and that in an apparent attempt to read Buakane's expression. At last he sighed in resignation.

"Well, at the very least you have offended my wife deeply," he said.

Buakane was genuinely surprised at this sudden turn of events. Her only intent had been to offend the headmaster.

"How did I offend your wife?" she asked. "I have yet to speak to her."

"You have questioned her ability to coax the flavor of this bird into the sauce—so that one small hen could share itself with many. It is like the story of our Lord and Savior, Jesus Christ, is it not?"

"I do not know this story, Headmaster."

"Then perhaps it is your job to shut up and listen while others speak."

"Yes, Headmaster."

Buakane shut her lips, but in her mind she spoke of everything that she saw and heard to her mother. Now and then she made pointed comments to her father as well. *See what a* dikenga *you have gotten me into, Bad Odor,* she said. The fact that Bad Odor could neither talk back nor strike her across the mouth—these were trade-offs that made the white man's girls' school somewhat bearable.

Then she remembered the *real* reason that she was there: *Oh, you stupid, stupid Buakane,* she said to herself. *How soon you forgot that Chief Eagle is a violent man who does far more than strike his wives across the mouth. What a fool you are to have forgotten that when this cruel man dies, then you and all his wives must be buried alive with him. Even that hen that you are about to eat possesses more intelligence than you.*

Aiyee! Now the Headmaster was speaking, and she had not been listening. When he was finished, he puffed up like a sun-bloated corpse and put his face close to hers.

"So what do you make of this Jesus?" he rasped.

"I have not yet made up my mind," she said. "I must hear more."

Born Without a Neck grunted. "You surprise me, Buakane. If I could not see that gap where your two front teeth should be, I might, if I squinted, take you for a Muluba. Except that you have very black skin—too dark for me. All you Bashilele are so black. Nonetheless, and I say this truly, I think that you will learn quickly."

"Thank you, Headmaster," Buakane said.

"Now," said the Born Without a Neck, "we have come to your hut, and it is time for you to get out of the box on wheels." Then he summarily dumped her out on the ground.

Immediately a pack of little children appeared from nowhere and had themselves a good laugh at her plight. As the only words she heard were Tshiluba, and the accent was exactly like the Headmaster's accent, Buakane deduced that at least some of the urchins were his. She decided to milk the situation a bit for their entertainment.

"*Aiyee,*" she cried. "Oh my leg! Children, come see what your father has done."

Five little heads, three of them with necks, peered down at her with worried expressions.

"*Katuka!*" Born Without a Neck shouted and the children scattered.

Buakane pulled herself erect. She was shaking with anger.

"You are not a nice man," she said. "What is it that I am supposed to learn from you? Besides cruelty?"

He stared straight ahead for a long time while Buakane struggled to stand on her injured leg. "It is not a good day for me," he said. "You are not the only one with problems. Now listen to me, child. Eight girls share this hut. Your bed is the one with a package wrapped in banana leaves on it. Follow me."

They went inside, but he left the door wide open, so Buakane was not afraid. This hut was built in the Baluba style, and it was something truly to marvel at. The walls were made of mud that had been packed into a framework of crisscrossed bamboo. This meant that the house could not be disassembled, then picked up and carried away in a single night like a Bashilele hut. At the same time, with the thicker mud walls and the higher-pitched thatch roof, this hut was considerably cooler inside than Buakane had expected it to be.

"*Bimpe be,*" she said. Very nice.

The headmaster pointed to the bed with the banana leaf package. "Open it," he said.

Buakane had never had a gift, much less been given the privilege of opening something tied with a bow. "Yours are a primitive people," the headmaster said as he untied the *lukodi* bow for her. "This is not judgment on my part; it is merely fact. The point is that you must never be ashamed to ask for help. That is the only way you will learn. Of course, a woman can never hope to become civilized, but you need not remain a savage, either."

She said nothing.

"Look, you little heathen, when I speak, you must acknowledge it."

"Yes, Headmaster." *If you were in my village,* she thought, *and my father heard you speak thus to me, your head would soon be his new drinking cup. So this is what I will do to survive your voice, which grates on my ears; your breath, which is rank; and your words, which are cruel: every time you speak, I will call you Head Drinking Cup in my mind.*

"Now open your package," Head Drinking Cup said.

As she did so, certain items spilled out that brought to mind a goat being sliced from sternum to anus. These, however, were no entrails, but strange gifts, the likes of which Buakane had never seen, or perhaps she had seen them but had not been given the opportunity to use them.

"This is soap," said Head Drinking Cup, and he picked up something as long and thick as her forearm that was speckled with the color of the sky on a sunny day, and white. "Take a small piece of this down to the spring when the other girls go and rub this on your body while you stand or sit in the flowing water. Observe how they do it. Do the same with your hair. That will cleanse your body."

"Yes," Buakane said, as if she were a simpleton. She knew what soap was, but except for old Diamba who had a record hemp crop one year, or Chief Eagle, who stole from everyone with his levies, no one in the village of Mushihi could afford this white man's invention.

There were many marvelous things in that bundle, including two cotton dresses with bright African scenes printed on them and a pair of plastic sandals the color of water in which cassava leaves have been boiled. But the thing that pleased Buakane the most was the palm-size mirror with the picture of King Baudouin on one side and reflective glass on the other. Old man Diamba with his hemp crop had been the first person in the village to acquire one of those. Buakane had heard a rumor that Chief Eagle's stable of wives shared two more of those mirrors (although one of them was cracked). So now, should Buakane return any time soon, she would have only the fourth mirror in the village. That would certainly make her popular among the girls her age—or any age for that matter. Even old women would come with little gifts—

"Buakane, why do you already cease to listen?" Head Drinking Cup demanded, snapping his fingers in front of her eyes.

"*Aiyee!* I have not ceased, Headmaster."

"Then what were my last words to you?"

"They were words of wisdom, Headmaster, such as only you are qualified to say."

Head Drinking Cup beamed, as only a vain, inglorious man can beam, which is to say, quite brightly. "I will leave you to rest now until the girls return from school. The privy is the round building behind the hut. We use corn husks; you get a maximum of three per day."

Then Head Drinking Cup departed, and after marveling over her many treasures in private, Buakane grew sleepy and spread her new blanket out upon her springy bamboo slat platform, one that she did not have to share, and soon fell fast asleep. When she awoke, it was only after a good deal of dreaming, wherein her younger brother was poking her foot with his toes. It was not a welcome disturbance; thus Buakane awoke disoriented and out of sorts.

"Stop that," she said.

"The chief's wife commands me," a girl's voice said, and many other voices outside the hut laughed.

Buakane rubbed sleep from her eyes and sat up. Her heart began to beat faster. Her hut was crowded with girls, and she could hear more of them outside. How many were there altogether? Thirty? Perhaps forty of them?

"Look," Buakane said, "I was sleeping. I did not know that I had guests. It was not my intention to offend. I wish only to do what I am supposed to do."

"You think that you are special because your husband is the chief, is that not right?" said a big girl with wide shoulders and no waist.

Buakane recognized this girl as Hermaphrodite, who was also from the village of Mushihi but was several years older than Buakane. Hermaphrodite was named thus because her body parts were both male and female. It was said that as young child, Hermaphrodite had behaved as any other Mushilele girl, but as she approached womanhood and her body changed, so did her personality. Hermaphrodite developed small breasts and bled, but she was prone to fits of anger, and her large size and muscular build intimidated many people. Needless to say, her bride-price was set very low. She was bought by a young man from a faraway village and was never heard from again.

"Hermaphrodite," Buakane said happily, "how good it is to see you once more, and to know that I have a friend here."

"Shut up," the big girl said, and, reaching down, she dug her thumb and forefinger into the Achilles' heel of Buakane's good leg. "I have never seen you before, and here you are supposed to call me Brings Happiness."

"Aiyee," cried Buakane in pain. Then she let the pain be funneled into anger so that it would work on her behalf. "But I have seen you. It was you who taught me how to braid a proper grasshopper paddle—not my mother, even though that is her name.

"And it was you who taught me how to dig clay and work it into a pot that would stand up to the baking. You, and not my mother. Do you remember how lopsided my first effort was? You made me destroy it and start over. I cried then, which you said was a good thing, because the clay was starting to dry out too much and a little bit of my snot and tears were what it needed to stay moist enough for another try. And of course you were right!"

"I said, shut up," Brings Happiness said.

"E," Buakane said.

"Come, we will eat."

Buakane followed in silence. In front of the headmaster's hut, where the cooking fires lived, most of the girls quietly squatted in two concentric semicircles with a piece of banana leaf on the ground in front of each child. Because the act of squatting pulled at the stitches in Buakane's leg, she gasped in pain. It was an involuntary response that she regretted immediately; nonetheless, it caused Born Without a Neck to shout at one of his little daughters.

"Bring a stool for this heathen Mushilele," he yelled. "And hurry up about it, too. Do you not know that her father drinks his beer from the heads of little Muluba girls like you?"

The girl commenced screaming, and although she was of an age where she was still new to walking, she staggered over, while yet maneuvering a wooden stool as big as she was. To their credit, none of the other heathen Bashilele girls laughed at this pitiful sight.

When the girl reached Buakane, she pushed the stool at her, screamed even louder, and then toddled away as fast as her chubby bowed legs would take her. They did not take her far, however, before the little legs gave way and the toddler sat down with a plop. That seemed to be what stunned the child into silence. A slobbery silence. It was only then that her mother ceased laughing and, scooping up her daughter, held her close.

"You have delayed my meal," said Born Without a Neck, and he clapped his hands twice. "*Buasha, buasha,*" he said in Buakane's heathen tongue. It was clear by his tone what he meant: *Serve me my dinner immediately—or else!* Since Born Without a Neck was the headmaster of the school, and in charge of keeping the girls' husbands out of the stockade, the two words *or else* were of great importance.

Immediately, several girls who'd been assigned to help the headmaster's wife cook on that particular day jumped into action. They began by making rounds, first plopping a fist-size lump of stiff cassava porridge on the leaf, a spoon of carefully prepared cassava leaves (for they too contain strychnine), a ladle of palm oil gravy, and a pinch of stinging green chilies.

Where was the chicken? Buakane wondered. Fortunately, she did not ask, because when she glanced over at the headmaster's plate, she saw half of the bird perched on his lump of cassava. Looking around, she saw that the other half of the chicken appeared to be have been divided among his four sons in proportion to their ages. His four daughters received no meat, and his wife a piece no larger than her thumb.

When the headmaster's wife saw that Buakane's eyes were upon her, she looked away quickly. Buakane felt pity for the woman, but anger as well. A Mushilele wife would not watch her girl children grow into weak women because they ate no meat. After all, it is the lot of Congolese women—Bashilele, Baluba, and Bapende—to work in the fields. And it is the privilege of the men to sit on their stools in the communal hut and tell stories of their brave exploits. The men would have you believe that the telling of stories requires more energy than hoeing fields, digging up cassava tubers, and pounding the cassava tubers into flour. Let it be known that the tubers are pounded in wooden mortars as big around as a fat man's belly, and the pestles are as hefty as a fat man's thigh.

"Headmaster," Buakane said, addressing him in a most respectful tone, "is it true that the chicken only flew over the pot of gravy before landing on your plate? For behold, these forty students of the Bashilele tribe, and your four daughters of the Baluba tribe, not one of them has as much as one bite of that delicious meat that we can see on your plate, and the plates of your handsome sons."

Buakane had much more to say on the issue of fairness, and the division of limited resources. She was no expert by any means, but coming from a noble clan, she had been privy to palavers around her hearth that dealt with these issues. Buakane was a woman of the royal court; she had been raised to be a skilled conversationalist. Although her tongue had been designed by the gods to converse with women, it had been honed by Paddle, and it had often been said that she was clever beyond measure.

But much to her dismay, her small joke about the chicken flying over the pot was met with hoots of laughter from many of the girls, and fits of giggles from the rest. Even the headmaster's wife had to cover her mouth with the corner of her wrap cloth, so as not to give herself away.

Only the headmaster was not amused. "*Tangila weh!*" he said as he stabbed the air with his finger. Look you! He had used the shortened form of "you," the threatening form; there was no need for him to say more. Besides, his entire body was shaking; it was as if he had taken ill with a sudden case of malaria.

After that, stillness descended over all the compound. Except for the sounds of chewing—for one must chew with an open mouth to enjoy the aroma along with the flavor—the meal was consumed in silence. Buakane ate slowly, because for her the end of the meal was problematic. It was customary to belch at the end in order to express one's satisfaction, but how could one be satisfied with a meal in which the chicken only *flew* over the pot?

Yes, there had been only *one* small chicken, but a fair person would have cooked that bird in a small amount of water, in a covered pot, until the meat fell off the bones. Then she would have shredded the meat before adding it to the gravy. In truth, Buakane had never seen it done just this way, but only because Paddle had never had to feed forty growing girls at one time.

Still, there had been lean hunting times, when Paddle had had nothing better to add to the gravy pot than a handful of dried caterpillars. Or perhaps a sparrow or two. Yet Paddle had always been fair about the way in which she rationed available protein. *E,* no doubt about it, Paddle would have shredded the meat!

One by one, the girls who were finished belched, stood up, and quietly left the family compound. It occurred to Buakane that she had better not be the last girl left eating. As she pressed a wad of *bidia* between her thumb and forefinger to form a scoop for the gravy and chopped cassava leaves, a solution came to her. The *bidia* was really of an excellent quality. It alone was deserving of a hearty burp.

So Buakane burped loudly and all but jumped to her feet. It was possible that the headmaster cleared his throat to call after her, but if so, by then she was already back inside her hut.

The hut, which she was to share with seven other girls, already held sixteen. When Buakane entered, some ululated softly, others clapped, while still others danced. Then in one voice they began to chant.

"Buakane, Buakane, our hero is Buakane!"

All this behavior was shocking to Buakane, for she had not meant to stick her head above the grass. But what surprised Buakane the most was that it was Hermaphrodite who chanted with the greatest enthusiasm. From now on, in Buakane's mind, she would forever be known as Brings Happiness.

FIFTEEN

Every summer when she was a little girl, Julia's parents would take her to the Butler County Fair. The three memories Julia promised herself she would never forget were the two-headed calf, the fear she felt at the top of the Ferris wheel, and the wonder she felt as she watched the knife sharpener advertise his wares. This man would sharpen a knife, and then he would slice a piece of paper down the middle—presumably attacking it edge-on. People said that it was a trick, that it was physically impossible to do this. Yet it was being done in front of their eyes—or so it seemed. At any rate, they felt deceived, so they became angry.

One fellow accused the knife sharpener of rigging the paper, of gluing two pieces together. This fellow demanded that the performer slice open a sheet of paper that had been given to him by an outside source. The knife sharpener agreed to do this, and again he was successful. Another guy—a man whose face was red from drinking—said that this didn't prove anything. He said that if the guy who sharpened knives wanted to be taken seriously, then he had also to be open to using a knife supplied to him by an outside source. The knife sharpener agreed to do this as well, provided he could first sharpen the blade.

When the drunk heard this simple request, he exploded with

rage. He said many choice words to the knife sharpener and the growing crowd before being ushered out of the state fairgrounds by two burly police officers. With him, of course, was his little daughter, Julia, and his small son, Willard.

That day was particularly significant for the Newton family, because it was the day that Mr. Theodor Newton, Julia's father, hit rock bottom as an alcoholic (although it would still take several more months until he sought treatment). For Julia, personally, this lesson taught her that even the slimmest edge can be reduced to something even slimmer. But when one is hanging on by one's proverbial fingernails, then what?

For Julia's entire first day at Mushihi Station, she felt like she was clinging by her fingernails to a chunk of balsa wood about the size of a breadbox while adrift in a sea of sharks. After chapel, she'd been dumped at her new home by Henry and told to "settle in." That was her job for the day—that, and that alone.

But "settle in" with what? Unlike most other missionaries, Julia had not arranged to have her household furnishings shipped in crates or barrels. In fact, everything that she owned was contained in the two rather large suitcases she'd brought with her.

Because her arrival coincided with the end of colonial rule, it was impractical for her to plan for a term of any particular length. Therefore, her house was to be furnished with the basics—whatever that meant—including the kitchen, and the latter would be stocked with three months (the time it took to get more supplies) of dry and canned goods. However, when Julia took a peek into the pantry cupboards, she burst into tears. Nothing—not one item looked familiar!

She saw full-fat powdered milk labeled KLIM, and wieners in tins canned by Plumrose, whole heads of cauliflower in tins, courtesy of Libby's, ditto peas, and SPAM, SPAM, and more SPAM. Fortunately Julia liked the luncheon meat, just as long as there was ketchup to be had—and there was—but she would have to train herself to down the many tins of kippered herring, and sardines, which had been stacked neatly in alphabetical order.

There wasn't much to say about the rest of the house. It was separated from the kitchen by a covered breezeway and was composed of three small rooms, plus the bathroom. The first room, the one behind the front door, was the common room, so it would serve as Julia's dining room—especially during inclement weather.

In the back were three doors. The two on the outside opened to reveal two very small bedrooms, each with a single bed and nightstand. The bedroom on the left also contained a small desk, whereas the one on the right laid claim to a chest of drawers. Tucked between the bedrooms was a utilitarian bathroom that was so tiny, one could theoretically be sitting on the john while brushing one's teeth *and* simultaneously soaking one's feet in the tub. That was only a *minor* exaggeration, Julia thought.

The bedroom with the desk would, of course, be Julia's study. She chose not to sleep in this room because it had a rear door. Despite the fact that such a door might be beneficial should the house catch fire, it bothered Julia that this door opened onto the *tshisuku*, the elephant grass. How easy it would be for a heathen headhunter to slip in unnoticed and slip out again, with a new wine cup. To ensure that this didn't happen, Julia took the small bed that was in that room, tilted it on end, and leaned it against the door. If anyone tried to come in, she would hear it crash to the floor.

In the second bedroom, the one that she would make her own, there was no rear exit to worry about, just a small window that appeared to have been painted shut. This bedroom also contained a small bed, but unlike the first, this one was already made up with linens and a coarse blanket. There was a pillow on the bed that was stuffed with barley chaff—some of which poked through the burlap inner case. Julia immediately stripped off the pillow's cotton outer case and tossed the pillow in a corner. She would much rather use her dirty laundry to stuff the pillowcase than that hideous thing.

Beside the bed stood a simple stand, on which a kerosene lamp and a box of wooden matches awaited the night. Upon spotting this rough, but somewhat cozy setup, Julia felt the unmistakable sensation of pent-up adrenaline wash from her body. She nearly collapsed onto the bed, not even bothering to take off her shoes or bobby socks.

When she awoke, the light in the room was dim. Her head ached, her mouth was dry, and her tongue felt like a bundle of broom straws. At first she thought that she'd only been dreaming of Africa, which was, frankly, a huge relief. Then from outside her window she heard the query call and then answering call of a pair of francolins, a bird resembling a large quail. Julia had always hated napping, because instead of waking refreshed, she invariably felt even more tired and horribly depressed after sleeping during daylight hours.

That afternoon was no different. "Oh, Julia, you stupid, stupid fool," she said aloud. Then she started to shout, and why not? Who was there to hear her emote at her pity party, except the quail and possibly some baboons? The Muluba woman, Cripple? Nah. That clever little manipulator had probably already talked Henry into giving her a ride back to Belle Vue.

"I'm stupid!" she shouted to the four walls. "I've done it again! Crown me Queen Precipitous of the Kingdom of Dilettantia. I'm always rushing around, hungry for adventure, and I never stop, and I never consider the consequences."

At that point, just by chance, Julia stopped ranting long enough to hear rapping at her door. Her first impulse was that her brother was pestering her; that was his favorite sport. Pester, pester, pester. There were times when she just wanted to haul off and—

"*What?*" she cried, and then remembering where she was, and that she was supposedly alone, her heart raced.

But then the door opened and to Julia's utter astonishment, the woman named Cripple stood there, brandishing an iron fire poker from the wood-burning stove. Over her head the strange little woman wore an upside-down metal colander.

"Were is the intruder?" she demanded without a preamble.

"Uh—"

"*Mamu*, I have come to your defense. Who is it who wishes to inflict harm upon you? Show me, that I might skewer him like a grasshopper on a broom straw." The really scary thing was that Cripple somehow managed to say this with a straight face. Like she really meant it.

This woman was nuttier than a Christmas cheese log. Surely she couldn't *really* have supposed that Julia was being attacked in any way. Because if she had, what good could *she* possibly hope to effect, armed with an ember poker?

"I am alone, Cripple," Julia said. "Sometimes I experience bad dreams."

"It is precisely in our dreams when we are never alone," Cripple said. "Have you not heard, *Mamu*, that it is our dreams which are our doorways to the spirit world? That is the real world, Mamu Whose Name One Cannot Be Bothered to Remember. This world is but an illusion."

"No!" Julia shouted, for now she was angry at Cripple.

"But it is true, *Mamu*. It is you Christians who are in need of—"

"Stop it! Stop preaching at me. And stop calling me that terrible name: *Mukashiana*. I know what it means now. That was very cruel of you, Cripple. Just because you have received much torment in your life, that does not give you the right to torment others. You have undoubtedly heard of Yesu, have you not, Cripple?"

"*Eyoa*," she said as she leaned on the fire poker. "This is the son of your God who had no wife and no *lubola*, because he was a spirit. Yet even without this manly part, he put a young unmarried girl in the family way."

"Cripple, never has anyone been so wrong and yet so right at the same time. Anyway, our Yesu said that we should treat others the same way that we wished to be treated."

"Truly, truly?"

"I do not lie."

Cripple cocked her head to one side, and that's when Julia became aware that, as usual, she had the baby with her, strapped to her back with a wrap cloth featuring a torrid jungle scene of brilliantly colored parrots, stalking black panthers, and tropical foliage. When the baby saw Julia, she began to scream bloody murder. Without skipping a beat Cripple untied the cloth, took the baby into her arms, and stuffed a nipple into its month. Instantly the baby was soothed.

Julia smiled despite herself. "You came to defend me with a baby strapped to your back?"

"*Mamu*—you shall get your new name. In the meantime, it will be my pleasure to assure you that at no time was my baby in any harm. Now come, *Mamu*, we talk too much and supper gets cold."

"I-I don't understand," Julia said. "There is no supper; I never made one."

"Perhaps you were so busy in here that you forgot." Cripple turned and limped from the room, as if she expected Julia to follow.

If that was indeed the case, then Cripple lucked out. But it was only because Julia needed to use the toilet in the worst way. After that, Julia was able to focus on the main room and to see that not only had the table been set for supper, but that water had been poured and that a pair of mismatched candles—one blue, the other orange—flickered cheerfully on the small table.

"What the heck," said Julia. She hurried over to the table just as Cripple pushed through the front door bearing a tray on which sat an enamel plate heaped high with food.

"Sit," Cripple said, as if she were speaking to a small child.

Nonetheless, Julia sat obediently as she'd been directed.

"Now put *serviette* in lap, if you please."

At last Cripple set the steaming plate on the table and stepped back, but she did not leave. "I made you Spam and elbow macaroni bake, with melted cheese on top, and peas and carrots. There is chocolate pudding for dessert."

The smells coming from Julia's plate were making her stomach suddenly clench with desire. Her pity party had come to a screeching halt. But just as she was lifting the first heaping forkful up to her mouth, her upbringing, along with Cripple's prying eyes, prevailed upon her to do the right thing.

"Have you eaten?" she asked.

"*Nasha.*" No.

"When will you eat?"

"When you are through with me for the evening, *Mamu.*"

"*What* will you eat?"

"I brought with me a cup of rice and a small piece of salted fish. It should last me two or three days until I find out where the market is."

"Cripple, there is no market here, because here is the middle of nowhere." They were speaking in Tshiluba, and Julia was hoping that her American idiom made a modicum of sense when translated into Tshiluba.

It must have, because Cripple's eyes widened. "*Aiyee,*" she said. "Then I shall have to buy food directly from these headhunters."

The delicious aromas continued to call to Julia's stomach. "Cripple," she said, in desperation more than anything else, "you must sit and eat with me."

"No, *Mamu,* I cannot!" Her expressive eyes now registered horror.

"Where I come from it is very rude to refuse an offer of food. Is it not the same here?"

"*E,* but we are not equals, *Mamu.*"

"Cripple, in just a few months you Congolese will receive your independence and you will become a free people. It is time that you begin to think of yourselves as our equals."

"*Mamu,* do you forget that I am a Muluba, and as such, I am far superior to any white, man or woman? However, I cannot sit at your table, because it is still against the colonial law, and if the Belgian officials—the Rock Breakers—find out, they will beat me with the hippo hide strip."

Julia swallowed back a combination of mirth and indignation. The fiery little woman had chutzpah, as her Jewish friends at college would have said.

"This will be our secret, Cripple. Now go to the kitchen and fetch another plate for yourself. From now on we will eat together."

Cripple did not budge.

"Go on," Julia urged.

"*Mamu,* I not wish to offend, but I find that your food tastes disgusting, and it is not filling in the least."

"You have tasted this Spam and elbow macaroni bake?"

Cripple shrugged. "A good cook must always taste her work, is that not so?"

"Yes, I suppose so."

"But what does one taste tell a person? Perhaps two tastes, or even three tastes, are a better basis on which to form an opinion. *Mamu,* it occurred to me that if you were to threaten me with a punishment even *more* severe than the Bula Matadi's if I did not join you at this table, then I would have no choice but to obey your orders."

"Threaten you? Punish you? Cripple, I do not want to do that."

"But you must; it is for my own good. And for the good of my child. Do you wish my breasts to grow flat and shriveled, and that my child should starve?"

"No, of course not!"

"Then say that you will beat me with this fire poker, and that when you are through doing that you will take my child and raise her as a Christian."

"And that is such a terrible thing?"

"Truly, truly, it is the very worst thing imaginable."

"Eat all your meals with me," Julia said with a straight face, "or I shall beat you with a fire poker and then snatch that baby from you and raise it up as a Christian."

"*Aiyee!*" Cripple cried and shuffled off to the kitchen as fast as her halting feet could carry her.

When at last they had eaten their fill, and Julia had watched a woman hardly more than half her size eat twice as much as she, Julia insisted on helping with the dishes. It was the right thing to do; it was the Christian thing to do. After all, Julia was not only younger, she was strong and healthy. If Cripple had been a white woman, she wouldn't have hesitated to give her a helping hand, so what difference should her dark skin color make?

Yes, Cripple was a servant, but a servant making under a dollar a day, plus room and board. Even if she didn't do anything but complain, Cripple's company would be worth every penny of it.

With the kitchen work completed, the two women took a pair of folding chairs out on to the breezeway to watch the sunset. This time Julia hardly noticed as Cripple untied her infant and clasped her to a swollen breast. The day had been hot, but without rain, and the banks of clouds that had been slowly building contributed to the most spectacular sunset that Julia had ever seen.

But that close to the equator the sun doesn't slip behind the horizon, it plummets like a red hot orb that has burned through a crepe-paper sky. In the next minute the clouds would be in silhouette, rimmed with gold; then the gold would melt and the blue sky deepen into indigo blue. Yet even before the last traces of the sun were gone from the clouds, the planet Venus would proudly take her place in the sky, the first of the night beings to do so.

"Look, *Mamu*," Cripple said, pointing to Venus, "there is the moon's wife."

Julia smiled. "Is that so? Well, in that case the moon is very much bigger than his wife."

"*Eyoa*, this is true. This is true, but as you will soon see, they have many, many children, so it must not be too bad a thing to be his wife."

Cripple was right. The clouds on the horizon stayed put, and soon there were so many stars in the sky that Julia actually began to despair of coming up with an adequate way of describing them to her mother. Every phrase she could think of sounded hackneyed and trite.

In the end she decided to do a very un-Julia-like thing; she sat there at peace with herself and with Cripple, and simply enjoyed the night sky.

SIXTEEN

Nurse Verna Doyer despised tattletales. No, that was too strong a word. Nurse Verna strove mightily to love everyone as God had commanded her to do so in Leviticus, chapter nineteen, the same book and chapter in which the Lord had commanded her to stand up in respect every time she saw a gray-haired person, and which also forbade her from getting a tattoo. Nurse Verna tried hard—exceedingly hard—to be a good Christian, so she merely disdained tattletales. She did, however, make one broad exception to her rule: anything that might affect Mushihi Station was not to be considered gossip.

That afternoon, Verna, having felt somewhat guilty about her feelings toward the newcomer, Miss Julia Elaine Newton, had left instructions for her cook to bake a batch of brownies from a recipe she'd translated from the *Settlement Cookbook*. It was one that her cook had made only a few times before, because it used valuable ingredients, like cacao powder and a fresh egg. For Nurse Verna, this was carrying the commandment to the extreme; it was practically like throwing her arms around the interloper and calling her "daughter." Perish *that* thought!

The brownies were delicious, as anticipated. Following their own supper, after Reverend and Nurse Verna had each eaten two, they stacked the remainder on a dessert plate, covered them with a used but nicely smoothed piece of aluminum foil, and set out to deliver the delicacies. Reverend Arvin Doyer carried a flashlight to use on the way back, in case the young woman prevailed upon them to come inside and eat yet another of the delicious treats. Should dusk fall before their return, there was the ever-present danger of poisonous snakes waiting for small prey in the open path.

But there are many kinds of snakes in Eden, are there not? That is one of the many thoughts that raced through Nurse Verna's mind just minutes later, as she and her husband waited impatiently outside the Hayeses' door for someone to answer. Reverend Doyer pounded this time, and finally Henry opened it slowly, but looking none too pleased.

"It is the dinner hour," he said. "Missionaries generally eat between five thirty and six. *We* always have; you know that."

"How do you know it isn't an emergency?" Reverend Doyer said.

"Because your wife is holding a plate of brownies, but she's wearing a scowl."

Nurse Verna heard the Great Distraction snicker from behind the door. It wasn't the child's fault that she was being raised like a hooligan. In a proper environment she might have stood a chance. Clearly, *that* was no longer an option.

Nurse Verna could either demand that the impudent little brat be suitably punished or that the real purpose of their visit be addressed. Ever the pragmatic and prayerful woman, Nurse Verna chose the latter.

"These brownies aren't intended for you," she said while thrusting the goodies at him anyway. "They have been poisoned by Satan, so you might as well give them to the Great Distraction."

"Nurse Verna, if I weren't an ordained minister, and you weren't a—never mind. I should not have said that. I am sorry for my words."

Now it was Verna's turn to feel sorry. Whether or not Henry Hayes meant what he said, Nurse Verna truly regretted her hateful words. However, she just wasn't ready to take them back. Stewing over the continued presence of the distracting waif was like scratching a mosquito bite; it felt good to do so, even if it was the wrong thing to do. The Great Distraction belonged either far away at a boarding school or in the United States, living with a set of her grandparents.

"Reverend Hayes," Nurse Verna said—which was practically an apology, given that she almost never used his ecclesiastical title—"we have come to lay upon you a very disturbing piece of news. We do so in order that the three of us might then join together in earnest prayer."

Much to Verna's relief Henry stepped outside completely, pulling the door tightly shut behind him. He motioned his visitors to follow him back down the path a few paces.

"What is your concern, Nurse Doyer?"

"It concerns us all," said Reverend Doyer. "In the spirit of Christian charity, my wife had the cook bake these brownies, which we just now tried to deliver to our newest coworker, Miss Julia Newton. But when we arrived at her house—well, as you know, the path from our house passes directly in front of her main room. Her dining room. You will never guess what we saw in there."

"A partridge in a pear tree?" Henry said.

"As usual, Henry," said Nurse Verna, "I shall have to swallow my irritation, and so again I thank the Good Lord above that he has chosen to set only a minor stumbling block in my path."

Henry bit his lip and nodded. "Go on, please."

"Well," said Reverend Doyer, who could be quick with the words when he wanted to, "as one might expect, Miss Julia Newton was eating her supper—some horrible red-and-yellow noodle glop—but she wasn't alone."

"It was a Spam and elbow macaroni bake with cheese, and you love it," Nurse Verna snapped. "But about the alone part; she was dining with a black! An *African,* no less. It was that same crippled woman who you brought with you last night from Belle Vue. I think she is supposed to be Miss Newton's housekeeper. They had no idea that we were watching, of course, because we stood stock-still, like we do when we're hunting and the game is being driven in our direction."

"That's not all," Reverend Doyer said. "When they were finished with their meal, that African woman casually reached under her blouse and pulled up a b-r-e-a-s-t and proceeded to nurse her infant. Right there in a white woman's dining room! Can you imagine that?"

Henry smiled. "You don't need to spell the word *breast.* Your wife is a nurse, and I am a widower, and we live among a tribe that goes topless to church. But yes, we aren't allowed to entertain Africans in our houses. And we certainly are not allowed to eat with them at the same table. The Mission Board should have made this very clear to her. We can lose our lease if word of this gets around."

"Think of all the sheep that will be lost," Reverend Doyer said, for he was ever the good shepherd.

"Think of all the sick and hurting who will go untreated," Nurse Verna said. Her heart ached at the thought of any of Arvin's lost sheep suffering needlessly, all because of some college girl with liberal ideas and a point to prove.

"You needn't worry yourselves," said Henry. "I'll go over just as soon as I've finished eating and speak to her."

"Oh, no," said Reverend Doyer, "that would be exactly the wrong thing to do."

"How so?" Henry said.

"Have we not just established that she is a young woman—one who is pleasant to behold, in fact? Does not Bathsheba come to mind?"

"Bathsheba committed adultery with an old coot named David," Nurse Verna said.

Henry chuckled, so Nurse Verna gave him her sternest, and much practiced, glare. Unfortunately, in the gathering gloom it lacked much of its full potential.

"That is my point exactly," said Reverend Doyer. "I have no doubt that you can be trusted, Henry, but it is *she* who worries me. You happen to exude a certain—well—animal magnetism that I am told certain women find to be quite irresistible."

"He didn't hear it from me," Nurse Verna said quickly.

"Putting the two of you alone together in the postdinner hours could be like putting the goat in with the bear."

Even though they were now standing well away from the closed front door, completely off the front porch as a matter of fact, Nurse Verna was positive that she heard someone snicker. And since there weren't any bushes behind which to hide—just a border of scarlet amaryllis flowers, the obnoxious, mocking noise had to be emanating from inside Henry's house. The Great Distraction was living up to her name yet again!

"Did you hear that?" Nurse Verna demanded.

"Did I hear what?" Henry said.

"Don't play games with us, Reverend Hayes," Reverend Doyer said. "We all know that it is the Great Distraction."

Henry let out a loud sigh that was obviously packed with meaning, most probably a message intended for that elfin child of his. Why on earth Henry continued to coddle the girl a full two years after her mother's death was beyond Nurse Verna's ken. The fact that he allowed her to wear her dead mother's clothes was not only ridiculous, it was downright unchristian.

"We will wait right here on your verandah," Nurse Verna said, "until after you have eaten your evening meal, and then the three of us will walk over there together. Then in unison we shall confront the new arrival and her lame housekeeper."

"Cripple," Henry said in Tshiluba.

"*Tch*," Nurse Verna said. She had served the Lord in Africa so long that at times she wasn't even aware of the Africanisms she'd incorporated into her lexicon. This time, however, was an exception. Nurse Verna was not going to stand quietly and be corrected while there was still a chance that the Great Distraction was listening in on the other side of the door.

So many little battles fought, and for what? Most of these battles weren't even for the Good Fight; they weren't part of the war against Satan. The battles for which Nurse Verna girded herself in armor—both physical and spiritual—at the start of each day were battles that Nurse Verna fought in order to control the people, environment, and events happening around her. They were Verna's personal battles, not God's battles.

Yes, mercifully, every now and then one of Verna's battles and one of God's battles would coincide, and when that happened, Nurse Verna gloried in the moment. It was then that she felt no guilt whatsoever, only empowerment.

Take this evening's mission, for instance. The Parliament in Brussels had decided that the white race and the black race should not mix. That was the law, and missionaries were to be law-abiding. By having this woman—a common *housekeeper*—dine in her house, Julia Newton was jeopardizing all the work that had been done on Mushihi Station.

So you see, the battle to get Miss Julia Newton to publicly confess her sins and begin towing the line was righteous in nature. The outcome would affect the future of Mushihi Station.

However, it was her ongoing struggle to dominate Henry that worried at the edges of Nurse Verna's conscience. Where did that come from? What did that mean? It wasn't something that she could ever talk about with Arvin. In their thirty-three years of marriage, Nurse Verna and Reverend Doyer had never once had a conversation that even came close to bordering on intimacy.

Well, there you had it; Nurse Verna couldn't even finish her thoughts in peace before Reverend Paul Henry Hayes slammed the door one more—this time behind him—and placed himself in the lead.

"Just follow me. Flashlights off, please. No talking, of course."

Nurse Verna wanted to speak up, maybe even shout something, but of course that would have defeated the purpose of their mission. All right, *her* mission. That of making Miss Julia Elaine Newton play by the rules. It was only fair.

If Nurse Verna had to play by the rules, then so did the others. During the thirty-three years in which they had been missionaries, there had indeed been occasions upon which Nurse Verna wished she could have invited certain Africans into her house to share a meal. She could think of several African men whom she had found to be rather stimulating conversationalists.

There had even been a woman patient whose mind was sharp as a tack. Her name was Kukema, which means To Doubt. One day, while slicing manioc tubers with a machete, Kukema put a gash in her foot that required seventeen stitches. Not once during the procedure did Kukema as much as whimper.

Nurse Verna later learned that Kukema had astonishing powers of concentration and had been busy reciting the Gospel of John to herself the entire time. For years after that, Nurse Verna often daydreamed scenes in which she and Kukema were friends—regular American-style friends, who could visit over a cup of tea. Perhaps even gossip a little.

Of course that was not to be. And so neither was Julia Newton's alliance with this misshapen Muluba woman from Belle Vue. Henry had taken forever to finish his supper and do whatever he did next behind that closed door. So who knows what those two lawbreakers were up to now.

Frankly, nothing would surprise Verna. One couldn't have been a nurse in Africa for thirty-three years and not have seen it all. But one could be sorely disappointed. Especially if one was completely honest with oneself, which Nurse Verna was. Sadly, this condition was almost as rare as Antarctic malaria.

"Shhh," said Henry needlessly when they got close to Julia Newton's house. Then after some time he whispered over his shoulder. "What do you see through the window?"

Nurse Verna stepped adroitly around the much younger man. Her stomach roiled and her head throbbed in rebellion. She couldn't help the loud gasp for air that escaped.

"Do not be so dramatic, wife," Reverend Doyer said, as he pushed past Henry. "Well, look at that" were his next words. "Look at how we have misjudged her. She is on her knees praying with that woman."

"But in the *house*," Nurse Verna said. "Convert her on the verandah, fine! Just not in the house!"

"I will speak to her first thing in the morning," Henry said. "I will even get a written apology from her if that is what you want."

Nurse Verna forced a laugh. "Oh, don't be silly, Henry. What kind of woman do you take me for?" Of course she didn't want him to answer. She wasn't the kind of woman that she wanted to be; she wasn't even close.

SEVENTEEN

Julia and Cripple did not tarry under the night sky. Their star-gazing ended abruptly when Julia casually inquired about infant care in the Belgian Congo. What prompted this question was that whenever Cripple untied the wrap that held the baby to her back, Julia could see that baby girl was naked.

"Cripple," Julia said, "in my country we wrap our babies' bottoms with thick strips of cloth, and then when they make water—or the other—we remove that cloth and wash it. Of course, we first put another clean cloth on before we wash the dirty one. However, we are very fortunate, in that we have water available to us all year. What do Congolese mothers do during the dry season?"

"*Kah!*" said Cripple, immediately taking the offensive. "How long must your babies sit in their own filth?"

"Well, that depends. If it happens at night—Cripple, why must you turn all my questions back around to me? I want to learn your customs."

"*Tch,*" Cripple said as she rocked to and fro, even though her folding chair was quite stationary. "Behold, I will share some of our traditions, but only because you have been kind to me. This way you may return across the great waters to that faraway place to teach other whites a better way to live. During my employment as a housekeeper, I have observed that many of your customs are truly disgusting."

"*Aiyee!*" Julia said. She was only pretending to be upset. By now she knew that this was just the kind of response that Cripple was hoping to get.

"*Eyoa,*" Cripple said, and stopped rocking. "Truly, truly disgusting. Your cement floors cannot absorb the urine of an infant. Our traditional houses all have dirt floors. As soon as the baby starts to urinate, the mother holds her child above the floor. Every morning the mother sweeps the top layer of the soil out the door with a broom made from the stiff spines of a palm leaf. There is never any smell, nor does any problem develop on the skin, such as the itch and the red bumps that grow on the white babies at Belle Vue."

"It is called *rash* in English," said Julia. "What about the feces, the *tuinvi?*"

"The *tuinvi* is dog's work, *Mamu.*"

"Did you say *dog?*" Julia barked a couple of times before remembering that all the local dogs were basenjis, a breed that was naturally incapable of barking.

"Are you in pain, *Mamu?*" Cripple asked.

"No, most certainly I am not! Where I come from dogs make lots of sound—I am told that some baboons make similar sounds."

"*Tch,*" Cripple said, with a tilt of her chin. "I am traditional, and I am a heathen, but I am not a savage. How would I know the sound that a baboon makes. Do you think that I roam about the jungle like an animal? But, yes, I speak of the dogs that wander about the village, and which the men take when they go hunting. *Dog,*" she said, as if she were speaking to a person who was intellectually impaired.

"I still do not understand," Julia said. "How do dogs help clean up feces?"

"*Aiyee,*" said Cripple, shaking her head. "You are like a small child in your thinking. Dogs lick the baby's bottom. They lick it cleaner than soap, water, and cloth. The feces is good food for the dog as well, and therefore one does not need to feed one's dog. Everyone benefits. In some traditions, every baby gets its own puppy."

"But then those puppies grow up to have puppies, and soon would there not be more puppies than people?"

Cripple resumed her bizarre rocking. "Such a simple woman. We are a practical people, Mamu Mukashiana. We do not possess your untold riches, stolen as they are from others through forced labor on their own land. When we face hard times, we eat our dogs. That is what they wish us to do, in return for the good life we have given them, by offering them the fruit of our babies' bottoms."

Julia felt both insulted and angry. She'd come to Africa with as open a mind as possible, determined not to be as judgmental as the previous generation of missionaries. This, however, was one cultural difference about which she could not remain mute. Julia adored dogs. She had been raised with dogs—*properly*, of course. Her second dog, Felix, had needed to be put down at age eleven when Julia was a freshman in college. That was four years ago, and the memory of that day still brought tears to her eyes.

"That is the most disgusting story I have ever heard!" Julia shouted. "It is wrong to eat dogs. Do you hear me? Wrong, wrong, wrong."

Cripple stopped rocking again and swiveled on her chair. "*Mamu*, would you rather that my people starve when famine strikes?"

"*Kah?* No, of course not. But from what I have been told, you also have chickens and ducks and goats. Sometimes even sheep. Is this not so?"

"If we have those animals, *Mamu*, it is not yet famine."

Julia Elaine Newton, there you go again, rushing to pass judgment, and again, without knowing the first thing about the topic. The only famine you've ever experienced was having to go to bed without your supper one night when you and your brother wouldn't stop fighting and your mother had to call your father at work in order to get you two to shut up.

"*E*, Cripple," Julia said simply.

Cripple cleared her throat. "*Mamu*, it is good that you understand, because now we can discuss the matter of acquiring our dog."

"*Our* dog? We are not getting a dog, Cripple. Put that out of your mind."

"That is unfortunate, *Mamu*, because this house and the horrible little shed where you wish to stuff Pierre Jardin and her weary old mother—these places have the hard concrete floors. They will not clean up like a sensible dirt floor."

Julia pretended to pound the sides of her head with the palms of her hands. "*Aiyee!* Who is Pierre Jardin?"

Cripple laughed. "Pierre Jardin is my baby." She pulled the infant from her breast with a loud, wet pop and held it forth for inspection. "Yes, she is very much a girl as you can see for yourself. She was given this name because the first Pierre Jardin, who is the chief of police at Belle Vue, has been kind to my family. That Pierre Jardin is brave, strong, and very intelligent. Are these not qualities I would wish for my daughter?"

"They are indeed," Julia said.

Cripple smiled with satisfaction, her point made. "*Mamu*, were you aware that this little one burned with fever yesterday and today?"

"No! Cripple, how sick is she? We must get her to see Mamu Snake at once!"

"*Yala*, do not concern yourself to this great extent, *Mamu*. Do you not see that she is better? Mamu Snake has already given her some of your white man's medicine. Much to my great surprise it appears to have had some effect. Her appetite has been fully restored. But now, *Mamu*, let us return to the matter of the dog, for we have need of one now in the big room in which we just ate."

Julia rose from her metal folding chair. "Explain—please."

Cripple hopped to her feet and deftly managed to tie Pierre Jardin to her back in a matter of seconds. Then like a one-legged sparrow she dipped and hopped, hopped and dipped, leading the way to the dining room.

"*Mamu*," she said, "it was you who said, 'Yes, Cripple, please go back in and see if any crumbs have fallen to the floor, and if so, please sweep them up. Because as you know, crumbs will lead to ants.' Do you not remember saying this to me, *Mamu*?"

"*E*, but—"

"So I returned with a broom and a strange flat pan that is frankly quite useless for cooking, and I began to sweep. And indeed, there were crumbs around your chair, *Mamu*, so you were correct to worry. However, around my chair there were none. At any rate, no sooner did I began to sweep than Pierre Jardin began to squirm like a piglet carried to market in one's bare hands. This I knew to be a sign that a dog was called for, so I removed my child from her sling and set her on the floor. Now, whatever nourishment my daughter had managed to siphon from this poor, twisted body of mine lies in that room next to your chair." Cripple pointed across the room.

It took a moment for Julia to translate and then decipher the clever woman's words. To be sure, she was careful to pray before speaking. Julia had once come to the conclusion that it was words spoken in anger that were responsible for at least half the suffering in the world.

"You must go and clean up the *tuinvi*."

"*Kah!* But, *Mamu*—"

"Now!"

"*Che-che-che-*," Cripple said, or were her teeth just chattering? Whatever it was, the housekeeper now sounded as pitiful as she looked.

"*Yala*," said Julia, "then I will help you." And so she did, but she made sure that Cripple remained with her at the scene of the crime.

At least that was her intent. But they had no sooner got down on their knees with a rag Julia found in the kitchen and some soapy water when the door flew open, and Nurse Verna burst in.

"*Katuka weh!*" she shouted at Cripple, which means "get out" but in the rudest possible way.

Cripple struggled to her feet. It was apparently a lot harder for the poor woman to rise from a kneeling position than to hop off a chair. Nurse Verna didn't seem to take this into consideration.

"Do you not have ears? Get out now! It is forbidden for you to be in the house of a white person."

Then an even more incredible thing happened. Henry came rushing in, grabbed Nurse Verna by her narrow shoulders, and marched her back outside. *Someone* pulled the door shut behind them, and there followed the sound of angry voices. This went on for an embarrassingly long time, although it did allow Cripple ample time to regain her feet. She was even able to readjust her wrap and the precious bundle it swaddled.

"It is time that you received a new name," she announced suddenly. Her head was cocked, but whether it was because of her deformity or as an expression of sarcasm, Julia couldn't tell.

"*Now?*" Julia said.

"Especially now, *Mamu*. It is most appropriate."

Julia sighed. "Please. Tell me."

"From now on your Tshiluba name will be Mamu Ndolo."

Ndolo: a helpful, kind, even-tempered person! Mamu Kindness would be the short English translation she would use when writing home to her mother. And all because she'd fed Cripple a meal, *and* because Nurse Verna had turned out to have a bat loose in her belfry.

However, the latter was not a kind thought; therefore, Julia immediately asked the Lord to forgive her in the privacy of her heart. The fact was that Jesus could return from heaven at any moment, so it behooved one to remain in a state of "high alert" as it were, with a clean heart.

"*Mamu,*" Cripple said, tugging gently at Julia's skirt, "does this name displease you?"

"*Kah?* Displease me? It is a wonderful name. Thank you, Cripple. I will try very hard not to disappoint you."

"Do not worry, Mamu Ndolo. Because you are white, I have already assumed that you will disappoint me—many times even. Thus, nothing will really change, and you can continue to keep your new name."

"Are you not special?" Julia said. It was a phrase she'd learned from a girlfriend at college who hailed from Georgia. Cora Beth had said—in the strictest of confidence—that it was a southerner's way of being snide while still appearing to be polite. Truth be told, it came across a little different in Tshiluba.

"*Tch!* Already you offend me, *Mamu,* because I am a cripple. But as I have said, it was to be expected."

Julia felt like tearing her hair out—but figuratively of course. She wasn't going to be like Great-Granny Thompson, who literally did just that, before she was secretly committed to a special kind of home. Thank heavens Henry burst back into the room before she overreacted and stuck her foot in her mouth yet again.

"Julia," he said, his thick dark curls plastered against his forehead with perspiration, "please don't be too quick to judge Nurse Verna. She loves Africans, she really does. She spends her life caring for them; you wouldn't believe some of the sacrifices she's made, the things that she has done for the Bashilele.

"You also need to understand that Nurse Verna is—well, she's stuck in her ways. She has a need for rules and protocol—*her* way, of course. In regard to segregation of the races, she follows the Belgian law. It's not because she agrees with it, but because she believes that as a Christian, she must obey the law."

Julia unconsciously put her hands up in a defensive posture while at the same time stepping back until she was up against the table. She was practically snorting with rage, and she knew it. Julia was also very much aware that she was being closely scrutinized by Cripple, that highly intelligent, thorn-in-the-side heathen who knew English. *Just calm down, girl, and get a hold of yourself,* she said to herself, putting her mother's voice inside her head.

Then, feeling a bit more in control—certainly more like an adult—Julia looked Henry square in the eye. "Now would be the perfect time to put to test that phrase: agree to disagree. For Nurse Verna's information, and perhaps peace of mind, my housekeeper was cleaning the floor under my supervision."

Henry looked at Cripple. "Is this so, *Baba*?"

"*Eyoa*," Cripple said, but she didn't stop there. "Master, do you have a wife?"

"*Kah!*" Henry said, and then chuckled. "No. Why, do you want me?"

"*Tch!*" Cripple rolled her eyes in disgust. "Do not take offense, master, but you are ugly."

Henry chuckled again. "*Me?* Ugly?"

"Master, surely you have seen your reflection in a water basin. Pinched nose, no lips—truly disgusting. But it is not for me that I inquire; it is on behalf of this poor woman, who is herself even more hideous than you."

Henry's eyes twinkled. "So you think that she is even uglier than I am? If that is the case, why should we marry?"

"*E*, look at her hair. It is like dried elephant grass. Is it any wonder that her parents sent her here, rather than pay a dowry in their faraway land? But she is a kind woman, master, with wide hips and full breasts. And I think that she may still be young enough to bear a child, although with white women, their age can be quite deceiving. I have been told that white women often lie and say that they are younger than their Belgian years. Is it shameful to survive—to become old and wise? In any case, this one is not wise, so I doubt if she is old. *E*, I believe that she is still young enough to bear you a son."

Henry roared with laughter. "Why, you little matchmaker!"

Julia was fit to be tied. "Now stop it! Just a minute ago the conversation had to do with evicting Cripple because she might be down on her knees praying after working hours, and now you joke about marriage?"

All signs of humor drained from Henry's face. "Actually, there was a lot more to it than that; the Doyers happened to see the two of you eating together earlier this evening. Eating is practically the penultimate kind of fraternization—it's almost worse than sex."

Sex! Julia felt her cheeks burn. She couldn't believe that an ordained missionary had said the S word. She had never once heard her parents use it—not once.

"Wow" was all she could think to say. That must have made her seem even more stupid, if that was possible.

"So," Henry said, "good night then."

That was it! Just like that, he turned and left. Either he was embarrassed as well, or else he didn't care to be caught in the middle of what was sure to be a heated discussion. After all, she had already made a reputation for herself as a woman of passion—or perhaps in Henry's eyes, an argumentative college girl.

"Mamu Kindness," Cripple said, "I too will be going to bed."

"Sleep well," Julia said, then caught herself. "No, you will stay until we have cleaned the floor."

"Good," Cripple said, "but in that case I must bring up a matter of utmost importance."

Uh-oh, Julia thought. *Not now. Whatever it is, not tonight. Please, Lord, allow me to get settled with the minimum of problems. I already know that I've bitten off more than I can chew. You've already made that abundantly clear.*

Having armed herself with the power of prayer, Julia faced Cripple with a smile. "What is this matter of great importance?"

"Mamu Kindness, when I am finished with this labor, I shall return to a room that has no bed."

"Do not be frivolous at this hour, Cripple. Of course there is a bed. I saw a sleeping platform in there this morning."

"*Tch*, did the white *mamu* sit upon this platform? For if she had, then she would have discovered that it was riddled with termites, and it would have sent her crashing to the hard concrete floor. Perhaps if the white *mamu* was a cripple like myself, and possessed as many years as surely I must, then her twisted and painful body would hurt even more."

"*Aiyee!*" Julia cried sympathetically. "Cripple, is that what happened?"

Cripple looked away, but not before Julia saw that she was blinking back tears. Julia was shocked. It had never occurred to her that someone as feisty as Cripple would cry in public. Maybe this was an act, yet another example of the housekeeper's manipulative nature. Of course, it had to be an act. Julia hated being played, so she waited it out while Cripple took her own sweet time to answer.

"*E*, Mamu Kindness," Cripple said at last. "I do not wish to complain, for if you fire me, I have nowhere to go; these are not my people. But when I fell through the bed, not only did I hurt my back, but had I not been holding Pierre Jardin in my arms, she too would have come to harm. Perhaps something even worse would have happened, *Mamu*."

Now it was Julia who bade her time. "Fine," she eventually said. "Then you will sleep in this house, in that room over there." She pointed to what was to be her office. "It has a proper bed with a soft top. But you must never, ever, speak of this to anyone."

Then the most disturbing thing happened. Cripple hurriedly wiped her eyes on the backs of her balled-up fists and fell to her knees. Grabbing Julia's feet, she began pressing them to her forehead and rubbing them along her cheeks.

"Mamu Kindness," she crooned, "you are truly my everlasting

friend. Pierre Jardin and I will always be in your service. We will follow you even to this America of which others speak so much about, although I have seen no convincing proof of its existence— perhaps a colorful headscarf from your land might be enough."

Julia literally bit her lower lip to keep from laughing. Well, they did say that when God closed a door, he opened a window. As it turned out, she wasn't going to be friendless after all. And one thing was for certain, she certainly was not going to be bored.

EIGHTEEN

No, Julia was certainly not going to be bored. They—the little family of Julia, Cripple, and Pierre Jardin—were still eating breakfast when a pint-size visitor showed up uninvited, just inches from Julia's elbow.

"A ghost!" Cripple screamed. She fled the table, knocking her chair over behind her.

"Hi," Clementine said, coming around to where Julia could see her. "It's me again."

"I see," Julia said, although there wasn't much of the child to see. She was wearing a white cotton dress that had clearly belonged to her mother, and it was bunched up around her waist, with the excess material held in place by a man's worn brown leather belt wrapped twice around her waist. Along the edges of the neckline and short raglan sleeves were pink hand-embroidered roses. Set atop her mass of dark curls was a straw hat with a five-inch brim, which hid all her face except her delicate chin. Around the brim of the hat was a wide pink ribbon, and affixed to one side was a tired pink bow.

"Auntie Julia," Clementine said as she righted Cripple's chair, "do you suppose that we could be cohorts? I should like that very much—of course, if that's all right with you. Cohort Clementine sounds ever so much better than Accomplice Clementine, don't you think?"

Julia was stunned. And amused. Then mortified. That's what she should be: plain old mortified. Now her stubbornness—make that her willful disobedience—was leading this innocent child down the path of sin.

"No, you're not," said Clementine as she reached for a piece of toast.

Now Julia was back to stunned. "I'm not *what*?"

"You're not a bad influence—because that's what you're thinking, isn't it?"

Then before Julia could even cry out in disbelief, the child prattled on. She was like a little windup toy.

"It's not like I didn't already know what you were up to," Clementine said. "See, when Papa got back last night, Uncle Arvin and Auntie Verna were still with him. They were articulating a mile a minute, in a most disagreeable tone, so I made myself scarce. Well, you can guess what they did next."

Julia smiled inwardly at the child's adult, if somewhat stilted vocabulary. "I'm not sure that I can."

"They prayed, of course, Auntie Julia. That's what grown-ups always do when they disagree. Papa and the Doyers got down on their knees and they held hands and then they just really let God have an earful. I bet you can guess what it was about."

"This time you might be right."

Clementine had been trying to transfer an overloaded teaspoon of marmalade from the jam bowl to her toast. She managed to get the spoon halfway there before dumping its entire contents onto the clean white tablecloth that had been so kindly provided for Julia's use.

"Rats," she said. "Yeah, it was about you, Auntie Julia, all right. Auntie Verna thinks that you aren't dry behind the ears yet and need to be seasoned spiritually. Papa said that her analogy made you sound like an ear of corn." She giggled. "Both Auntie

Verna and Uncle Arvin want the Home Board to send you back to America because you can't play by the rules. They said that you are only going to cause big problems now that independence is coming."

Julia rested her forehead in her hands. "What did your papa say?"

"He said that they should ask God if you were a fresh wind blowing?"

Julia straightened. "A fresh wind blowing *what*?"

Clementine shrugged. "My nose started itching then and thought I was going to sneeze, so I went to my room. Auntie Julia, I think I want to be a linguist when I grow up. Just not a missionary linguist."

"Uh-huh," Julia said absentmindedly.

Oh Lord, tell me what to do, Julia prayed. And then the answer, the right answer, just popped into her heart—or her head—or wherever it was that God spoke to her. What would Jesus do? Didn't he tell his followers to sell everything that they had and give it to the poor? Strictly speaking, the food and the extra bed weren't hers, but Cripple was as poor and needy as Julia could possibly imagine anyone being.

She took Clementine's sticky hand gently in hers. "Listen, Clementine, I am not going to keep this a secret."

"Aw—"

"Do you know why?" Julia asked.

"No!"

"Because you and I are warriors," Julia said.

"We *are*?"

"Oh yes," Julia hastened to say. "We fight for what's right; we don't need to slink around in the shadows, now do we?"

"We're good warriors! But I don't want to kill anybody, Auntie Julia."

"No, no, we're not that kind of warrior. We just battle things like fear, and we stand up for our principles."

"But I'm not scared, Auntie Julia. Just ask Papa. Once I heard him tell Uncle Arvin that I wasn't afraid to stir up a hornet's nest."

"Is that so?" It wasn't hard for Julia to see how that might have come about. Then in the far distance Julia heard what sounded like drumming.

"That means it's a half hour till chapel," Clementine said. "If you don't want to be late, you'd better *ela kahia*."

"I don't understand," Julia said. "Something about a fire, I think."

"It's an idiom," Clementine said. "And you better *buasha, buasha* too."

With that she was halfway out the door. Julia grabbed her hat and bag of supplies from a chair and followed the child. In the spirit of benign rebellion, she would refain from brushing her teeth that morning. For her, it was another form of bravery—an extreme one, breaking free of the "you musts" of childhood imposed upon her by her mother. Even in college, when living in the dorm with no one to look over her shoulder or feel her toothbrush, Julia had tried mightily to toe the party line. She had always been the obedient child, as the Bible commanded.

Outside it was another glorious morning. A long dirt path led straight from Julia's house to the church. The dew was still glistening on the short grass on either side of it, weighing down the grasshoppers. The long-tailed birds were out in force today, and seeing them flitting about filled Julia's heart with unexpected joy.

"I think I'll try catching one of those birds," she said to Clementine. "You know, by putting salt on its tail."

Clementine snickered, perhaps in pity. "It can't be done, Auntie Julia. If it could, there wouldn't be any there for you to see now. The boys of the school all board, and they are starving for protein. That's why Papa brings in barrels of dried caterpillars that he stores for them in the shed behind our house."

She caught up with Clementine long enough to glimpse her face. The child was serious. Dead serious.

"Ugh."

"They're good, Auntie Julia—but you have to fry the caterpillars in palm oil with hot chilies."

"I'll take your word for it."

Approximately halfway to the chapel, the path took them near a clump of bushes. Clementine, who was again well in the lead, steered into the verdant hedge and virtually disappeared. Of course Julia felt compelled to follow.

From a very narrow gap in the foliage, the bushes gave way to a small clearing, hardly greater in scope than a king-size bed. This small space was taken up by two concrete slabs, separated by three whitewashed stones. Atop each slab lay the wilted remains of flowers, perhaps picked over a long period of time. In addition, a single plastic flower lay in front of each whitewashed stone.

Inscribed on the slab to the left were the words:

Elizabeth Rose Hayes
Cherished wife of Henry Hayes
Beloved mother of Clementine Hayes

Inscribed on the right-hand slab were these words:

Jonathan Allen Hayes
Our son, our brother

The stones were unmarked.

Julia stopped just in time. She had always been told not to step on a grave, yet the little side path opened right at the foot of these graves. It was very awkward, not to say a bit shocking. And suddenly there was Clementine sitting on the ground in the small clear space at the end of what was surely her mother's grave.

"Auntie Julia, may I present my mother, 'who never should have had children to begin with.' These three stones represent three years of Mama's life when she should have been dedicating herself to winning more souls over to the Lord, instead of succumbing to morning sickness, which as we know is God's punishment to all women, 'because Eve didst bite into the mango, which the mamba didst offer her in the Garden of Eden. And had it truly been God's will that these three little ones should be born alive on this evil place called earth, then the angels would not have snatched them away at the hour of their birth.'

"Oh, Auntie Julia, you should have heard Mama cry—I just know that *she* didn't take a bite from any mango dangled out to her by a snake. And she had such hopes for this next one—the named one. I don't remember everything that clearly, but I do remember that Papa cried so much after Mama and the named one both died that he took forever getting back to saving souls. Auntie Julia, why did God Almighty let *me* live? Aren't I the greatest distraction of them all? It's me who is the bane of Auntie Verna's existence."

"Clementine! Where did you hear that horrible stuff?" It was a rhetorical question, the kind one asks when one is taken aback.

The little girl under the hat, the one swallowed on the ground in her mother's clothes, wasn't listening. "Mama," she was saying, "this is Auntie Julia, your replacement. She's very young, Mama, and I've only just met her, but I think she's going to work out okay. Nobody likes her just yet, except for me, so you know that's a good sign.

"What's that, Mama? Oh, well, Papa thinks that she's sassy, and that she doesn't carry any meat on her bones, but that's exactly what you predicted he'd say. And Auntie Nurse Verna doesn't like Auntie Julia because she's so young, which means that she is bound to be both pigheaded and obstinate. *Plus,* since Auntie Julia went to a secular college, she might even harbor Darwinian thoughts. Oh, the horror of it all."

Clementine paused for perhaps a minute, although it seemed much longer. When she spoke again, it was clear that she was addressing Julia.

"Is there something special that you wanted to say?"

Julia gulped. How do you meet someone's dead relatives? That was one topic that had not been covered in her missionary orientation program.

"Ah—sure, that would be great. *Muoyo wenu*," she said, which is the traditional Tshiluba greeting that Mrs. Hayes would have used every day of her stay in Africa.

But when Clementine reacted with the giggles, Julia realized exactly what her mistake had been. How thoughtless of her to wish "life to you" to five lifeless corpses.

"Hello, Mrs. Hayes and Jonathan—and the nameless ones," she added. "Clementine is a delightful daughter and sister."

"Amen," the child said and performed her usual magic trick of standing while clothed in yards of excessive material.

It wasn't until she was out of the little cemetery, having rejoined the path, that Julia beheld the strangest element of that entire experience. Julia was in the lead now, with Clementine lagging slightly behind as she said her good-byes to her family. When Julia turned, she was startled to see Clementine reach into the bushes and withdraw a wooden stake. The stake wasn't much longer than a yardstick; however, for some bizarre reason, a large ceramic doll's head had been securely taped, as well as glued, to one end.

The head came from the sort of doll that had glass eyes—in this case, brown—that could open and close depending on the positioning of the head. In addition, the eyes were trimmed with long dark lashes—very much like Clementine's. Had the head been just a size larger, at first glance one might even think that it *was* the Great Distraction!

Julia stopped in her tracks, shocked and bewildered. "Clementine, what is the meaning of that?"

The child looked around, just as innocent as a lamb at play. "Of what, Auntie Julia?"

"Of that hideous thing! Of your head on a stake!"

Then the child snickered. "Oh, that! It's just a doll's head; it's not my head. Look closely. Her nose is way too petite."

"Hmm. The two of you look—I mean, you and *it*, look very much alike."

"Really?" Clementine said. She held the stake even closer, so that the head rested against her hat brim.

Julia was flabbergasted by this behavior. "Isn't this silly game more than a bit disrespectful? What would your papa say if he saw you doing that?"

"Papa put it there, Auntie Julia. And it's not a silly game; it's to scare away the natives. They think that it is a real human head."

Oh, please, Julia thought. "Why would the Bashilele rob graves?" she said. "It's not like missionaries are pharaohs, and they're buried with heaps of treasure. Anyway, I thought they were afraid of ghosts and spirits."

Clementine's eyes narrowed as she raised her delicate chin. "It's to protect my Dearly Departed from a cult, Auntie Julia. And just so you know, it isn't *things* that those cult people want. If you don't believe me, then ask Papa. And if you don't believe him, you can even ask Uncle Arvin and Aunt Verna."

Then it hit Julia like a truckload of coconuts. She remembered hearing from someone—perhaps her Tshiluba teacher back in Ohio—that there was a cult that used human brains in their rituals. More specifically, the cult members used the brains of whites. They procured the brains by digging up the remains of Caucasians. Not only that, but Mushihi Station was dead center in the middle of all this wickedness.

"Oh, Clementine, I'm so sorry," Julia said. "Please forgive me. Sometimes I don't think before I speak, and when that happens, I can be very inconsiderate of other people's feelings."

When Clementine pursed her lips, her mouth compressed to a pink bud no larger than the tip of Julia's index finger. "*E*," she finally said. "I know that I'm just a little girl, Aunt Julia, but you got to understand that I know a few things too."

"I do, honey," Julia said. She set her bag of supplies on the path and reached out to hug the motherless soon-to-be ten-year-old.

"No, thank you," Clementine said. "I only accept hugs from Papa now." Her lower lip trembled. "But feel free to check with me in the future."

"Fair enough," Julia said. "Spoken like a real trouper."

NINETEEN

By only the second day of her stay in the girls' compound, Buakane's wound began to show signs of healing. She could walk now with the aid of a crutch. This had both its advantages and its disadvantages. No longer was Buakane in need of a night gourd by her bed, but now that she was ambulatory, she was required to accompany the other girls to participate in the bizarre activities that composed their day.

First they lined up and filed into this very large palaver hut, where they sang songs and prayed to a strange god. This was supposed to be a god that was part spirit and part man, sometimes dead and sometimes alive. The only thing Buakane knew for certain was that this god was always fighting one of his former warriors.

The white man laid claim to bringing their god with them from the Faraway Place, but they denied bringing the evil warrior along. They appeased their sometimes god by singing and by much flattery. Even the words to their songs were filled with flattery such as one might say to Paddle's mother, who possessed the finest copper bracelets that Buakane had ever seen. *Tch*, but the tunes of these songs were akin to parrots being strangled.

All told, there was nothing about the white man's bizarre rituals that truly made sense to Buakane. Instinctively, she knew that this religion was not for her. She also realized that if she wished to remain at Mushihi Station, she had best fit in. But what if she could not, if only because the white man's god saw through to her heart and became angry at her deception? After all, she had been warned by several girls that unless she put her faith in this strange new god, she would be severely punished.

Aiyee! One could not be confused *and* continue to heal well at the same time.

"How severely does this Jehovah god punish?" Buakane asked.

The girls all became very serious. "You will be cast into a fire that will not consume you," their leader said, "and there you will burn forever and ever."

"*Aiyee!* This cannot be! For what reason will this strange new god punish me?" she had asked. "I have done nothing to offend him; truly, I have never met this man."

"Because of your badness."

Buakane thought back to the worst thing that she had ever done. While still young enough to prance about the village stark naked (six or fewer Belgian years) she'd stolen some fried plantain cakes, called *mikata*, from the hearth of an elderly woman whose back was turned.

The tasty cakes were simply treats to Buakane and her friend, but to the old woman, they represented hard labor and much needed calories for her and her ailing husband. But let it be remembered, Buakane had been but a child at the time of her crime.

So it was that on her first visit to the white man's palaver hut, Buakane decided that the white man's god, Our Father Which Art in Heaven, was most unfair. Thus, she was not in a receptive mood when she was thrust into a line of girls much younger than she was; these girls would still be free to go naked in Buakane's home village. They were definitely not the same girls from the day before.

"Why am I in *this* line?" she asked the man in charge. "Do you not see that I am older?"

"Quiet, girl. You are with the first-year students, and I am your teacher, Monsieur François. Can you say François?"

"*Flançois,*" Buakane said. The letter "r" was unfamiliar to her tongue, and thus it wanted to flip over it, rather than ripple.

The other girls laughed. "Stupid chief's wife," someone said.

"This one thinks that she is so special," another sneered.

Things went from bad to worse when the actual teaching began. Monsieur François scratched some marks on a blackboard with a white stick, and then he pretended that these marks had meaning. Buakane was astounded when the other girls began to play along with him. One by one they too pretended that those chicken scratches had meaning.

Around the room, quite like a children's game, they played. Finally it was time for Buakane, who was seated in front, beneath the window, to give meaning to the marks.

Hitherto the girls had said things that were at least somewhat related; all of them had to do with a boy, a girl, and a soccer ball. The boy runs and jumps and kicks the ball. The girl sees the boy running and jumping, but she does not kick the ball. She cries out "run, boy, run," and "jump, boy, jump."

"Buakane, now it is your turn," Monsieur François said. He wore eyeglasses with thick black frames, although they lacked lenses.

There were other details about him that Buakane's curious eyes had been busy observing, such as the dark brown ring around the inside collar. And then there was matter of the gray-and-white strip of cloth tied around the teacher's neck. It hung down across his belly like a noose. What was its purpose? Was he aware that it bore a bright orange palm oil stain, about a third of the way down?

"Buakane," Monsieur François said. "It is your turn; you must show us how well you can read."

Of course Buakane stared at the marks and thought, *Why not?*

"The boy kicks the ball into the *tshisuku*," she said in a clear, loud voice.

The silence was palpable, something that Buakane, who had always been praised for her stories, took to be an encouraging sign. This encouraged her to continue.

"The boy runs after the ball, and the girl runs after the boy. The girl cries out, 'Come back, boy. Come back, boy.' But the boy cannot come back, because he has been caught and eaten by a pack of fierce hyenas."

The silence was replaced by Monsieur François's heavy breathing. The veins along his temples—at least those not obscured by the empty eyeglass frames—twitched like worms when a clod of moist earth has been overturned by a *lukasu*. His fingers gripped the slender tip of his palm branch switch. His entire body began to tremble.

"Buakane!" he seemed to bark, his voice suddenly not unlike that of a baboon. "Get out of your seat."

Buakane rose as regally as she could from the silly little bench that was befitting a child, and not the wife of great chief— although she would no sooner return to her marriage with Chief Eagle, and a future that involved being buried alive, than she would being fed piece by piece to a pack of hyenas. Only then did Buakane notice that all the other girls were already standing; some of them were trembling as well.

Not only that, but the white woman—she of the hair the color of dried *tshisuku* and eyes the color of a cloudless sky—was running toward the classroom, her skirts gathered up in her long slender hands. Imagine that: a white woman running! Who knew that such a thing was possible? They were said to be as feeble as the oldest of grandmothers, and beyond that, so lazy that they shunned even the easiest of tasks, such as sorting through rice to pick out small pebbles.

Buakane's first thought was that the white *mamu* was running to scoop up the little white girl—the one who spoke Buakane's language and who had shown her such kindness the night before last. The girl had been sitting—or perhaps even squatting like a real Mushilele—beneath a young mango tree that grew midway between the buildings containing classrooms. Somehow, despite her strange and cumbersome apparel, the girl turned into a chameleon and slipped into the lower branches of the tree unnoticed.

"Aiyee!" Monsieur François cried loudly, forgetting to bark. This was just before he dove under his desk. Monsieur François was a Muluba, so such cowardice was to be expected.

Most of the girls were Bashilele, and so they remained standing. The few who represented other tribes also cowered, but they had no desks, only the low wooden benches upon which they sat. Therefore some tried to take cover with Monsieur François, who rebuffed them viciously.

One girl stripped off her clothes, threw herself on the dirt floor, and wiggled under the bench at the rear of the building. There, covered in red dust, she lay as still, and *un*remarkable, as any dark log.

Throughout the chaos Buakane stood as still and remarkable as the finest ebony carving. Yet she knew that it was only she who was in danger. For the source of such great terror was none other than her rightful husband, Chief Eagle, he who had been unjustly shamed on her wedding night.

There was nothing for her to do now but to accept his wrath—but on her terms. She would never, ever, give him the pleasure of conquering her spirit. During her brief sojourn into the world, Buakane—the good, the kind, the beautiful—had grown wings more powerful than an eagle's and had soared to heights that this cruel man could not even imagine.

Buakane had seen things that he would never see, heard things that he had no ears for. Even the hyenas were on her side, for they had chased Buakane into the white man's path so that she might take a ride in the metal beast that roars, and as a result encounter all these wonders.

TWENTY

As director of the girls' school at Mushihi Station, Julia had many tasks. For the first week, however, she was to take things slowly: sitting in on the various classes, observing the teachers and their methods, getting to know the students, and perhaps introducing some new teaching materials.

She would have preferred to sit in a class with the youngest girls first, but Monsieur Gaspar (all the teachers had taken French names) had taken great offense at this. The oldest girls had sacrificed the most to learn their lessons; therefore, they should be the first to show off their achievements. Monsieur Gaspar had a high-pitched nasal whine that sounded not unlike a wood borer, so Julia quickly appeased him.

It was during a recitation from the Book of Ecclesiastes, in French, that Julia looked out though an unscreened window opening. In the far distance she noticed what appeared to be a band of men carrying a litter. This *is the* real *Africa,* she thought, but as the group approached, others noticed it too, and a spell came over the room. The girls all stood and crowded the three open windows, all at the same time, as they vied not to be the one most exposed.

Monsieur Gaspar, on the other hand, who had struck Julia as being somewhat fastidious, was clucking like a hen who'd just laid an egg. He was also pacing furiously, and Julia practically had to chase him around the room just to have a conversation.

"What is it?" she demanded. "Who are those people?"

"Can you not see, mademoiselle? That is the great chief of the Bashilele, Chief Eagle. He rides upon the shoulders of eight slaves, and he is surrounded by ten warriors. He is coming here on business."

"Business?" Julia asked. "What kind of business?"

"*Tch, tch, tch,*" Gaspar said. "Did the new girl, the one with the wound on her leg, did she not tell you that she is the chief's wife?"

"Gaspar, she is no one's wife! She is a child—a *muana mukese*. A small child even. She ran away from the chief because he is a cruel man. Now she is my student, and here she will stay."

Gaspar threw back his head as if to laugh, but no sound came out. "*Baba wetu, babe wetu,*" he finally said in a squeak. Then he ran to the corner of the room to hide behind a movable chalkboard.

For better or worse, Julia had never been one to play dead. Even as a small child, when she thought that she heard a noise under her bed, instead of hiding under her covers or crying out for her parents, Julia would lean over the edge of her bed and dare the boogeyman to come out. When it didn't—which, thankfully, was always—Julia would jump out of bed, grab her walking stick (it had once belonged to her grandpa), and vigorously poke at the darkness.

"Take that and that and that," she'd say. Only then could she sleep. Yes, sir, Julia Elaine Newton confronted her problems head-on; she did not hide from them.

But what differentiated Julia from so many others of the post-modern generation was that the young missionary remembered to ask the Lord's protection and guidance when the going got rough. However, this did not prevent her heart from pounding as the men and the litter drew nearer, and she could make out the scowls on their faces and smell the rancid odor given off by men who had been drinking palm wine for two days.

Julia had never been that close to half-naked men, except for those wearing swimming trunks at the swimming pool in Oxford or at nearby Acton Lake. Any stories she'd heard about the Bashilele men being so attractive now seemed like only so much fiction.

The litter came to a stop about ten feet in front of her. The slaves—muscular men with downcast eyes—slowly assumed a squat. They continued to hold that position, even after Chief Eagle disembarked. On either side of the litter stood five warriors, clad only in their palm fabric loincloths. These "cloths" hung from leather thongs slung low around their wearers' waists. Although she tried not to look, Julia caught sight of what were surely human ears strung along the leather thongs.

In his left hand, each warrior held a bow, approximately six feet in length. In each warrior's right hand gleamed a machete with a freshly sharpened blade. Over the right shoulder of each man was slung an animal skin quiver, filled with arrows that had been notched with the feathers of a guinea fowl.

Chief Eagle was clearly a man unto himself. He stood a head taller than any of his guards, and that wasn't counting his headpiece—half crown, half bishop's miter. The base of this headpiece was trimmed in leopard skin, rather than ermine, and its body was constructed of ebony and ivory, instead of gold. Also, it was studded with precious cowrie shells, and clusters of red and cobalt beads, but the idea was the same. This was a unique hat, one that was bestowed upon the wearer because of his inherited position, and everyone agreed that it was a symbol of certain over-arching powers. This was a "listen to me or else" hat.

Julia had no doubt that on that particular day, Chief Eagle was wearing it to impress—and possibly intimidate—the missionaries of Mushihi Station. *Well, good luck with that*, she said to herself. Outwardly, she was all grace and goodness—at least she hoped as much.

"Life to you, Chief Eagle."

At the mention of his name, Chief Eagle started. Perhaps the teensiest bit; Julia was sure of it. This gave her hope that victory would be hers.

"*Mamu,*" said one of the warriors, taking a single step forward, "Chief Eagle does not converse with women—even white women."

Well, that was uncalled for. So much for grace and goodness.

"In that case, life to you," Julia said. "What is it that you want?"

"Chief Eagle has come to retrieve his property."

"His *property?*" Julia echoed shrilly. "Tell him that *she* has a name; it is Buakane."

"The name of his wife is not your business, *Mamu.*"

"But you did not tell him," Julia said.

"Nevertheless, for your sake, it is best that you remove yourself from this matter," the warrior said.

For Julia the time had come to grab hold of Grandpa's walking stick and give the monster under the bed a few vigorous pokes. While her mind reviewed her first couple of moves, her eyes took in the remainder of Chief Eagle's royal garb.

Apparently Chief Eagle had some prowess as a hunter, for around his neck hung a necklace of leopard claws. These had been interspersed with precious cowrie shells. At the end of the leopard claw necklace dangled an uncut stone of exceptional brilliance. It was about the size of a small hen's egg and had been encased in a delicately woven copper basket. Julia assumed it was a diamond.

The chief had a powerful physique, there was no denying that. His particularly low-riding loincloth advertised that to the world. Unlike his bodyguards he carried neither bow nor quiver. Instead, he wore a complete leopard skin over his left shoulder like a cape, the preserved head of the dead animal angling down toward the small of his back. Julia thought it too bad that the big cat was incapable of biting the tyrant's buttocks.

"Tell this man," Julia said to the warrior as she pointed at the chief with her chin, "that in your village he is the chief, but here on the mission station it is *I* who am the chief."

"*Aiyee,*" said the man, "I cannot tell him this."

"Why not?" Julia said.

"Because then I will have him severely beaten," Chief Eagle said. "I might even have him killed."

"In that case," Julia said, speaking to the evil man directly, "you are beneath my contempt. Now, go away."

Even as the words were coming out of Julia's mouth—in fact, even before the signal got from her brain to her lips and vocal cords—Julia knew that they were a mistake. But by then it was already too late. The lever releasing the trapdoor had been pulled, and she, and possibly others, were going to suffer, and all because she couldn't keep her big fat trap shut.

What on God's green earth was she to do now? Henry could advise her. Cripple would be delighted to weigh in with a half-dozen opinions. Heck, even the Great Distraction could probably come up with a wiser solution than anything that the newcomer, Julia, could dream up. With all her earthly options unavailable, that left only God. Please, she told her conscience, do not as much as *think* about the Doyers!

"Oh God," she said aloud in English, "you know that I ask for almost nothing on my own behalf. Therefore, please help me now. Help me to get out of this jam."

"*Ha-chrumm,*" the chief growled. "*Ha-chrumm.*" He sounded like a motorcycle being kick-started.

"I was speaking to my god," Julia said.

"Why did he not answer?"

"He did—inside my heart. He said that I should not have spoken so harshly to you."

"*Tch,*" Chief Eagle said, and then spat so close to Julia's feet that she reflexively stepped aside. "You tell only lies, missionary; your god speaks to no one. Now you will listen to me. Return my property to me, and return all the property of the Bashilele warriors that you protect within those walls, and I will not kill you."

That's when God spoke to her. That was her Joan of Arc moment, her Daniel in the lions' den encounter, her David versus Goliath fight, if you will. Julia was never going to willingly give up the girls, one must understand. Either God was going to step in and do something miraculous on their behalf, or not. But either way, Julia Elaine Newton of Oxford, Ohio, was prepared to die that morning in the service of the Lord.

Perhaps one of her students—or even a teacher—witnessing her death would be inspired by it. It was even possible that one day that student or one of the student's descendants might visit America. Then they would have the opportunity to seek out Julia's still grieving parents, to tell them what a shining witness she had been. They could share with Julia's home church in America the story of her bravery, and how it led them, savage Bashilele headhunters, to believe in the Lord.

Julia knelt, clasped her hands in front of her, and bowed her head. "Kill me," she said bravely. She was not afraid, for God was on her side.

"*Kah?*" the chief said, and then he laughed. Rudely. Loudly. Then his disgusting, bare-chested warriors in their low-slung, provocative loincloths joined in the laughter. Eventually even the slaves laughed.

"Stop it," Julia cried. "Stop it now!" The time for submission was over. Having her head lopped off with a razor-sharp machete in the service of the Lord was one thing, but mockery was just cruel.

"Stop it, stop it!" Chief Eagle said in a screeching falsetto.

Instantly all the men imitated him. They began hopping about like robins on hot asphalt, their hands flailing at the air while they kept their elbows tucked in at their sides.

Meanwhile Julia was keenly aware of the dozens of pairs of eyes watching from open-air windows of the four classrooms in the two main buildings. She sensed that as comical as this scene might appear to the casual observer, no one there that morning, besides the chief and herself, was laughing. Yet again she had let her big mouth lead her astray.

The chief seemed to be a mind reader. In an instant he was again his regal, imposing self. Even without his miter he would have towered over Henry.

"White woman, you speak only words of foolishness. Why should I kill the *thing* that is to become my next wife?"

Julia was only momentarily confused, thinking perhaps that she had heard wrong. The *thing*? Did he mean *her*? Was *she* to be his next wife?

"*Eyoa*, I speak of you," Chief Eagle said, making his intentions crystal clear. "When our independence comes and the Belgian masters have been driven from our lands, then I will return and I will take you for my wife. You will bear children for me. These children will have the knowledge of the machines that the white man possesses, as well as the courage and strength of the Bashilele. Then the people of Mushihi Village will rise up, and they will conquer all the surrounding tribes. Behold, the descendants of Chief Eagle will be recited in the palaver huts of every village in Kasai Province for all time."

"I will never be your wife," Julia said through clenched teeth. "I will never bear your children. I would sooner lie with a dog than with you!"

What made her say that? Was it Satan? It had to be! Satan was trying to sabotage her witness. Maybe if she had just kept her mouth shut at that point, the egotistical giant would have returned to his village feeling like he'd made a good trade: Buakane for Julia. Then just before independence, Julia and Buakane both could hightail it out of there. Better yet, she would report what just went down to Henry, who would call it in on his short-wave radio to the Belgian police—assuming that there were any still around—and they would go to Mushihi Village, and they would arrest the lunatic. Just not bloody likely.

At least Julia's cruel words made the chief blink. "Very well," he said. "I will kill you, white woman—but only after I have had my use of you. And, of course, after all my warriors are through with you. Then, if you are still alive, I will give you to my dogs. Perhaps one of them will choose to lie with you—before he eats you.

"But do not think that you have stopped me from retrieving my property or that which belongs to my men. On independence day, justice will prevail."

Chief Eagle snapped his fingers and the litter came to him. All he had to do was to step into it sideways. The coordinated movements of the eight slaves, as well as the ten warriors, was astonishing. Julia tried to focus on that scene for as long as she could, because reality was simply overwhelming.

TWENTY-ONE

Nurse Verna had never felt such rage. Anger, yes. Nurse Verna had always been an angry person—except for right after praying. During prayer Nurse Verna habitually turned great chunks of anger over to the Lord. She'd grown up in St. Louis, along the banks of the Mississippi, so she visualized that emotion as one might see a block of ice, bobbing its way downriver from Minneapolis during the spring thaw. But if one wasn't in the habit of regularly heaving these heavy blocks up onto the very capable shoulders of Jesus, then one's soul—to mix metaphors—might get clogged with sin and freeze over altogether.

Nurse Verna had no idea where her anger came from. Frankly she really didn't want to know. It had been suggested by a social worker, at God's Precious Lambs Orphanage, that it might have to do with the early childhood trauma she'd experienced—blah, blah, blah. Nurse Verna didn't believe in psychiatry. When she was in nurses' training and had to serve for a semester on a psych ward, she had felt nothing but contempt for the patients. They were weak; they hadn't gotten on with their lives as she had. They certainly had not found a source of release for their pain and anger as she had. They had not found redemption through the Lord. They needed to hoist their blocks of ice up onto Christ's shoulders.

Oh, but if it was only that simple. If only Nurse Verna's anger would stay away. Wasn't that how it was supposed to work? To whom could she turn for advice? Certainly not her husband, Arvin! Reverend Arvin Doyer was an excellent missionary, a good preacher for the *natives,* but he was no theologian. Arvin was miles away her intellectual inferior. She wasn't judging him as a human being, mind you; she was merely thinking a fact. Surely God, who was omniscient, understood.

For instance, Arvin had struggled through a mediocre seminary, one that hadn't even required its students to learn ancient Greek, Aramaic, or biblical Hebrew. It was considered to be sufficient if they could read the Bible in King James English without stumbling. In fact, the True Gospel Seminary claimed that King James English was the "language of heaven," and that it was the language in which God dictated his Holy Word less than six thousand years ago. Arvin firmly believed that the so-called ancient languages like Aramaic were inventions of the devil. They were languages that God permitted to be mentioned in the Bible as a way to test the faithful.

To put it bluntly (why did no one ever ask for her to put it bluntly?) Nurse Verna had married an imbecile, because beggars couldn't be choosers, and Nurse Verna had a dream of her own to fulfill. Ever since she was six years old, Nurse Verna longed to be a missionary doctor. A surgeon, in fact. It had been her dream to come to Africa and repair harelips and perform skin grafts—and oh, there was such a need for medical personnel of any kind in the Belgian Congo.

Yes sir, little Verna Johnson, as she was known in those days, became quite an expert on overseas mission work, thanks to the This Little Light of Mine Program that the orphanage held every year, the Saturday before Christmas. That was when a real live missionary couple, ones who had actually lived among the natives and wild animals and all manner of exotic diseases, came and put on their dog and pony show, as Miss Claussen, the headmistress, called it. Although much to little Verna Johnson's disappointment, the missionaries never once brought either a dog or a pony.

At any rate, they always brought lots of gruesome Kodak picture slides, which actually turned out to be a much better idea. In return, the orphanage handed over the "offering jar," to which they had been their adding pennies all year. Once there was over fourteen dollars in that jar, and that wasn't even counting Canadian money.

The highlight of the missionary visits were always the "altar calls" at the end of the presentations. Before these solemn occasions the children were permitted to ask a few short questions. Perhaps it was because the missionaries came too regularly, or perhaps it was because Miss Claussen had a glare that could melt the paint off a Buick, but every year the same thing happened. It was only little Verna Johnson who went up to get saved, and only little Verna Johnson who dared to ask a question.

"Now that I'm saved," she'd say, "do I have to get me a husband to be a missionary doctor to deepest, darkest Africa?" Only a new kid to the orphanage would be stupid enough to laugh at Verna Johnson.

"I'm afraid so, Verna," the missionary lady would say. "You see, life in the Belgian Congo is so difficult that a wife needs a husband to survive."

"Uh-huh. But I don't want to be someone's wife; I just want to be a missionary doctor." And still, there wasn't a soul at God's Precious Lambs Orphanage who dared to laugh at little Verna Johnson, for her anger—backed up by her teeth and fingernails—were legendary.

Verna's quick wit, fiery temper, and flailing limbs put her at the top of the orphanage's food chain. This started with day one. Margaret, a fat, unhappy twelve-year-old and current resident bully, had tripped the six-year-old Verna as she was lining up for her very first chow line. Instantly, there followed a blur of arms and legs—all of them Verna's—and screams of pain—all of them Margaret's.

Then like two cats, the girls went their separate ways, the incident having been apparently forgotten. The only thing that changed was that Margaret never again tried to bully little Vera, and in private, Miss Claussen referred to little Verna as the Threshing Machine when speaking about her to other staff members.

The visiting missionary was always very patient with little Verna. "My advice to you, Verna," she invariably said, "is to turn this problem over to the Lord."

"Do you mean I should pray?" said little Verna.

"Exactly," the visiting missionary lady said. "The Bible tells us to pray without stopping. And you know what? God answers all our prayers too. It might not seem that way, but that's because we might not like the answers and we refuse to hear them."

"Like what?"

"Well, like what we were just talking about. What if God said to you: 'Verna Johnson, I like the idea of you becoming a missionary doctor to Africa, but you need a helpmate.'"

"What is a helpmate—exactly?"

This time, however, the missionary lady said something different. In fact, her words were so surprising that little Verna almost didn't hear them.

"Well, I suppose that in your case it might be sort of an ordinary husband, one to help you meet the official requirements. And if a tree falls across the jungle path, he can help the natives move that tree out of the way while you do the important medical tasks."

That was Verna Johnson's—hitherto little Verna Johnson's—defining spiritual moment. *That* was the last time that she had to go up and get saved, because *that* time she knew that her conversion had finally taken. God had finally spoken to her, and his words were these—more or less.

You, Verna Johnson, have been chosen to be one of my medical missionaries to Belgian Congo, Africa. Work hard, study hard, pray hard, accept donations, and marry whomever I, your Lord God, wilt send along—no matter how ordinary that man might be.

So Verna Johnson was faithful to the Lord God Jehovah, even if God slipped a little bit when it came to keeping his side of the bargain. Nurse Verna fumed inwardly when she heard other folks making excuses for God, because a fact was a fact. Besides, Nurse Verna had already made a ton of excuses on God's behalf, and of course she'd heard the same ones a million times from other so-called faithful Christians.

Nurse Verna had worked two part-time jobs during college and graduated with a 4.0 (the highest score imaginable in those days). But no medical school in the country would risk offering a scholarship to an orphaned girl with a reputation as a hothead. That went double for an Ivy League school. However, Nurse Verna Johnson's work ethic and good grades did get her a full scholarship at a church-funded but state-accredited school of nursing, located halfway between St. Louis and Springfield. And for what it was worth, Nurse Verna Johnson received her R.N. degree and M.R.S. certificate on the same day.

On this part of their covenant, the Almighty came through: Reverend Arvin Doyer was dumber than a plate of cold macaroni. In a way that was a shame, because his intellect was by far his strongest feature. Nurse Verna understood and agreed that such thoughts were unkind, perhaps even unchristian, but they were her *private* thoughts. Everyone has unkind, private—even ugly— thoughts. People who deny having such thoughts are hypocrites, and they are in need of intense self soul-searching. There would never be any pulling the wool over Nurse Verna Doyer's eyes.

One of the very few benefits of having been orphaned at age six was that by then Nurse Verna had already experienced the worst of humanity, and she was ready for a clean slate. Orville, her father, was a "professional gambler," a clean-cut second-generation

Norwegian who worked for the St. Louis mob as a shill at a back-room gambling table: the local yokel seemingly hell-bent to lose the family farm while in town on a drinking binge. Meanwhile, Pussycat, aka Verna's mother, slithered among the players passing out "drinks on the house" to everyone except to Orville, who was served iced tea.

The money was good, but it was oh so much better for the "house." Finally, Orville and Pussycat came up with a surefire way to sneak a few bills unnoticed past the house, and why shouldn't they have? They were doing all the work, after all! Their scheme paid off. At least it paid off for several months—until the urge to show off their wealth got the best of them and they purchased a brand-new 1910 Model T Ford. Barely a week later, they were found dead in this car, their bodies riddled with bullets.

The cops surmised that they were the target of a hit man, who had rightly presumed that they were dead when the Model T Ford strayed from the road and then over a high bluff above the Mississippi. The killer had either been unaware that a six-year-old was asleep on the backseat when the shooting began or didn't care. It was a riverboat captain who first spotted the automobile perched in the branches of a giant sycamore, but he didn't report it to the authorities until he had exhausted every harebrained scheme he could think of to get the automobile down on his own.

Little Verna Johnson had no next of kin, and in 1910 there weren't a lot of folks lining up to take in a mean-tempered girl who looked "as if she'd done wrassled with the devil and lost." God moves in mysterious ways, does he not? So when a name-less benefactor stepped up to the plate and promised to make an annual donation to God's Precious Lambs Orphanage if the facility would take in a certain six-year-old—anonymously, of course—was *that* one of God's mysterious ways? Even the grown-up Nurse Verna Doyer, who had an opinion on virtually everything, was stumped when it came to thinking about that. Obviously Orville and Pussycat weren't "saved," and thus they were doomed to spend an eternity in hell. The same went for their killer. Yet if Nurse Verna had not been orphaned, she might never have been the recipient of salvation.

She certainly never would have come to Africa and performed hundreds of surgeries—yes, real surgeries that would have required a doctor to perform them in the States. She had delivered thousands of babies and wrapped tens of thousands of wounds.

But now, because of the humiliating words spoken to Chief Eagle by one neophyte woman—a woman who didn't deserve the *title* of missionary—all this was about to come to a screeching halt. The missionaries might even lose their lives over this, become martyrs. Martyrs! Like St. Stephen! Well, yes—there would be glory in that . . .

Then the Lord, as he was wont to do, ripped that savory morsel of daydream from between Nurse Verna's teeth. These days it was the RCs—the Roman Catholics—who were big on martyrs. Real Christians, like Protestants, just quietly died in the Lord, and for the Lord.

Thus far Nurse Verna had served the Lord as a missionary nurse to the Belgian Congo for thirty-three years, which just happened to be the same amount of time that Jesus had spent on his mission as both God and man. The bulk of the Doyers' time had been spent on other mission stations, since Mushihi Station, their present posting, was only ten years old.

However, the Doyers, along with Henry and his now-deceased wife, had been at Mushihi Station from the very beginning. They were like the pioneers of yesteryear in that regard; they were pioneers for the Lord.

They'd staked out a virgin plot of land, high up on a plateau, applied for, and received a lease from the Belgian Crown. They'd cleared away the elephant grass—the *tshisuku*—built houses for themselves, a medical dispensary for her, a church for Arvin, a carpenter shop/garage for Henry, and of course a school. The Mission Board back in the States was adamant about that. Education was to be their main thrust—otherwise the Roman Catholics, who had great schools, would steal both the bodies and the souls of the Africans.

Nurse Verna had her own opinion, thank you very much, but the Mission Board was composed exclusively of men. As everyone knows, men are not inclined to listen to a charity case, especially one who, rumor had it, was descended from the "criminal element."

Fortunately Nurse Verna knew the Bible backward and forward; she knew that often the first thing that Jesus did on his travels was to heal the physical afflictions of the locals. If he happened to have been somewhere with a synagogue when it was Sabbath, then he preached. However, you can scour all four Gospels, and you're not going to find one example of him teaching a conversational French class, and absolutely, positively *no* examples of him explaining math problems!

Not that any of this mattered anymore. The wannabe missionary, Miss Julia Newton from Ohio, had just gone and ruined everything. For *everyone*. Oh yes, Arvin, for you too. No more stars in your crown—one for each soul saved—when you got to heaven.

And what about you, Reverend Paul Henry Hayes? What about the school for runaway child brides that your wife worked so hard to establish? *Well,* Nurse Verna said to herself, here's what: *the dilettante with the willowy figure and bottle blond hair has destroyed all your wife's work in one day.*

If Henry hadn't been so busy flirting with this pretend missionary, he might have—well, he might have done something different. Frankly, even the Great Distraction would have made a better director. Ah, but Henry's chickens were about to come home to roost. Tonight was Wednesday night prayer meeting, and it wasn't only the Almighty who stood a chance of getting an earful.

TWENTY-TWO

When Buakane heard the white *mamu*'s response to Chief Eagle, her heart coalesced, becoming smooth and hard, like a lump of polished ebony within an ebony shell. For a flicker of time she had been led to feel hope, excitement, a stirring of the mind. Perhaps—who knew how, but perhaps—someday she might have been be able to ignite that feeling in Grasshopper Paddle as well! But such foolish thoughts those had been. What a vain, selfish girl Buakane was, to even have thought that she could have a future here under the white man's protection. How could she have possibly imagined living so close to the man whom she had shamed and betrayed?

As soon as she was certain that the chief and his band of warriors had turned for home, Buakane ran from the classroom building and threw herself on the ground beneath a mango tree. Each step, each movement, jolted her wound; she might just as well have been dancing on sword blades. Nevertheless, when she reached the hard-packed earth beneath the canopy, she commenced rolling on the ground. Was she oblivious to the pain by then? No. Did she welcome it? Yes.

She began keening in full, agonizing voice, as one would do when confronted with the loss of a parent. This was to be her last indulgence, this traditional expression of grief. It was to be false grief; hearts that are made from ebony are so dense that there is no room in them for anything. Not even for manufactured grief.

"Buakane, stop it," the young white *mamu* commanded as she swooped in low like a bird of prey. Like an eagle.

"Get up," the white woman said. "Everything will be all right."

Buakane got up. But first she rolled free of the white woman's hands so that she stood beyond her reach.

It was Buakane's cowardice that was to blame for everything that had gone wrong. If she had submitted to her father's will and gone through with the marriage, there would have been no hyena attack. No gaping wound. No promise of knowledge, no hint of meanings attached to secret symbols in things called books, and then to have these promises snatched away.

If Buakane had not acted like such a quivering child, the white *mamu*'s life would not be in danger. The only way to save the innocent—yet stupid—creature was for Buakane to return to her village posthaste and to prostrate herself at the feet of her husband, her master, Chief Eagle. But only a real fool, or perhaps someone not right in the head, might consider that Buakane actually had a choice.

The time for choices had passed. Perhaps at one point her freedom could have been purchased by Mushihi Station—at a great price, to be sure. However, when the white *mamu* declared that she would rather lie with a male dog than with one of the highest-ranking chiefs in the entire Bashilele tribe—well, an insult of this magnitude could be avenged only with goats and pigs and flocks of chickens. Perhaps even more of the same for many years.

Buakane glanced around and saw that the other girls were still inside the school building, their eyes wide with fear. For once they were silent. There was no sign of Monsieur François, the Muluba teacher. Buakane dipped her head in farewell to the white woman before speaking.

"*Mamu*, we laugh and we cry, for the healing help on my leg, and the food I ate, and places where I slept. However, the time has come for me to return to my responsibilities. Stay well." She turned and commenced limping away in the same direction that she'd seen Chief Eagle leave.

"Stop!" The white woman's voice rang out sharply.

Buakane eventually stopped, but only when the white woman, who had the use of two healthy legs, ran ahead of her and got in her way.

"Think of the other girls," the *mamu* said. "They were very brave to seek sanctuary here, but if they see you give in to the chief's demands, they could lose courage. Buakane, please think for a moment about what would happen to them if they returned."

"*Aiyee, Mamu*, did you not understand my husband's words? He will *kill* you if you do not return me to him."

The white woman shook her head. This set her long hair into motion of the most bewitching kind. Adding to the bizarreness of her appearance was the color of that hair: *mukunze*, which in this case was somewhere between that of dried elephant grass and gourd blossoms.

"Buakane, listen to me," the *mamu* said. "He cannot kill me until *after* independence day. That is still a long way off. Because if he did, the Belgians would send soldiers into the village and—and—I do not know the word in Tshiluba. But the soldiers would take him away, and he would never be chief again."

"Truly?"

"I speak only words of truth."

"*E*, but even so," Buakane said, "you know nothing of Chief Eagle and his ways."

"I have met Chief Eagle, and I have looked into his eyes. Tell me, child, have you looked into a Belgian official's eyes?"

Child? Buakane felt like she'd been punched in the soft spot behind both knees. Instead of making her angry, as it should have, being called a child made her feel like a child. Suddenly her resolve was gone, and she felt helpless and confused.

"*Tch*," Buakane said. "I will return so as to be a good example to the other girls."

"We laugh and we cry," said the white woman.

TWENTY-THREE

The white woman named Julia Elaine Newton stumbled back down the path to her house, her eyes blinded by tears. The bumbling outsider from Oxford, Ohio, hardly noticed the cluster of bushes that enclosed the five deceased members of the Hayes family. The silly, overeager girl who was always getting herself into a mess simply had no business trying to meddle in the lives of others, especially in such a foreign place, and at such a volatile time.

As Julia kept berating herself, the tears fell faster and faster, and her movements became more erratic. All she could think to do was to get back to the house that Henry had built and crawl back into bed. When she was a little girl, she used to believe that if she closed her eyes and wished for something hard enough, she could make that something happen. So she staggered on now, like a drunken sprinter, until the sound of chanting behind her caused her to turn.

A flock of schoolboys, some wielding sticks, had been following at a distance of about twenty yards. When she stopped, they also stopped, and their chants gave way to whooping and hollering. The fact that they had been mocking her did not make them bad, for this sort of behavior was the African way. After all, this is what she had signed up for. All things Africa.

"I'm game for anything," Julia had bragged to her closest friends back in Ohio. "Bring it on."

Never mind that she'd been warned about the cultural differences. "When you fall, the Africans will laugh first and then ask if you are all right. Or perhaps they will only laugh."

"American kids can be plenty rude too," Julia had said.

"It isn't just the children who will laugh," Mamu One of Us, her language teacher in Cincinnati, had tried to explain.

The thing is, when a hardheaded recent college graduate has already made up her mind about something, all the words in the world aren't going to penetrate her eardrums. Of course now Julia could hear! The truant schoolboys with their sticks were like salt in her wounds.

Julia cupped her hands to her mouth. "Boys," she shouted, "go back to school."

The boys found this hysterically funny. One young smart aleck, who was wearing a shirt that contained more holes than fabric, cupped his hands to his mouth and parroted the words back at Julia.

"Boy-eez, guh beck ta stool!"

On another occasion this same cheeky kid, who couldn't have been more than seven, would have had the opposite effect on Julia. On another occasion Julia would have thought him cute. Precious, even.

The thought of this reduced Julia to a red-faced, quivering blob of self-pity. Surely that is how she must have appeared to them. For from that moment they became even crueler in their taunts—and these were supposed to be *Christian* natives! These were not the half-naked little savages whom she'd seen along the road on the drive up from Belle Vue.

"I quit!" Julia screamed at the monsters in English. "I can't take it anymore!" She dried her eyes on her sleeve and ran as fast as she could in the dowdy missionary dress she'd been forced to wear. She did not stop until she had slammed the door to her house behind her.

Thank heavens Cripple was nowhere to be seen, because Julia might well have taken some of her frustration and anger out on her. As soon as she caught her breath, Julia shoved the little chest of drawers that Henry built against the door and threw herself upon the bed. There she sobbed herself to sleep.

The sun was low in the sky when she awoke to a fierce headache and a painful rapping at the door. She closed her eyes again, hoping to ignore the rapping and go back to sleep. Gradually her foggy brain began to recall why she was lying on her bed fully dressed and wearing her shoes. Meanwhile the rapping never let up.

"Julia, Julia, please, you have to open up."

It was Henry. Oh Lord, what should she do now? It was his mission station, his wife's legacy that she had bungled up, so he had a right to be angry with her. *Really* angry. Except that he didn't sound angry; he sounded concerned.

Well, concerned was almost worse. Henry should be angry because Julia *deserved* his anger. And so did the Mission Board. The Mission Board had no business sending an immature college student to perform such sensitive work—okay, so she'd graduated, but only recently. Nurse Verna and Reverend Arvin Doyer, they had both been acutely aware of that. Julia had read that on their faces the moment they laid eyes on her. Why couldn't the Mission Board have seen that she was unfit?

"Julia," Henry persisted, "I'm not leaving until you open the door."

"God, please help me," she prayed as she dragged herself off the bed.

Then vain, foolish woman that she was, Julia caught a glimpse of herself in her hand mirror. Her reflection displayed bloodshot eyes and a blotched face deeply indented with creases from her pillowcase. Her blond hair—which apparently disgusted the natives—looked as if it had been combed by an angry cat. There were even clumps of hair in her mouth.

"Henry," she called, "can you please wait in the dining room for me? And can you face the kitchen?"

"No. Not until I've seen that you're okay."

"Oh, all right," she said at last. She pushed aside her hair one final time before opening the door.

Immediately the lock of wayward hair fell back into her face, as if brushed there by an unseen hand. Was it possible, Julia wondered, that Satan used our bodies to help us fail at spiritual tasks? If so, that wasn't playing fair. But who ever said that Satan played fair?

Finally, Julia stood in front of Henry, stripped of all pretense. She looked hideous, she smelled bad, and above all, she was a miserable failure. She had ruined the one thing Henry prized most apart from the Great Distraction.

So then, when his strong arms enveloped her in a tender embrace, her first thought was that he meant to squeeze her until it hurt. Literally. Henry didn't believe in hitting, especially not women. How clever of him to find another way to enact physical violence upon her person. How deserving she was. She would not fight back,

"Praise God that you're all right," he said, and then released her from his arms.

Julia was dumbfounded. She stood there, mute and bewildered, gazing up into his eyes, until he remembered his half of the bargain.

"Yes, of course," he said. "I'll go sit in the dining room, facing the kitchen. Take as long as you need, but you will need to have an overnight bag and your passport."

"*What?*" Surely she had heard wrong.

"We're not sure it's going to be safe for you here. Not until we can sort this out with the Belgians. So tomorrow morning, first thing, I'm taking you over to Dikenga Station. It's about fifty miles from here, and in Baluba territory. Chief Eagle wouldn't dare try anything that far from home."

Julia's ears rang; she knew not whether it was from her head-ache or from having heard further of the enormous gravity of what she had done. It was probably the headache, morphing its way into a proper migraine.

"I was only trying to defend that child, to protect her from that evil monster." Tears flowed freely again. "I am so sorry for not holding my tongue, for not acting like a Christian." She turned her head away from him as far as she could.

Henri grabbed her shoulders and shook her gently until she looked at him. "I know. What you said could have slipped out from anyone. No one is blaming you, Julia."

"They're *not*?"

"No," Henry said. "Now hurry, get your things. You're bunk-ing with Clementine tonight."

Julia scurried. She didn't even bother to change into a differ-ent dress, although she did throw a clean dress and underthings into the bag. But it wasn't until she was about to pull the front door shut behind her that she remembered—with much shame—her new friend Cripple, and Cripple's curiously named baby girl, Pierre Jardin.

"What about Cripple?" she demanded.

"That's already been taken care of. As it happens, Nurse Verna has an assistant named Many Boils, whom she trusts with her life. Oh yes, I mean that literally. Many Boils is a Muluba—although not from Dikenga Station. I've already taken Cripple and Pierre Jardin over to stay with Many Boils and his wife tonight. They'll be riding along with us tomorrow."

"Oh. Henry, can I just—"

"No," he said. "It's going to be dark soon; we need to get over to my house." And that was that.

Except that it wasn't. Supper that night was fried Plumrose hot dogs—from a tin, no less—and pancakes served with Lyle's Golden Syrup and Blue Band Margarine—also from a tin! But it was a miserable affair because Clementine kept entirely to herself, unless forced to do otherwise. And what fun is there in talking to someone—especially someone as bright as Clementine—if you know that they are responding only because they have to say something back when spoken to?

Perhaps midway through the meal, Clementine dropped her fork on her plate so that it created a great clatter. When she was sure that she had her father's attention, she dabbed both corners of her mouth with a heavily starched napkin and cleared her tiny, bird-size throat.

"Yes, Clemey," Henry said, without looking up.

"Papa, if Auntie Julia really is blown up with arrogance like the Goodyear Blimp, and she decides to keep Buakane here, will you protect Auntie Julia with hunting rifles?"

"Darling, you know that I can't spill human blood."

"What if it was *me*, Papa? Would you protect me, your little darling?"

Henry emitted something between a sigh and a groan. "Clemey, please. You know the answer."

With that, Clementine stared back at her food and remained in stony silence for the rest of the meal.

At least all things come to end, Julia thought. Eventually, the little girl would be put to bed, and then maybe she and Henry could resume talking about this huge mess she had made. But oh, how unrealistically optimistic that was. No sooner had the table boy collected the last of the coffee cups than Julia heard a knock on the door.

Henry jumped to his feet. When he answered the door, Reverend Doyer and Nurse Verna practically mowed him over on their way in.

"Reverend Hayes," Reverend Doyer said, "a serious matter has been brought to my attention that concerns you."

"With all due respect, Reverend Doyer," Henry said, "did we not beat this dead horse well into the ground earlier today?"

"No, sir," Reverend Doyer said. Then with the authority of a much older man, he headed straight to the table and sat in Henry's vacated chair. "This matter has nothing to do with the most astonishing case of immaturity that the Mission Board has ever foisted upon us. No, sir, this has nothing to do with the juvenile delinquent, Miss Julia Newton; this matter concerns my wife, Nurse Verna."

"I see," said Henry, sounding as if he did.

Perhaps that was the case. Thank heavens, at least, it wasn't about the Juvenile Delinquent, who just happened to be sitting at the same table. Why, Julia thought, Henry hadn't said anything in her defense was—well, it was just indefensible! Then again, Henry apparently wasn't the sort who defended. Imagine telling his own daughter that he wouldn't defend her, even if her life was at stake.

"The child should not hear this," Nurse Verna said.

"I have a name," Clementine said. As usual she wore one of her mother's white cotton shirt dresses, bunched over a belt at the waist. Tonight she was also wearing a wide-brimmed straw hat with a wreath of pink silk roses around the crown. Unless she spoke, it was hard to tell that there really was a body under the getup.

"Of course you have a name, *Clementine,*" Julia said. "Clementine is a beautiful name."

"And Clementine," Henry said, "now that we are reminded of your name, I want you to go to your room."

That is all it took to get the girl to obey—just to have someone acknowledge her name publicly, maybe even vehemently, in the presence of those who would reduce her to the Great Distraction. Henry had Julia to thank for that. At least the Juvenile Delinquent was good for something.

As soon as Clementine had called "good night" from her room, Reverend Doyer told his wife to begin talking. "It's your story, Nurse Verna," he said.

"It's like this," she said. "You don't know how much I have

prayed about this very moment. That God would lead you to hear my words. To listen to my story from start to finish, before unleashing that fiery temper of yours."

"My fiery temper?" Henry said.

Reverend Doyer nodded. "Like the wrath of Jehovah in the Old Testament."

"Wait a minute," Julia said. "Jehovah was God, and God can do no wrong. Therefore the wrath of Jehovah was justified."

Both Doyers turned to stare at Julia. She may as well have been an alien from Mars or have spoken in some gobbledygook language of her own, judging by their expressions.

"Perhaps I should join Clementine," Julia said quickly.

"You stay right where you are," Henry said. It sounded like a cry for help.

"Well, then I shall," Julia said. "Now please, Nurse Verna, continue. I promise that I won't interrupt again."

Nurse Verna sat down heavily in Clementine's empty chair before speaking. "This is about the day Henry lost his wife, Elizabeth, and his infant son."

Henry slid into the fourth chair at the table. His deep tan looked noticeably paler.

"Go on," he said.

Nurse Verna did the oddest thing then; she turned to Julia and recounted the story to *her*. "We were on our way to our annual missionary conference," she said. "That was two years ago, so it was held at Ngandu Station—we rotate every year. Anyway, we were at the Loange River waiting for the ferry. Like many of them, the ferry there is just four dugout canoes lashed together with some boards.

"Anyway, it was an exceptionally hot day, and Mrs. Hayes—Elizabeth—was eight and a half months pregnant, so she decided to wade along the shore."

"Only one mustn't do that," said Reverend Doyer, "because of the crocs."

Nurse Verna patted his arm. "Shhh. But you see, Henry was with her, keeping an eye out. However, the water there is so muddy that an enormous crocodile was able to sneak up and pull Elizabeth under. First the beast grabbed Elizabeth by her leg, but Henry held tight. So the beast let go of her leg and grabbed Elizabeth by her arm—well, Henry still would not let go. God gave him the strength to not let go."

"Praise God," Reverend Doyer said.

"But you see," Nurse Verna said, "neither would the crocodile give up. In the end, Henry was able to pull Elizabeth from the river, but the price she paid was steep. She lost her left arm up to, and including, the elbow. In addition, she was in full labor. I am not a doctor, Miss Newton, I am merely a nurse. And I cannot work miracles; only God can.

"There was a Roman Catholic mission at Bakuabo, about twenty kilometers back the way we'd come, so I told Henry to drive like Jehu, and see if maybe they had a doctor who was willing to help—even though we are Protestants. Meanwhile, I did my level best with the knowledge that was mine, and the tools that were available to me."

"Praise God," Reverend Doyer said again.

This time Julia wished that she were sitting close enough to slap him. But why did she feel that way? Whatever the reason, it just proved that she was unfit to be a missionary.

Nurse Verna gave her husband a pitying look before continuing. "I will admit that saving the life of the mother was my priority," she said. "It is no secret that I believe that children have no place on the mission field. That they are distractions."

"Great distractions," Julia said. She couldn't help herself.

Henry started, but said nothing.

Nurse Verna actually seemed to smile. "Exactly. That said, Elizabeth was able to deliver an infant son, and although I cleared his air passage—and I have delivered hundreds of babies—he was never able to breathe sufficiently on his own. I had to revive him several times with my own breath, as the Prophet Elijah revived the widow's son, but eventually—well, eventually it was the Lord's call."

"Praise God," Reverend Doyer said.

"Oh shut up," Nurse Verna said, speaking to her husband, but she kept her eyes on Henry. "I came here tonight to clear the air."

"Clear the air?" Henry said, which was ironic, because he suddenly seemed lost in a fog.

"Yes, Henry. We heard about Chief Eagle's threat, and since these last few months before independence are dangerous to begin with—well, only the Lord knows what's going to happen next. Tomorrow we could all be up in Glory, worshipping at our Savior's feet."

"Praise—"

"Verna," Henry said, like a man waking up, "it's not fair of you to scare Julia like that."

"Fair? Henry, all these years I have toiled in the clinic to gain these people's trust, and in one day she has managed to bring the vengeance of a ruthless man down upon our heads."

"Please finish clearing the air, Verna," Henry said. That's *all* he said; there was not a hint in his voice of sarcasm at that point. No sir, he was not going to be contradicting Nurse Verna's claim that the immanent danger was all Julia's fault.

"Very well," Nurse Verna said, obviously happy to oblige him. "What I came over to say tonight was *this*: I did my very best to save that infant of yours the day that your wife died. I did not give up on him too soon. If there is anyone to blame for his death—and I am not saying that there is—then that someone would be the Great Distraction."

Henry was on feet. "*Who?*" he roared.

The Doyers rose as well. "Henry," Nurse Verna said, her eyes still on Julia, "I might have been able to save Elizabeth as well, if it hadn't been for the constant carrying on of that child."

"*Carrying on?* Her mother was dying, for Pete's sake!"

"She was a big girl," Reverend Doyer said. "She was seven years old, for crying out loud. I kept telling her to be quiet. I tried to get her to walk with me a ways back up the road so that Nurse Verna had space to work. I told the Great Distraction that I thought I'd seen a family of monkeys in the forest up there, but she wouldn't listen. I *lied* in order to save your wife and son."

"She is not the Great Distraction," Henry hissed. "She is a *child*. An innocent child. Now get out of our house. Please. You've had your say, so now please go."

"It wasn't my wife's fault," Reverend Doyer said. "We just wanted you to know. A lot of things have gone wrong, but that day was none of our doing. And neither was today."

"Today was all my doing," Julia said.

Nobody contradicted her. In fact, no one said anything after that. The Doyers left, and after Henry bolted the front door from the inside, he too went off. At first Julia assumed he was only going to check on the back door.

When about half an hour had passed, and he still had not returned, Julia took the liberty of turning the wick down on the kerosene lantern to its lowest possible position. Then she carried the lantern as she would a flashlight, returning it to Clementine's room.

Julia had supposed that she would endure a sleepless night, but that was not to be the case. Almost immediately she fell into a deep and dreamless sleep that saw her through until morning. The next time that she opened her eyes, Henry was standing over her, demanding to know the answer to something.

Apparently whatever Henry wanted to know was extremely urgent. He had a piece of folded paper in his right hand, which he kept slapping across the fingers of his left hand. His brow was furrowed, and his dark brown eyes were searching and desperate.

"*Yah?*" Julia said. "What? Again, please."

"Have you seen Clemey?" Slap, slap, slap.

"No. I was asleep until just now."

"You slept all night? Without waking up once?"

"Yes. No offense, Henry, but we young people sometimes do that."

"Do you mean to say that you slept right through it?"

"I suppose that I must have; but since I don't know what *it* is, it's hard to say for sure if I did."

"Julia, my little Clemey is missing."

"*What?*" Julia's stomach muscles clenched with fear. "She is such a vibrant, energetic child—tell me, who would do such a—I mean, but really, there has to be an explanation."

Henri sat on the bed beside her. "*This* is the explanation. This is the note I found on her bed when I came in to wake her for breakfast. I'm hoping that you can tell me something that I don't know."

Julia took the note over to the window where her still bleary eyes stood a better chance of reading Clementine's very Victorian, spidery handwriting.

Papa,

I have an idea that just might work, thanks to you, glory hallelujah amen. Tell Auntie Julia that she need not worry about sleeping with a canine. And please don't stay mad at her. It looks like she possesses little in the way of fortitude.

Love you mostest,
Clemey, The Great Distraction

Julia carefully refolded the note. "Oh, dear," she said. "I haven't a clue what this means. Not a clue."

"I was afraid so," Henry said. "But I was hoping."

"Now what do we do?" she asked softly.

"We do what we always do at Mushihi Station when the going gets tough."

"We pray," Julia said.

TWENTY-FOUR

The Great Distraction did not believe in the power of prayer. It had failed to keep her mother alive, and two years of it had failed to raise her mother from the dead. Ergo, a year ago the Great Distraction stopped believing in prayer, and shortly afterward, she saw no need for God, either. Being a fair-minded child, she did, however, give her father a good month's notice that she intended to fire his boss.

"You can't fire God," Papa had said. "He's not your boss."

"He's my shepherd, isn't he? And a shepherd is the boss of his sheep. Well, God was Mama's boss too and he did a lousy job of watching over Mama that day by the ferry. Since Mama's not here to fire God, then I'm doing it for her."

And that's where Papa had let the subject lie. Well, for a while. He brought it up once to his brother, Uncle John, who said that if Clementine was his child he'd spank her little bottom until he'd spanked the devil out and spanked God back in. That's what any normal parent would do with any ordinary child. But Clemey was no ordinary child, no siree, you could say that again.

Why, you could spank Clemey's little bottom all the way over to Kenya, but that wouldn't make her eat one spoonful of broccoli, if eating vegetables was your goal. Clementine was a miniature

Elizabeth, they all said that, except for the Doyers, of course. The Doyers didn't approve of Mama, because she was forever trying to conceive babies.

Papa once said that one of the things that he'd always liked best about Mama was that she was forever drawing lines in the sand. He said that's what he admired about his Clemey too. Not just that, but Clementine's lines were never drawn willy-nilly either, but based on her understanding of principles.

You gotta have principles. You gotta stick up for what you believe in, for the people you love, even if you are afraid. You can't just say that you love your little girl; you have to be willing to protect her. If someone was going to kill your darling Clementine, and you had a house full of guns that you used for hunting—well, shouldn't you use those guns to protect your little girl?

By sticking to the main road, Clementine Hayes took only two hours to walk to Chief Eagle's village. She arrived at the break of dawn as the cocks crowed and the women stirred to light the cooking fires. Clementine was wearing the same outfit from the night before—her mother's dress, straw hat with pink flowers—but in addition she carried an embroidered canvas bag over her shoulder. Clementine knew that her arrival would cause an uproar, so she was determined not to flinch.

She was not disappointed. The first woman to see her dropped a clay pot and staggered backward.

"Ghost!"

"White woman's ghost," another woman cried.

Hut doors slammed shut. Children screamed. The cocks stopped crowing, and the dogs, which should have been growling, crouched low to the ground outside their owners' huts and whimpered.

Unimpeded, Clementine followed the spiral that is the layout of the traditional Bashilele village. It begins with those people of lesser value living on the outer circles, that is, servants and trusted slaves, and ends with the chief's hut in the center. Clementine made it as far as the wives' quarter before she was intercepted by two warriors armed with gleaming machetes.

"If it please you, white thing, are you a ghost?" one of them said.

Clementine was careful not to smile. "No, I am not a ghost. Wait." She slowly removed her hat. "You see, I am real—a real girl. Most unfortunately, I am a white girl." All this she said in their native tongue of Bushilele, and with a perfect accent. It was the language that was supposedly so difficult that no white man was capable of learning it.

The men made no response of any kind.

"I am the daughter of Muambi Gets Much Done. I have come to see Chief Eagle."

The warriors began discussing their options. Should they bring this matter to the chief's attention or lead the girl to see him straightaway? A third option was to kill her on the spot and have one of them claim her skull and the other claim her clothes.

"Stop your women's talk!" Clementine said in her bossiest tone. "I can hear you. I have very powerful magic in this bag, and I will put a curse on you, one that you will surely regret forever, unless you take me to see your chief at once!"

The warriors looked stunned. "You can understand our speech?" one of them asked.

"*E*. Did you not hear me speak to you just now? Did you not hear me tell you who I am?"

"But—but no one except for a Mushilele can understand our language. We did not think—"

"*E*, you speak the truth. You did not think. Now take me to see Chief Eagle before I cause your goats to die and your wives to be barren."

So they took Clementine straightaway to see Chief Eagle, who surprised the girl by appearing at the door of his hut rather rapidly—especially considering that he was such a big-shot heathen, all full of himself and headed straight for hell. In fact, he seemed more curious about her highly unorthodox visit than he did annoyed.

One had to admit that he was a very handsome man, despite the fact that he was maybe thirty-seven years old and missing his two front teeth. Then again, every Mushilele man was missing his two front teeth. All in all, Clementine reckoned, sleeping next to the chief's muscular body for one night might actually be a better deal than spending it curled up next to one of the mangy dogs she'd seen on her way in.

"Life to you, little one," said the chief. "They tell me that you can speak our language like a human. Can this astonishing news actually be true?"

"*E*, Master, and now I am speaking it to you."

"So you are. Tell me, how did you travel here? These women soldiers of mine report that they did not hear a *camion*."

"King Eagle," Clementine said, for she had no problem with buttering his toast on both sides to accomplish her goals, "I walked here on my little worthless white girl legs. I did so because I have an urgent matter to discuss."

Chief Eagle grunted. "*Truly?*"

"Truly, truly."

"Now, before we discuss this urgent matter of yours, I must first ask you a very important question."

"Ask," said Clementine.

"Where is your father?" said Chief Eagle.

"He remains at our house. He does not know that I am here."

"Do you want to sit?" asked Chief Eagle, pointing to a chair.

By now Clementine was aware that a crowd had begun to gather. Undoubtedly, the first to watch this most unusual scene were some of the chief's wives and their children, and then the nobles and their families.

"No, thank you," said Clementine. "I prefer to stand. I have come only to present you with a gift. In exchange, I will request a particular gift from you."

As Clementine spoke in a soft, ladylike voice, reminiscent of her mother, Elizabeth—thank you very much—the chief, for his own amusement, repeated her comments by shouting them through cupped hands so that all assembled could hear. Then he turned back to her and shook his royal scepter practically in her face. The scepter, by the way, was an intricately carved piece of reddish-brown wood, capped with an ivory handle, from which sprouted the long black-and-white hair of a colobus monkey.

"You will start by telling me your request. You must understand that I am not a wealthy man."

"Your Majesty," Clementine said, "my request is that you sell me that worthless female child, Buakane. I would pay back her dowry."

"*Aiyee!*"

Clementine guessed that the cry which went up came from Buakane's mother, herself one of the nobility. As for the Chief Eagle, the look on his face was certainly fit to kill—figuratively, of course, not literally. Everybody used that word wrong—even Papa.

"What would you, a mere child, do with Buakane?"

"I would send her to another place so that her memory can be erased. Forgotten. Then perhaps King Eagle and the whites at Mushihi Station can live in peace."

Another cry arose from the crowd, prompting Clementine to continue. "With your dowry returned and my gift, life can continue without involving the Belgians."

The chief shifted feet. "I said that I would wait until after independence before killing the white woman, did I not?"

"*E*, you did. 'But one's machete grows thirsty for blood, as one's heart grows hungry for vengeance.' Is this not so?" Clementine had heard this saying more than once and hated it. In the Belgian Congo it was ever so true.

Chief Eagle smiled for the first time. "I will agree to sell you the worthless girl, Buakane, daughter of Bad Odor and Grasshopper Paddle. Now show me your gift. Is it in that sack?"

"Indeed it is, Your Majesty."

With great flair, worthy of the most famous magicians that you can imagine, the Overly Dramatic Clementine Hayes, the Great Distraction, Daughter of the Problematic Elizabeth, withdrew a doll's head. Although it was only half the size of Miss Julia's head, it had sapphire blue eyes that opened and closed and long blond hair.

"I killed that ugly white woman on your behalf, Your Majesty. Then I shrunk her head and preserved it so that it will not decay. Now you can display it in your hut, as a symbol of your eternal greatness."

Chief Eagle was speechless, but not the crowd. They made a great deal of holy racket as they beat a hasty retreat. Old *baba*s screamed, as did young children. Jumping Geronimo, if they weren't all screaming by the time the royal compound had been cleared.

"Go ahead, take it," Clementine said. "It will not harm you. In fact, it will do just the opposite. It will protect you from your enemies. If you put this in your hut, no one will dare to come in and do you harm. The preserved head of this white woman contains much magic power."

Chief Eagle, the bully master of so many wives and concubines, who was riding the express train straight to hell, gingerly outstretched an arm.

"Take it by the hair. Sometimes, however, you must lay the head down so that it can sleep."

"Sleep?"

"*E,* like this." Clementine grabbed the doll head in both tiny hands and held it flat. The blue eyes, surrounded by the long dark lashes, closed, causing the chief to gasp and jump back. "As I said, much, much power."

Chief Eagle reached for the doll's head again. "Tell me all that it can do," he said.

"Your Majesty, I cannot tell you what this head—your head

now—can do. That is for you to discover. And you must keep that information secret. If you do not, the head will crumble and become dust. Dust to dust. Have you not heard these words spoken, Your Majesty?"

"His Majesty is a heathen," said one of the two warriors. "But I have heard these words. I used to be a Christian in my youth."

"There, you see?" Clementine said. "Now, truly, I must commence my return, for the walk is long and my legs are but short."

"You will not walk from here," Chief Eagle said.

"*E,* I will," said Clementine. *Keep a stiff upper lip,* she told herself. *Then eat steak and kidney pies, and God save the Queen.*

Chief Eagle clapped his hands. "*Kippoi,*" he barked. Immediately, eight burly men appeared out of nowhere carrying a sedan chair, or as Papa called it, the "throne on two sticks." The chief motioned for her to climb aboard. "My men will carry you back as far as the entrance to Mushihi Station. From there you must walk to your house."

"We laugh and we cry," said Clementine.

"But let us laugh more than we cry."

"*E.* Your Majesty, may I ask you a question?"

Chief Eagle smiled. "I think that you already have."

"Do you think that a father should protect his children?" said Clementine.

"Always! That is his job."

"What if he has only a girl child?"

"Then most especially," said Chief Eagle. "A girl child will bring in dowry payments; a girl child has value." At that everyone laughed—except for Clementine. "Do not worry, small one," the chief said, "for if that is your worry, I will see that no harm comes to you."

"Amen and glory hallelujah!" Clementine said. Then, realizing that she had just spoken aloud in English, she told a lie. Just like the grown-ups. "Those words were how one expresses gratitude in my language," she said.

Chief Eagle beamed. "One more thing, little white girl."

"*E,* Your Majesty?"

"It is enough that you have given me that terrible woman's head, especially now that it has been imbued with so much magic. Therefore, I am refusing your offer to repay the dowry."

"But, Your Majesty—"

"*Yai,*" he said to the bearers. Go!

As the Great Distraction, aka My Darling Clementine, was being carried aloft on the shoulders of eight burly headhunters, her mind, as usual, was kept busy planning ahead. Might one even go so far as to suggest scheming?

After all, she would have to explain to Chief Eagle how the ugly white woman not only survived her own death, but managed to regrow a perfectly good new head. On second thought, that might not be too hard. The Auntie Julia he saw next time would be a ghost, one made to look superreal by the powerful magic of the Great Distraction. Ta-da!

No, the real scheming involved how to get Papa and Julia to see how brilliantly right they were for each other. But before that happened, Papa was going to have to choose between his principles and real live human beings. There'd be no use bringing Auntie Julie into their little family, For Which We Give Thee Thanks, unless Papa was prepared to defend her to the teeth.

Clementine had already picked out the dress that she would wear in her role as maid of honor. It would be the white lace dress that her mother had worn to Brussels when she received the Order of the Lion from King Baudouin. She would refuse to wear a belt with this dress. She would let the skirt drag like a train, unless Papa could see his way to have it hemmed. And maybe, just maybe, Clementine would forgo a hat so that Mama looking down from heaven could see the happiness in her daughter's eyes. Glory, Hallelujah, Amen, and pass the peas.

AFTERWORD

The young woman despised being cold. Each year, when winter arrived, she felt as if her soul had curled up along with the leaves that had turned brown and lay uncollected, caught in the naked shrubbery around campus. The icy winds that penetrated her coat blew down from Canada—not directly—but came screaming across the stubble of Indiana cornfields to the west. The border between Ohio and Indiana did nothing to stop the cold, and when it was funneled through the valleys between the steep hills of Cincinnati, it seemed to emerge magnified. It seldom snowed in Cincinnati, Ohio. At least not enough to make up for all the gray skies, with trees silhouetted against them like the claws of dead crows lying on their backs.

The young woman's name was Buakane, and she was an African from the Congo; more specifically, she hailed from a highborn clan of the Bashilele tribe. Her mother's name was Grasshopper Paddle, and her father's name was Bad Odor. At one time, when she was but a girl of ten—or thereabouts—Buakane was sold in marriage to a powerful chief named Eagle. That very night the girl who married Chief Eagle ran away, setting into action a chain of events, like dominoes, that would eventually land her on the frozen campus of the College of Nursing at the University of Cincinnati.

What was a child of the Southern Star, a young woman with the constitution of a tropical flower, doing in such a distant, inhospitable place as this? Ah, that is a fair question. But the Americans are fond of a saying that goes something like this: "If I had a dollar for every time someone asked me that question . . ." That is, the complete story of just how Buakane of the Bashilele, that once-fierce tribe known for their headhunting, came to be shivering on an Ohio campus would fill an entire book. Or it would take many nights around a hearth to even scratch the surface of such a story, and Buakane had neither the time nor the inclination to dwell on her past.

All that must be known is that after the Congo became independent, terrible tribal wars raged over much of the Kasai, but it was famine that was death's closest companion. Shortly after independence all the missionaries evacuated, although a year later, Tatu Henry and Mamu Julia (who were now married) returned, along with Clementine, to resume work at Mushihi Station. There they discovered that both of Buakane's parents, Paddle and Bad Odor, had perished in the famine.

The Hayes family remained in the Congo for only one more year. When they returned to the United States to stay, they took Buakane with them. They settled in Dayton, Ohio, not too far from Oxford where Julia had grown up, and Dayton is where Buakane came into her own. It was there that she learned how to speak English and about the strange American ways. Through hard work, and thanks to her formidable intellect, she was able to graduate from an American high school when she was just eighteen.

At one time Buakane had thought that all whites were rich beyond measure, far richer than even a thousand village chiefs. Now that she lived in their world she could see that wealth was a relative thing, and even knowledge came at a price.

The Hayes family was not wealthy. Tatu Henry was currently a pastor of a very small congregation, but did the occasional carpentry job on the side. Mamu Julia worked as a teacher. Clementine was a second-year student at Harvard University—which everyone said cost an "arm and a leg." However, that was only an American expression, not something to be taken literally.

Buakane's dream of becoming a nurse seemed like an impossible dream until she spoke it aloud. For the Bashilele had a saying: "Words spoken aloud catch the wind and turn into action." Now this Child of Beauty, Goodness, and Excellence, She Who Was Worthy in All Things was a first-year student at the College of Nursing at the University of Cincinnati. Who back in Mushihi Village could have imagined that? No one. But *eyo*, the words of Buakane's spoken dream had caught the wind, and "out of the blue," as it is said, a secret benefactor had stepped forward to pay for her entire course of study.

Earlier on this particular day, under feeble sunlight, Tatu Henry and Mamu Julia had dropped the young woman off at her dorm following her first Christmas break. Now the sky was as black as a zebra's mane, and the weather bitter in her mouth. Yet the girl had to go out, for she'd found a note slipped under her door, inviting her to meet with her benefactor at the student union. The signature on the note was illegible, giving the poor girl no information other than the time and place to meet. This unexpected appearance of her benefactor caused Buakane's heart to beat so fast that it felt like it might leap from her chest, and then gallop away like a giant kudu.

When at last Buakane stumbled into the tall brick building where her benefactor waited, she was so cold that her fingers clutching the note were stiff and her eyes immediately began to tear up. At first Buakane could see only students—most of them white—and a low moan escaped her lips. Was this yet another cruel trick played on her by fate? Or perhaps even a curse placed upon her by Nanabuka, the witch doctor of Mushihi Village? For despite her ten years in the United States of America, and her informal adoption by the Hayes family, the Mushilele prodigy remained a heathen.

"Buakane! Life to you, Buakane."

The young woman whirled. Standing within striking distance of her elbow was Mamu Snake, the great white healer, she who had sewn the deep gash opened by the hyena the night that Buakane, the girl, had married an eagle. Buakane had not seen the missionary for ten years; what's more, not once had she even asked after the old woman.

"*Mamu*," Buakane said with her first breath. "*E*, life to you."

Mamu Snake motioned to the nearest empty table. "May we speak in English, Buakane? I only have a few minutes before I have to leave for the airport, but I wanted to hear it for myself."

"Hear what?" Buakane asked in English.

"I heard that you spoke without an accent. It has been much remarked upon. Please, say something else."

"Now I am embarrassed," Buakane said, "so of course I can't think of anything to say. Well—except to ask why it is that you pay for my nurse's training. What I mean to say is, you don't even know me, except for that one night when you saved my life. Which isn't to say that *I'm* not grateful, because believe me, *I* am, but I didn't do anything for you after that, except bring you trouble. Loads and loads of trouble."

"Praise God in his highest heaven," Mamu Snake said. "You *do* speak English without an accent! You speak it perfectly, just like a native."

The old woman had a very deep, raspy voice, and she'd spoken loudly. Everyone was staring at them now, not that Buakane cared one whit—or one stick of *manioc,* as she would have said in her previous life. Back in Africa, where life was fraught with constant danger, old age was something to be revered, and Mamu Snake was surely the oldest woman that Buakane had ever talked with face-to-face. Even after having lived in America for half her life, Buakane found that she still could not estimate the age of a white person with any sort of accuracy. As for Mamu Snake, her age was incalculable, given that it was undoubtedly between fifty and infinity, a totally unfamiliar range in which few Bashilele women ever found themselves.

"Are all your expenses being covered?" the ancient missionary asked.

Buakane nodded as she struggled to hold back more tears. These fresh tears were different from those caused by temperature. As the daughter of Paddle, She of the Highborn Clan, it was not fitting that she succumb to such a public demonstration of emotion.

"*Mamu*, my heart overflows with gratitude."

Mamu Snake grunted. "How is your leg? Do you still feel the scar?"

"*Eyo*. It is twice felt." By that Buakane meant that her fingers could immediately zero in on her scar, even if she wasn't looking at her leg, as well as the fact that she sometimes dreamed about the night the hyenas attacked her.

"I was afraid you'd say that," Mamu Snake said. "I did the best I could. I'm only a nurse; I'm not a surgeon. I'm not even a doctor."

"You did a great job," Buakane hastened to assure her. "The doctors here all say so."

"Good. Buakane, I must ask you a question: Why do you wish to be a nurse?"

"*Mamu*, isn't that obvious? I want to do what you did; I want to return to my village and help my people. You know what it's like there; they must be hurting even worse now."

"Then why not go as a doctor?"

Buakane was flabbergasted. How was she supposed to respond to such a ridiculous question from someone who was being so kind to her? It was one thing to ask the wind to pay for nurses' school, but quite another to dream of medical school. Was this old woman playing a game of some kind? What was Buakane to think? After all, this was the same woman who had been so unkind to her friend and American "sister," Clementine.

Just when enough words had formed in Buakane's mind to come tumbling out of their own accord—perhaps in an unpleasant arrangement—the old woman spoke first.

"Yes, of course, you are right. You can receive your bachelor's degree in nursing in just four years. Medical school would take twice that long, including college, and then you'd have to complete your internship. You can go back to medical school later if you wish. In the meantime, go back to Africa and tend to your people. I'm going to arrange it so that funds are available for you to use whenever you're ready."

"We laugh and we cry!" Buakane said, without realizing that she was no longer speaking English. "*Mamu,* why do you do this for me?"

The old woman, she of the indeterminate age, looked away. "My husband, Reverend Arvin Doyer, passed away three years ago. I thought that he came from a very poor family—one that didn't have two nickels to rub together—but apparently that was not the case. There was some family money, not a huge fortune, but something that the reverend could have been spending on missions over the years and didn't. It is my intention to correct this oversight."

Then just like that, as the wind comes and goes, as fortunes wax and wane, Mamu Snake disappeared through the blur of Buakane's tears. Whether she stepped out into the bitter cold or melded into the throng of returning students, Buakane was unable to determine. But where once there was a girl who married an eagle, there was now a woman who would someday be a nurse.

BOOKS BY TAMAR MYERS

THE GIRL WHO MARRIED AN EAGLE
A Mystery
Available in Paperback and eBook

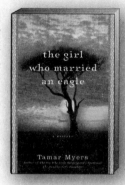

A riveting addition to Tamar Myers's Belgian Congo-set mystery series, this is the story of an all girls boarding school for runaway child brides, and features events inspired by Myers's childhood in the Belgian Congo.

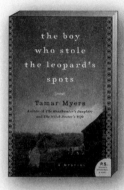

THE BOY WHO STOLE THE LEOPARD'S SPOTS
A Mystery
Available in Paperback and eBook

"Only an author with an intimate knowledge of the Congo—its people, landscape, and culture—could write . . . with such confidence and authority."

—Mary Alice Monroe, author of *Last Light over Carolina*

THE HEADHUNTER'S DAUGHTER
A Mystery
Available in Paperback and eBook

"Tamar Myers' mesmerizing novel of mid-twentieth century Congo plumbs passion, despair, and courage."

—Carolyn Hart

THE WITCH DOCTOR'S WIFE
A Mystery
Available in Paperback and eBook

"Myers draws on her own experiences as the daughters of white missionaries living in the Belgian Congo for this dazzling novel full of authentic African lore."

—*Publishers Weekly* (starred review)